"TONIGHT OUR BIGGEST FEARS WILL UNFOLD . . ."

With these words, Halina had the attention of the entire Den. She continued: "They are massing together right now for an attack on our Den. But we have help unseen and unheard of before in this strip of our world. We have the power of fear unmatched by anything ever conceived. Our great hope."

"What power is this?" sneered Syranosh. "Unless it is the power of fifty Toms, we should all leave here at once."

"I think not," said Halina. "We will stay and face our enemies. Do not be afraid. Do not run from here no matter what happens. You will smell and feel a terror beyond belief. It will come from the Canyon in the shape of Lady Farri to help us."

Yet even as she assured them of what was to come, Halina wondered whether her new and unexpected ally would fail her. . . .

CAT HOUSE

Michael Peak

A SIGNET BOOK

NEW AMERICAN LIBRARY

A DIVISION OF PENGUIN BOOKS USA INC.

PUBLISHER'S NOTE

This book is a work of fiction. Names, characters, places, and incidents either are the product of the author's imagination or are used fictitiously, and any resemblance to actual persons, living or dead, events, or locales is entirely coincidental.

Copyright © 1989 by Michael Peak

 SIGNET TRADEMARK REG. U.S. PAT OFF. AND FOREIGN COUNTRIES REGISTERED TRADEMARK—MARCA REGISTRADA HECHO EN DRESDEN, TN. USA

SIGNET, SIGNET CLASSIC, MENTOR, ONYX, PLUME, MERIDIAN and NAL BOOKS are published by New American Library, a division of Penguin Books USA Inc., 1633 Broadway, New York, New York 10019

First Printing, September, 1989

1 2 3 4 5 6 7 8 9

PRINTED IN THE UNITED STATES OF AMERICA

For Martha Lawrence,
who encouraged me while the fires raged,
and talked me out of everything else.

"IN THE BEGINNING . . ."

On the eighth day, God created cats.

All other creatures were either currently in existence, or on the drawing board for a future showing.

Cats were an afterthought.

"The creature man is my pet," said the Creator, "and so you shall be his. As man is to Me, so you will be to him."

"We will serve the man, then," answered Queen Farri, mother of all felines.

"Nay," said the Lord. "You will be as he is: arrogant, selfish, disobedient, and annoying. You will live with him, act as though you are far superior to he who feeds you, and he will love you."

"But how will he love me if I am all those things?" asked Farri, a little confused.

"Because he will see you as a mirror of himself. He will love you as I love him, while he is all of those things to Me."

Farri was confused, but knew the Creator sometimes seemed puzzling, yet was always right. Farri took a long look across the Kingdom, and saw the lords and ladies of every species ever created to inhabit the earth. Each had been given a specific task. Of them all, Farri believed hers to be the strangest.

Being so closely associated with the man could be a liability. They were the most destructive and least favorite of the entire family, although they were clearly in the Creator's favor.

Farri stood with the Creator on a huge rock at the edge

of an open plain. The other animals watched from afar, all of them eager to know what plans the Lord had for this newcomer. They all seemed nervous, as if they feared the arrival of another version of man. After all, the two of them did look an awful lot alike.

"You will have many children, Farri," said the Lord. "They will call you 'Queen,' as is your right. Some of your offspring will remain wild, and grow to enormous size and strength. Others will be small, yet will stay strange to man. It is their cousins who will live with him, comfort him, and frustrate him. They will call themselves 'farries' in your honor."

"Will the children, the 'farries,' be loved by their brothers and sisters in this world of animals?" asked Farri. "It is clear they have a mission tied to man. How will this affect them?"

She studied the Creator closely, hoping for a clue to His thoughts. It was an impossible task, since unlike all other members of the Kingdom, the Creator had no definable shape.

"They will walk this life alone," answered the Lord. "Especially the farries. They will be looked upon as man himself. Feared, mostly, and loathed by all others.

"They will be strong enough and cunning enough to be the most effective and ruthless predators on earth, yet small enough to be prey themselves.

"My krahstas, what the men call coyotes, will feast on them when they can. So too will kribas, the man's dog. The kribas are the krahstas' domestic cousins, and will be fiercely jealous of the man's affection to farries. Some will be stronger, and some weaker. Some will even befriend the farries as best they can, for they will be no match for the cat even half their size.

"But they are false friends, for the farri is alone on the earth. Everything else will be their prey."

Farri could see Lord Krahsta in the distance. He was clearly upset at the attention Farri was receiving from the Creator, and she knew his malevolent expression would get worse when he found out what her mission was. The plight of the krahstas was not so good. Man was destined to destroy all of Lord Krahsta's terrain.

Fearing the worst, Farri decided to try negotiating for allies.

"But the man will be their friend," said Farri hopefully.

"The man will be their provider," said the Creator, "although cats will certainly be able to take care of themselves. Just like man. And just like man, they will have no true friends in the animal world. They will have only themselves, and each other. . . ."

The
Den Mother

CHAPTER 1

Dahrkron had watched the cats near the edge of the Canyon for three consecutive nights. Hunger had driven him closer and closer to the man settlement, and tonight he would make his boldest move, before the moon grew in strength and gave too much warning light, and its maddening power drove the others in the pack to lunacy, possibly braving them enough to follow and share the kill.

The wind was in his favor for a change. He felt the light Southern California breeze caress his face, and walked, not loped, through the sage.

He had eaten cat before. A little spicier than rabbit or ground squirrel, for cats hunted too. And smart, they were. They were always aware of the nearest tree, and could get there before most of the pack could get started. But Dahrkron was not most of the pack.

No, Dahrkron was much smarter. Brilliant, in fact. Enough to be pack leader, although the stupid fool Trahkor was still running things. But tonight the others would chase the rabbits and squirrels long gone from the Canyon, and Dahrkron would eat farri.

He crept along the edge of the sage, nearest the common ground of Canyon and manroad. He knew it would not be much longer before the manroad stretched farther into the Canyon, robbing the krahstas of even more of their ever dwindling home. He breathed out an almost inaudible growl, loathing the farries who would befriend such a destructive beast.

There were five farries at the edge of the street, apparently holding a discussion of some sort. Odd, thought Dahrkron, farries don't usually travel in packs. When a male and a female broke away from the others, he made his move.

Like the wind he ran, out onto the road and toward the prey. Two of the three saw, and bolted in opposite directions. But the third was unaware! A female, she turned around just as Dahrkron was about to snap, and jumped to the right. Although it was normally a routine maneuver for the agile Dahrkron, his paws, accustomed to the forgiving turf of the Canyon, gave way on the hard blacktop. It was all he could do to keep from scraping his chin.

At a full stop, he regained his balance. He turned to give the hopeless chase, but stood dead in his tracks. The cat was still there.

Stunned, Dahrkron looked the cat over and then felt the laughter roll from his belly. His tongue flapped out of his mouth to the left side, then he snapped it back in with a grin.

"So, puss"—he smiled finally, when the cat still had not moved—"you will stand and fight, will you? Fool. You were born with no brains."

"You must go," the cat said simply. "There is nothing for you here. Go back to the Canyon or you will perish."

"Sure thing, puss," said Dahrkron. "I'll be glad to go back, with you in my belly." He would have laughed, but something was very strange. The expression worn by the cat was almost chilling. Well, *was* chilling for that matter. And what about the way the little bitch just stood there so defiantly? Didn't most cats turn over onto their backs when they fought? This was weird.

"Leave," said the cat, fluffing her tail even more. "Now."

"Right," said Dahrkron, and pounced.

Barely had he moved when the cat came at him. It had taken three swipes before Dahrkron could even open his mouth to bite. When his teeth came together, there was only air. When he landed and turned around, he could smell the blood.

His right eye was starting to swell. There were three

long gashes across his face, one nicking his eyelid. That was close. He looked at the cat and growled, but before he could move he felt the claw rip into his nose. He jumped and snapped, but got nothing. The wound on his nose was a bad one.

He took a step back and looked at the cat, who stood motionless in the dark.

"Back to the Canyon," insisted the cat.

"I could howl, you know, and a whole pack of coyotes will be here. How will you do then, brave puss? They will tear you to shreds."

"How will it matter to you?" answered the cat. "Is the knowledge enough to satisfy you? For surely they will feast on you as well."

"They would not kill another krahsta." Dahrkron smiled knowingly. He had opened his mouth too far. His bleeding nose poured in.

"No," said the cat, "they will not. But a dead coyote will only be more fresh meat. And dead you will certainly be."

The cat's delivery was so convincing, Dahrkron believed her. When the cat began to crouch as if to strike, he stepped back. The cat let go a fierce hiss, and Dahrkron knew he'd had enough. The Canyon was much safer.

Mahri watched the coyote lope off into the night. She had smelled the terror before actually seeing, and made tracks to the roof of the nearest house. From there she saw the unbelievable: Halina standing up to and chasing off the worst of fears. And even though the krahsta was gone, she still could not relax enough to contract her claws.

In time, however, she felt her wildly fluffed tail flatten out, and she climbed down to see Halina, who had walked over to their Den.

"You lucked out, dear." Halina smiled at Mahri. "You won't have to put up with Coron tonight. And a good thing. I don't think he had much of a reward for you."

"The reward is never worth it with such a slime." Mahri gritted her teeth at the mention of Coron. "He is so filthy and he bites so hard. Yuk. And look at what a coward he is, screeching off while you stood up to the krahsta."

"I must protect what is mine," said Halina. "Coron has nothing here, and has no reason to stay when there is trouble. He was right to run. I could not. I promised my girls I would protect them."

"We wouldn't have felt betrayed if you had run too," Mahri smiled. "My farri, how could you stand the smell? It was terrifying."

"There are definitely smells terrifying to me," answered Halina. "Krahsta is not one of them. There are farries around who do not fear the krahsta. I somehow know this to be so, although I've not ever met another farri who felt this way."

"Well, I'm glad at least you do," Mahri smiled. She had always admired Halina's strength and stunning beauty. Like the other girls who worked for Halina, there was nothing she would not do for her mistress. Mating with Coron was testimony enough.

Mahri had never encountered another farri as mysterious as Halina. Even her name was unusual. At a quick glance you'd swear she was just another tabby. But up close she was clearly something special. A face of true majestic lineage. Her lines were strikingly more defined than those of normal farries, and the orange—or was it brown?—flared in the most provocative pattern.

"The smell of krahsta will keep all the other toms away, tonight," said Halina sadly. "I doubt even your sweet calls could bring them out. At least Syranosh will do well, though."

"Yes," whispered Mahri.

Halina could see sad jealousy in Mahri's eyes, and smiled affectionately.

"Sharlo is quite a tom," said Halina. "He likes you the best."

"I wish he did," said Mahri. "He's so sweet. I don't know why he comes over here, anyway. He's so handsome and gentle, he could get any girl he wanted. And for free. He doesn't need to pay for girls like us."

"Sharlo comes over just for you, Mahri," Halina

smiled. "Sometimes you're already taken, because you're the most popular, so he takes Melena or Syranosh. But it's you he really likes. He's obviously trying to impress you, because he brings only the finest catches for payment."

"He must be a good hunter," Mahri smiled. She was glad there would be no business tonight. It was a rare treat to chat with Halina so candidly. The mistress usually spoke in puzzles, different from most farries, who were so direct.

"Should I be worried about my young Mahri?" asked Halina with a gentle smile. "Remember, dear, Sharlo is a customer. . . ."

"I know," said Mahri defensively. "He's just my favorite, I guess." She sat back and began to bathe her left side. She liked the long hair that accompanied a calico coat, but sometimes it was such trouble to keep clean. She spent far more time on her locks than did Syranosh or any of the other farries in the group save Halina. But somehow she rarely felt as though she looked quite as fresh. The toms in the area tended to disagree.

Mahri was the most requested of Halina's girls. Her face was almost delicate, a bright pink nose surrounded by a white mask with exceptionally long whiskers. And long whiskers were a coveted commodity. The shocks of black and orange began their battle around her big green eyes, and tangled in beautiful blends all the way through to her very fluffy tail. Mahri was lusted after.

"De Lilah!"

Mahri looked up at Halina. It was Halina's paladin, calling her in for the evening.

"He's awfully early tonight," said Halina, casually looking over at the house. "It's just as well. We'll have no more toms tonight. You might go home too, pretty Mahri. Although the krahsta should not return tonight, I fear he may in the future with others of his kind. They are cowards and hunt best in packs. It will be well for us to stay closer to our paladin's houses as a rule."

"De Lilah!"

Halina looked back toward her house.

"Maybe he'll have pizza tonight," she said, and trotted off.

"Here she is," said Roger mildly relieved. It was always good to have the cat around when he brought home a new girl. The cat could be such an icebreaker.

"Wow, she *is* pretty," answered Tammy, squatting down to pet De Lilah. "But she looks like a regular cat. I was expecting something bigger. What's she called? A. . . ?"

"Scottish wildcat," answered Roger. "They do look pretty much like regular cats, except she is a little bigger. Mean too."

"Yeah. Fierce." Tammy laughed as the cat rubbed against her knee and purred gently.

"It's weird. The guy at the zoo said she'd turn really wild when she got older. But she somehow stayed sweet. She's tough, though. I've had her for three years and she's never come home with even a scratch. She gets in a lot of fights too."

"Is it even legal to have a cat like this?" asked Tammy, remaining intent on petting De Lilah.

"No, it's against the law to have her. But you'd never know she's different unless you know."

"Then how did you get her?"

"Just know the right people," said Roger, a little smug. He sat down on the floor and scooted next to Tammy. De Lilah stepped over and began to rub against his leg.

"See?" said Tammy. "She wants attention."

"I'm saving my attention for the prettiest girl I know," answered Roger, and began to massage Tammy's shoulders.

"I'll bet you say that to all the girls," she smiled.

I'll bet you're right, thought Roger.

"No way, sweetie. Just you." It was going to be a great night.

CHAPTER 2

Syranosh found Mahri and together they walked toward the dead end near the Canyon. It was time again, when the sun began to lose its daily battle with darkness. When the moon would triumphantly gaze over the mountains in the east. When the cats came out.

The two farries walked in silence. Mahri never knew what to say to Syranosh for fear of saying the wrong thing. Syranosh seemed to be angry or ready to fight almost all of the time; she was the only one in Halina's group who tended to be unsocial. Gorgeous, there could be no denying, with perfectly patterned black and white, but beauty only runs fur-deep.

Halina was, as usual, already seated in the small burrow she called her den, which was made of the long, wild grass from the Canyon that tried to reclaim the street. It was Melena who Mahri saw first, sitting beside the mistress, blocking her from the others' view.

Mahri liked Melena. Unlike Syranosh, Melena was always a sweetheart. And she looked so good too. Black as night she was. Fluffy black, with her striking display of long shiny fur and those flashy long whiskers. And she didn't flaunt it, like so many of the others. Out of all the pretty farries Halina recruited, Mahri believed Melena to be the most deserving of her looks.

But today, Melena looked neither warm nor friendly, and the feeling was sensed by all the other farries immediately. Melena was scared.

When Halina stepped out from behind Melena to face

the group, there was an overwhelming gasp of dismay. Deep scratches lined both sides of Halina's face.

The reaction felt by Mahri was most alarming. She had unconsciously fluffed her fur to the fullest, simulating a battle stance. But there was no battle to fight; she was among friends. She began to relax, but was still upset about Halina. The mistress had *never* lost a fight. And if she recalled correctly, it had been nearly a year since another cat had even dared challenge her, and he was never seen again.

"My mistake," said Halina to the nervous and questioning farries. All eight of her girls were gathered around and giving their full attention.

"As you know," she continued, "it's been three nights since the attack by a straggler krahsta. Thank Farri we all escaped. But I am very afraid to just leave it at that and take a chance on leaving the danger unchecked.

"What a fool I was!" Halina looked skyward and then walked a nervous circle. "A fool. For I believe I may have placed us in a greater danger. A danger unthought of before. But who could have known?"

Mahri stole a glance at some of the other farries and saw, to her horror, the fur on several tails standing on end. The group was extremely nervous.

"It was early this morning when I set out into the Canyon. Yes," Halina said, acknowledging the wide eyes, "I went out alone to seek news. There are few sources these days. Most animals who could be prey are gone. The krahstas and the hawks have multiplied furiously in recent seasons, and their food supply is getting critical. They have come closer and closer to the Canyon's edge, forcing at least one krahsta to brave the fear of man enough to rush the street.

"There are whispers about the krahstas. There is dissension in their numbers about how to handle the food problem. While the group prefers the safety of the Canyon, there are members who feel farries are easy game and close enough to the Canyon to make it worth the gamble."

"Who told you all this?" asked Syranosh. "Sounds

like there are not many animals out there who'd wanna talk to a farri.''

''No, dear Syranosh, not many. But there are some. There are hawks whom I have met before in passing. They do not fear me, yet realize I would be a strong enough foe not to be worth the risk. They will talk, sometimes. And there are others, although it is not important.

''No, my dear Syranosh, what is important is our danger. Not only from the krahstas, but from our very own cousins.'' She sat down in the Den and remained silent for a moment.

''I met with a lynx,'' she said finally. ''There are at least two of them close by, though I saw only the one. It is from her I received these wounds. I did get information from her, but at what a price! And now she knows we are here, and I fear for our very existence if things get worse in the Canyon.''

''Why would you approach a lynx?'' asked Mahri.

''For help,'' said Halina. ''I wanted her help in fighting the krahstas. I thought she and her mate together, along with myself and some others, might drive them off. Instead, she drove *me* off.

''I could see it in her eyes, though. It wasn't me. Something else was of great concern to the lynx. She was afraid of something. Afraid. Just like the rest of the Canyon was afraid. There were whispers of a new terror amidst the sage. Something so horrifying . . . Yet no one would speak of it openly. And they didn't really have to. I could feel something. It made me quake all over, every hair on end. But I couldn't smell it or see it. It was just—'' She paused, trying to think of the right word. ''I don't know. It was just there.''

When Coron arrived and asked for Mahri, Halina, to the surprise of all her girls, told him Mahri was already taken.

''What the hell are you talking about?'' thundered Coron. ''She's sitting right there. Are you going blind?''

''You should know by now, Master Coron, I always know the exact whereabouts of my farries. This is no exception. And as I told you, Mahri is already spoken for this evening. You may certainly pick another girl.''

Mahri was shocked, and a little nervous as she began to feel the gaze of Halina's other farries. One of them was going to have a miserable night.

Coron stalked around the group, looking over the choices. He knew them all well, much to their disgust.

Coron was the most despicable farri imaginable. He lived alone somewhere, everywhere. It was widely believed his paladin had abandoned him years ago, and he was claimed by no other. To farries everywhere who had come in contact with him, there was no doubt why.

Huge he was, and filthy beyond belief. His coat, sparkling white in days gone by, was now a tangle of every possible crud. There were scars crossing several patterns about his face and forehead from the countless fights both won and lost over the years. Two of his front teeth were broken at the midway point, somehow adding to the look of permanent fierceness. And he was feared by them all—all except Halina.

Coron started to make a second circle around the girls, walking with a noticeable limp, compliments of an air rifle fired from the two kids whose rabbit pen he happened to be raiding at the time.

Melena's whiskers dropped with contempt when Coron stood next to her and began his mating call. Looking over and seeing the stern gaze on Halina's face, Melena turned dejectedly and walked away with Coron.

''Halina, we must stop dating Coron.'' Mahri was the first one brave enough to speak up on the matter of the ugly stray. ''Melena's gonna be lucky to get a grasshopper tonight. And for what? We started this whole thing because we missed the fun of mating when we got the changes scar. There's no fun involved with Coron.''

The group sat nervously hushed for several moments. No one had ever dared question the mistress before, although the issue of Coron had been whispered throughout the Den for weeks.

''Dearest Mahri,'' answered Halina, ''I admire your courage for speaking up with your troubles. As you know, we have never refused a tom for any reason, as long as he could contribute fresh game of some kind. None of us need the food, for we all live with good paladins who provide well for us. But the paladin cannot provide mates for us, and since we have become scarred and no longer go into season, we must be aggressive and often take what we can get. Rejection of a single tom could instill fear in other potential clients that they too might at some time be rejected.''

Mahri sat back and looked around at the other girls. Their faces told it all. Defeat.

''In this particular case, however,'' said Halina, also scanning the group, ''I believe you are correct. Coron is bad for us in many ways, and I am sure his expulsion from our list of regulars will only please the other toms in the area. They find Coron as revolting as we do.''

''And what about Sleron the Slink?'' asked Syranosh, referring to Coron's only known friend.

''For now we will continue to deal with Master Sleron,'' answered Halina. ''Although I don't trust him fully, as none of you do, he has yet to do anything too objectionable.''

''Other than bite too hard,'' added Syranosh.

Krahstas, lynxes, and Coron were forgotten. And so was the fear; at least for now. Mahri walked with Sharlo, and things would get better.

Sharlo lived with an old female paladin in a regular house down the street from Mahri. The paladin raised Sharlo as a show cat, with remarkable results. Sharlo was a very handsome silver tabby; his strong features seemed almost chiseled. His eyes flashed bright yellow, with whiskers reaching the perfect, sexy length. His nose was deep crimson, bordered with black.

''Halina's quite a farri,'' said Sharlo, a bit nervous. They strolled toward the hedges around Sharlo's house. ''I was able to sneak out early this afternoon. I tracked her down and asked her if she would hold on to you until I could get back out tonight. You're usually gone by the time my paladin falls asleep and I can get out.''

''So that's why she told Coron I was already taken,'' Mahri said with wonder. This was the first case of a tom actually making an appointment ahead of time. "Pretty clever."

"Well, it's just been frustrating lately. Oh, I shouldn't say such things. The other girls are all very nice, but I really only come out here for you. It's disappointing because you're usually taken, so I go with whoever is there, just so they won't feel bad. But there's no doubt who my favorite is, pretty Mahri."

"How sweet," Mahri smiled, wondering about the slight hint of sadness she heard in his voice.

"Do any of the girls mate when they're not with Halina?" asked Sharlo. "I mean, can you just take it upon yourself to mate whenever you want? With whoever you want?"

"It's not so easy," Mahri said reflectively. "For some it would be impossible if not for the group. We all have the changes scar, so none of us ever go into season. Without the smell of season, it's pretty hard to attract toms."

She thought about the day her paladin had brought her back from wherever it was. She was very tired for some reason, and unsure of where she had been. Things were strange and hazy that day. But one thing was very clear; her stomach had been injured somehow, leaving a terrible scar. And she never went into season again.

"There are a couple of us who can still call the toms effectively, but some have forgotten how," said Mahri. "They only went by their feelings before, and now those feelings are gone."

"Then why do you all do this?" asked Sharlo.

"The feelings of season are gone," Mahri said, "but not the feeling of mating. Nor the memories of how nice it is. We had to band together to make the toms notice. And it's still hard, when we have to compete with the farries who do go into season. And then we get nervous because a really great tom like you comes along, and we wonder why he does. You could mate with any farri in the area."

"The ones in season turn mean after we mate," Sharlo laughed. "They just want a daddy for the kittens, and then forget it." They approached the house of Sharlo's paladin, and he smiled gently. "I have something for you," he said. "It's in the hedge."

Mahri stepped over the layer of brick surrounding the perimeter of the bushes. She smelled it first, before being able to see it behind the leaves. Fresh dove.

"Sharlo! Really? They're so hard to catch!"

"You're worth much more, pretty Mahri." He smiled.

"It's so much. Will you share it with me?"

"If you don't mind," said Sharlo, "let's share something else, first."

"I'd like that," said Mahri, closing her eyes. She felt the firm, gentle grip at the nape of her neck, followed by a warm rush all over her body.

It was going to be a wonderful night.

CHAPTER 3

Roger peered through the front door and reached for the morning paper. It was already hot; it would probably reach the low nineties by midafternoon. The cat scampered between his feet and bounded out the door, reminding him he had forgotten to feed her again.

"That's it, ya little bitch," he grumbled. "You wanna eat? Go out and hunt."

Roger watched De Lilah trot across the street and head toward the dead end. He wondered what she did with herself all day. He figured she was probably still embarrassed about the scratches on her face. He had initially been concerned when she had come home bleeding. As far as he knew, she had never lost a fight before, or had even appeared to have been in one. She was, after all, a Scottish wildcat. She had remained perfectly still while Roger cleaned her wounds with hydrogen peroxide, although now she acted as though it had never happened.

Tammy was still lounging in bed—his bed, for the second time in one week. A new record, if Roger could recall. Normally it was once at her house, once at his, and then bye-bye baby. He'd have to go in and take another look at this chick. See what the attraction was.

He walked back into the bedroom, hoping she was still too sleepy to open her eyes. He hated the way he looked in the morning, the way his hair stood straight up to a point. And he should have bought stock in Visine years ago. At age thirty-two, he feared it had only gotten worse.

"Morning, babe," Tammy groaned, rolling over.

"Hi there. Go back to sleep."

"Okay."

He glanced through the front page of the paper, scanning the most recent foreign policy blunders by the administration. Passed by the local section to check out the Padres and Dodgers in sports.

Something caught his eye, and he turned back to the local section. Something about a mountain lion.

"Jesus," he said quite loud, looking at the accompanying picture.

"Huh?" mumbled Tammy, who had dozed off again.

"There's a fucking cougar in the area."

"A what? What's a cougar, babe?"

He took a sideways glance at Tammy, then rolled his eyes.

"A mountain lion. It attacked a five-year-old boy about two blocks from here. Right on this street! He was walking with his parents right along the rim of the canyon, and a mountain lion came out of nowhere and grabbed him by the shoulder."

Tammy sat straight upright. "No. You're joking again."

"No, really. Look." He pointed at the paper, complete with photo of the victim. "Dragged him away, until the father caught up to it and started beating it with a stick. It says he had teeth marks and gashes all over his face and head, but miraculously, he's gonna be all right."

"God, how horrible," said Tammy. She leaned over and looked at the paper. There was a file picture of a mountain lion next to the article, but it was not the one who had been involved in the attack.

"I saw a bobcat once, over in the canyon by the dead end," said Roger, resting his chin in his palm.

"Is a bobcat as big as a mountain lion?" asked Tammy.

Roger rolled his eyes again. "No. A bobcat weighs about thirty pounds. A mountain lion can get close to two hundred. A mountain lion could easily eat a bobcat for lunch."

"I didn't know it was so dangerous around here," said Tammy. "Is there anything else in the canyon I should know about?"

"God knows we have enough coyotes around here,"

said Roger. "Ya can't even sleep at night when there's a full moon because they're yapping so much. But a mountain lion? Give me a break." He looked back down at the paper and began to chuckle.

"What are you laughing about?" said Tammy, rolling over to get a better look at the paper.

"It's kinda funny, in a way. Take your kid for a walk and it gets grabbed by a fucking mountain lion."

"Yeah, real funny," said Tammy, not knowing how to take Roger's remark. "How would you like it if the cougar had gotten De Lilah?"

"That little terror?" Roger laughed, forgetting about the scratch marks. "De Lilah would have kicked its ass."

CHAPTER 4

There wasn't even a breeze to fan the oppressive heat. Mahri had remained curled up under a hedge for the entire afternoon, completely unwilling to move. She was shocked to see Melena, who had braved the heat and wandered all the way down the street to where most of the girls never went, save Mahri, who lived there.

"You must be burning up with such a dark coat," said Mahri. "Get out of the sun. Here. What brings you all the way to my house?"

"Oh, just lonely," said Melena. "Well, I wanted to talk, is all. And this isn't what you can talk about with a lot of the other farries in our group. Ya know?"

"I understand," answered Mahri. "I'm worried too. About a lot of things. About Coron, and what's gonna happen tonight when he shows up and Halina tells him no."

"Yeah, and this Canyon stuff," answered Melena. "I haven't heard any of the others ever question what we're doing. Have you?"

"Like how?"

"Like is what we're doing right," said Melena, not asking a question. "We've got the changes scars for a reason. I'd always heard Lady Farri gave us these scars when our time was up, and it seems like continuing to mate is against her wishes. You'll notice we never hear from any toms who have the scars. They just stay home and keep to themselves."

Mahri rolled over on her back, looking skyward with thought.

"I've had the same concerns, before," she said. "I even brought it up to Halina."

"Really?" asked Melena. "I'm surprised. Well, I mean, you know how she is and how terrified everyone is of questioning her."

"Yeah, I wonder why? Have you ever seen her do anything nasty to one of us? No. She treats us so well. It's just the air about her, and how stern she can be. She's a good farri. I think most of us just read her wrong because she's so, well, different is the only word I can think of.

"Anyway, she said the scar is just a kind of random thing, and it sometimes hits kittens who have never mated. And some farries live long lives without ever getting it. It's not fair. And I think Lady Farri would have punished us by now if it was wrong for us to keep mating. At least, Halina thinks so."

Melena stared through the branches of the hedge and said nothing.

"There's more, isn't there?" asked Mahri, afraid of what the answer might be.

"Yes," said Melena finally. "There's more. There are other farries outside our group. Two of them approached me last night and were looking to fight. They called me names and said what we were doing was unnatural and wrong."

"Were you with a date?"

"I was, but when they showed up, he vanished. It would have been me against both of them."

"Good Farri! Who was it? He couldn't have been afraid of two females. Especially with you there to help him fight."

"No," said Melena, "that wasn't it. I think he just didn't want to be seen with me."

"Are you kidding? You're gorgeous. Most toms would love to be seen with you."

"It's not my looks," said Melena. "Or yours. It's who we are. Those farries were angry last night. Angry at us for taking their toms away from them. They said we were going against the wishes of Farri by taking toms away from breeding females."

"Oh, I get it," said Mahri. "Your date still wants to mate with breeding females too, and being seen with us might ruin his chances."

"Yes," said Melena. "It kinda hurts too. I didn't like being called names and left feeling like an outcast."

"Hey, it was just two jealous farries," said Mahri, hoping to convince herself. "Nothing to worry about. Wait till they start calling Halina names." Mahri laughed at the thought, but knew she sounded much better about the whole thing than she felt.

"They said there were others," said Melena. "Both toms and queens who were banding together to put a stop to us. Apparently there's lots of farries who think what we're doing is wrong."

"Great," mumbled Mahri. "As if we didn't have enough troubles." She thought about the night before with Sharlo, and refused to believe something so wonderful could possibly be wrong.

Reading Mahri's thoughts, Melena said, "Let's just hope Halina is as strong and clever as we think she is."

"Yes," said Mahri. "But I believe we will find her to be more so than we could ever imagine."

When Coron approached the Den, most of the farries looked away with fear, dreading the certain confrontation between the scraggly tom and Halina. Mahri too was terrified, yet stood beside her mistress and faced Coron.

"I see you have your favorite pretty baby for me tonight," said Coron. "Mahri is my favorite too, and I'll treat her fine tonight."

"No, Coron," answered Halina calmly. "You will leave here."

Passing the remark off as just a joke, Coron began to step forward, and was greeted by a fierce shriek. His eyes fixed on Mahri, who was wildly fluffed and in combat stance, hissing and baring teeth.

"So, the little queen doesn't like me anymore," Coron laughed. "I think we can fix that."

Forgetting all about Halina, he fluffed up and walked toward Mahri. He expected the smaller farri to bolt immediately, giving him liberty to chase her down and have his way.

"I said you will leave here." Halina was right in Coron's face, having leaped between the tom and Mahri.

Mahri continued to stay fluffed and hissed again, trying to show aggression and not fear. She was amazed at how calm Halina was during all this; she had not yet raised a single hair.

"I came here for your services, mistress," said Coron, emphasizing the "mistress" with a sneer. "I don't wish to shred the whole lot of you to bits."

"You are no longer welcome here, Coron," said Halina. "You are filthy and foul smelling and offensive to my farries. You will leave this street and not return."

Coron was visibly angry at Halina's insults, stepping forward with the beginnings of a deep, throaty growl. "I'll go where I—"

Halina's claws reached Coron's cheek with invisible speed, leaving the stray gashed and awkwardly off balance. The follow-up bite to the chin pushed him reeling back, searching for secure footing. Regaining his balance, he instantly turned back toward the attacker, expecting another assault. He saw Halina standing calmly in her original space. Calmly and fluffed.

Fully alert now, Coron was ready to strike. Ignoring the rumors of Halina's strength and cunning, he began one of his most successful fighting maneuvers. Despite her unnerving stare, Halina was just a female and would be no match for *him*.

Suddenly he pounced. Airborne and claws opening, he was stunned by impact way short of his intended striking point. Halina had guessed his move. Meeting him halfway, she scored more flesh. Coron missed.

He landed square, and faced Halina directly. The wounds on his face were open and bleeding, he knew, yet he remained completely intent on Halina. He hadn't even decided on his next move when he felt the teeth sinking deep into his flank. He had forgotten about Mahri.

Coron turned quickly but Halina was already there to assist and the old stray had no other choice but to bolt. He made it across the street in three hurried strides and stopped when he realized the others were not giving chase.

"Okay, mistress," said Coron. "You and your group of trash cats can push me away tonight. But beware! You are not always a group. And not all of your little trash farries can fight like you. They will each suffer for your mistake."

"If you come back, you will die," said Halina simply, and watched Coron slink away in the night.

CHAPTER 5

Most of the other toms in the area either heard the scuffle or somehow sensed a problem. The night was very quiet after the departure of Coron, and a quiet night was usually the result of trouble. Only two toms showed up requesting dates, leaving most of Halina's farries to sit and gossip. A few voiced concerns about how Coron's expulsion would affect business.

It was not too long before Halina dismissed the farries and began walking home. Mahri walked along beside the mistress and Melena. Halina's house was the closest to the Den, and they reached the driveway without speaking.

"You two have questions," Halina said, sitting down on the pavement. It was fairly early and her paladin was not yet home.

"Not really," answered Melena. "We all wanted Coron chased away."

"Not about Coron," said Halina. "You both have had questions in your eyes recently, about other things, I guess."

The two other farries sat silently for a moment, and then Mahri spoke. "We've had concerns about what we're doing," she said gravely. 'We've heard nasty things from other farries, who say what we're doing is wrong. They say it's wrong for farries with the scar to mate, and especially wrong for any farri to demand food for the privilege."

"Only female farries without the scar would say such things," answered Halina. "They can mate constantly when they're in season, so what do they know? They aren't aware of the pain involved when a handsome tom just passes you by without even looking, or the pain of not ever having.''

Mahri was surprised to see Halina's unusual openness. Halina was always one to think and reason before divulging any feelings.

"Yes, they talk about us," said Halina sadly. "They are forming a group to put pressure on us to stop. They want enough farries, both female and male, to be able to constantly harass and scatter our Den, making it impossible for us to mate. They say it's because we are going against nature and disgracing Lady Farri. But those are lies, thinly veiling the truth.''

Halina could see the puzzlement in the eyes of Mahri and Melena. Most farries never lied. It would not occur to them to do so. Only in rare cases did a rotten one like Coron change the truth. Discovering a conspiracy by several well-kept farries was unbelievable.

"We are honest in what we do," said Halina. "We only want the attention of the toms like all other queens. But they will put pressure on the toms to avoid us.''

"I know," said Melena. "It's happened to me already.''

"I can see you two love the toms as much as I," continued Halina. "And I know you two are loyal to me. I think we will all need to be loyal in the future. And for a lot of reasons.''

Mahri could sense a sudden change in Halina. She had seemed sad through most of her words, which was very uncharacteristic. But now she was back to normal, speaking through wisdom instead of emotion.

"We have many problems far more serious than jealous farries," said Halina. "Indeed, we must all start fearing for our lives." She paused a moment to let her words sink in.

"As I told the group," she continued, "the krahstas are about and getting more daring. The obvious validation is the one who stormed our Den the other night. I fear it is only weeks, possibly days, before he will convince his brothers to come with him. If not this coming full moon, then certainly the following. It will depend on how well they eat in the Canyon.

"In addition, we have the two lynxes in the area to fear. Although they are distant cousins, I don't think they would hesitate to eat farri. When you're hungry, you'll eat anything.

"Coron is another of our fears. Yes, my dears, we hurt him badly tonight, and he will certainly not approach our Den in the future. But we must take stock in his words. We are not always together, and although he would not dare face me again, I fear there is no other farri in our group who could match him alone in a fight."

Mahri thought about Coron and how helpless she would be should he strike. She shuddered at the thought, and winced when picturing the possible results. She wanted to gag just thinking about his breath.

"There is also the unknown terror I told you about," said Halina. "Something ferocious beyond words, and I'm not just saying this to scare you. Truly, every contact I made in the Canyon would not even name the beast, let alone speak of it."

Mahri had a feeling all of this was leading up to something, and something very strange. She looked at Melena, who appeared nervous, and back to Halina, who seemed almost hesitant.

"This is not to be discussed with the others," said Halina finally. "I'm going back into the Canyon tomorrow. Something, I don't know, I just have this feeling. Something tells me it's in our best interest to find out what it is in the Canyon."

"Why?" asked Mahri. "And what could be so bad? It can't be much worse than a lynx or a pack of krahstas."

"The pack of krahstas may be no match for this beast," Halina said flatly.

"You don't even know what it is," said Melena.

"I'm going to find out," said Halina. "And this is a lot to ask, and I'll understand if you refuse. I want you both to go with me tomorrow. I'll be all right on my own, but if you go with me, I won't have any questions to answer when I get back."

"I'd love to go," said Mahri, who felt secure when Halina was around, no matter what. She honestly believed her mistress could handle anything in the Canyon.

"I'll go too," said Melena a bit nervously. Melena had mixed feelings about going, but did not want to be left out.

The three farries scampered off the pavement when the huge car of Halina's paladin roared into the driveway.

"Tomorrow morning," said Halina, and scampered toward the door.

Mahri stretched and watched the sparkles of morning light stream through the window. The youngest paladin's room faced the sunrise, and Mahri always stood on the pillow next to the young girl's head and watched the soft light sprinkle through the trees on mornings when the curtains had been left open.

Of the three paladins Mahri lived with, the youngest was by far her favorite. Mahri was unsure if the girl's name was Sandra or Sweetie Pie, so often was she called both by her parents. And it was the parents who originally began calling Mahri "Blazer," in the early days before Sandra was able to talk.

Mahri really enjoyed being with Sandra. She was playful, yet gentle enough, and loved Mahri with a passion. And she always offered a warm and cuddly bed, unlike the parents, who tossed Mahri out of their room instantly when the lights went down, following her with a closed door.

Sandra rolled over the slightest bit, momentarily interrupting the soft, fluid pattern of her breath. Mahri glanced at the girl and then began to groom. She began with her left side, bathing the countless strands of remarkably long hair. It was quite an inconvenience, being as thick as it was, but Mahri was glad to have it and quite proud at how nice she was able to keep it and how the toms often mentioned how good she always looked.

The noise in the kitchen told her that Daddy was about ready to leave, as he usually did this time of the morning. He would let her out, so she could meet up with Halina and Melena and go on about their search of the Canyon.

Mahri trotted into the living room, where Daddy was standing, staring at the papers he stared at every morning. She rubbed up against his leg, and he bent down to scratch behind her ears, an affection he would only display when Mommy and Sandra were sleeping. He patted her on the bottom, then stood back up.

The door opened and she stepped outside, instantly struck by the heat of the morning. It was already in the low eighties, and Mahri hoped Halina and Melena would both be ready early so they could head out before Brother Sun got too fierce.

Melena was at the Den when Mahri arrived, and it was only minutes before Halina showed. They walked over to the edge of the brush where the street ended and stepped into a world Mahri had never seen.

There was life and noises everywhere! Insects, lizards. Things they couldn't see. Smells far more intense than the usual drafts of the streets and houses. Every sense was at its peak, absorbing more than Mahri thought possible. She was torn between watching where to place her feet on this wildly uncertain terrain, and watching the brush and the sights and things that might be there if she looked hard enough.

Mahri followed Halina's lead. The mistress was marching forward with a determined pace, and Mahri hoped she would remember where the houses were. Until they walked into an open grassy area, the entire trip had been over narrow paths through brush.

"This is fun," said Melena, smiling. After trailing Mahri through the brush, she now stepped beside her and walked briskly.

"Let's find some shade and sit for a while," said Halina absently. "I think we're in the right area. We just need to do some watching."

There was plenty of shade around, although it was not as protective as it might have been. The Canyon was brown. The hot temperature and dry air had decimated the lush foliage and made it crumbly and hard.

The three farries found a large hunk of sage and stretched out on their bellies in its shade. They remained still for several moments, taking in the vastness of the Canyon with all their senses.

"Do we know what we're looking for?" asked Mahri. Her hunch was Halina knew exactly what they were searching for.

"We're looking for everything, my dear Mahri," answered Halina. "And nothing."

Mahri looked at Melena and received the same questioning look.

"But Halina," said Melena, "what will nothing tell us? And how will we know what nothing is?"

"Nothing is everything we've seen so far," answered Halina, looking at the sky. "When I was here the other day, there were fresh signs of many animals. There were birds in every tree and bush. Something is truly amiss, for today we have seen nothing."

Mahri reflected on Halina's words and continued to look around. It had not occurred to her earlier to check for something missing. She had noticed the insects and lizards, but nothing of substantial size. Nothing a true predator might be interested in.

"Well, *we're* here," said Melena, a bit uneasy.

"Yes," said Halina, and became quiet.

The three farries began to relax after nearly an hour in the shade. The heat still pounded away at the Canyon, making even the small shelter of the sage a rough stay. The lack of any breeze added to the swelter.

Mahri began to doubt the wisdom of the trip. Not just because of their suffering—and she had it the worst with her long and thick fur. But if the sun was affecting them in such a way, so would it affect all other creatures of the Canyon. And since they would be hiding in cool places as well, spotting any other wildlife would become less likely as time went on.

"I've been thinking about your questions," said Halina finally, after watching a hawk for some time. "The questions about what our group does, and if it's right." She sat pensively for a moment, and Mahri knew she would choose her words very carefully.

"As most of us reflect the paladin we live with," said Halina, "so often do I try to reflect mine. Of course, there are many things the paladins do that we don't really understand. It's pretty clear, though, how they're feeling, and what sort of mood they're in.

"My paladin does not live with a mate, as both of you live with paladins who do. But no, my paladin does not go without, as we did before our group formed. Indeed, he brings home different females constantly. So many different females, I have lost count. Not every night, but quite often.''

Halina shifted to lie on her left side, and fiercely licked her right side for a moment. Mahri smiled inwardly at Halina, whose fur was half the length of her own, yet bathed at least twice as much. Mahri knew of no other cat in the world who groomed herself with such frequency.

''I think what's interesting about my paladin,'' said Halina, looking back toward the ever-circling hawk, ''is how he feels about the females he mates with.''

''What do you mean?'' asked Melena. ''Surely he must like them or he wouldn't mate with them.''

''Well, you'd think so,'' said Halina. ''But *we've* sometimes mated with toms who weren't our favorites, which is why we started our group. We missed mating so much.''

''So you think he may be with a group like ours?'' asked Mahri, thinking about how scums like Coron made Halina's remark about mating with nonfavorites a gross understatement. ''Maybe a group of paladin males who have some kind of scar like ours? But males don't go into season, do they?''

''No, but good Farri! The way the female paladins smell when *they* go into season,'' said Halina, looking absolutely disgusted. ''They smell a lot like vinegar, or something really unpleasant. I don't know what could possibly be so attractive to the males, but they must like it, because my paladin sticks his nose in it so much.''

All three farries made a brief grimace, and then broke into giggles. The paladins did such strange things.

''How can you tell if Roger likes his mate or not?'' asked Melena.

''Oh, you know,'' said Halina. ''I can usually tell if he's happy or not. And just by comparing how he acts with them while they mate, and how he treats them in general.''

''Paladins mate for a lot longer than we do. No wonder some of the females howl so much. They sound like fighting toms. But not all. Some are real quiet and don't make much noise. I think Roger generally likes these mates a little better. Although sometimes you never know, because there's no way to be positive about what they're really saying.''

A breeze, ever so slight, began to stir the brush throughout the Canyon, and the farries raised their noses instinctively to taste it.

"There's this one female who comes over every now and then," said Halina. "She is truly a special creature on this earth. There is something very magnetic about her. I run to her whenever I see her, and I even let her hold me. She radiates an energy I have never before felt. Roger likes her the best of all. He really likes her. But it's curious because he never touches her. They've never mated.''

Suddenly Mahri felt a strange tingle creeping up her spine, and she saw the fur on her arms begin to rise. It was rising all over, she could feel it, but had no idea of the cause. Her face was tightening and she felt a hiss beginning to swell in her throat. There was no scent or sound of anything threatening, and nothing in sight. Yet involuntarily she was on her feet and completely fluffed. Her two friends were the same way.

Melena began to growl in a tone never before heard by Mahri or Halina. Mahri's claws were fully extended, and she quaked all over. But still, nothing.

The three farries cautiously began to move their tail ends together, for protection from all sides. Then the smell. Wild and primitive and ferociously ruthless beyond words, it shook the three farries to the deepest caverns of their souls.

"Three of my pretty little cousins," came the voice from the brush. "How pretty they are with all of those different colors.''

The exotic and smooth-flowing accent made the voice sound almost sensuous, so savage and yet remarkably peaceful.

"Puma," said Halina hoarsely, speaking the universal name. She stood between Mahri and Melena, and watched with horror as the brush began to move and out stepped a full-grown mountain lion.

CHAPTER 6

The newspaper offices were fairly close to Roger's house, allowing him the luxury of a lunch break at home on most days. He would slap some cold cuts on plain bread and sit with the stereo, taking time to check the mail and see which new and exciting mailing lists had discovered his existence.

Roger sold advertising space. He had some good accounts for a not so good paper. Well, it was okay, if you were into community rags. The *Los Angeles Times* or *San Diego Union* it was not. Readers didn't even have to pay for it. The *Courier* was one of those on-your-driveway-once-a-week-like-it-or-not papers. It was even dumped on Roger's driveway, before he, like most of his neighbors, dumped it into the trash. But it paid the bills, and someday it might be a stepping-stone to better things. So for now, Roger was content.

He sat back, munched on a particularly tasteless sandwich, and absently wondered where the cat was. On hot days, she usually lounged around under the hedge at the side of the house. Although normally she would slowly stroll out to greet his T-bird, today she had failed to make an appearance. Roger figured she had probably finagled her way into someone's air-conditioned living room.

When the doorbell rang, Roger was certain it was a salesman of some kind, or somebody collecting for God only knew what charity. He normally ignored the bell in the middle of the day, pretending to be out, especially if he wasn't expecting someone. But today he had left the front door open, and he could hear a man's voice coming through the screen.

"Good day to ya," boomed a man with a huge Texas cowboy hat. He looked far too casual for a salesman, although the heat had reduced everyone to short sleeves and open collars.

"Jerry Radcliff," the man said. "I'm your neighbor from down the street."

"Oh, hi. Roger Anderson." He leaned up against the doorframe and watched the man named Jerry Radcliff take off his hat and wipe the brow of an incredibly high forehead. Guessing the man's age at about thirty-five, Roger could see why he wore a hat. What little hair he had was very light brown. His piercing blue eyes sat deep inside his rugged, yet almost cold-looking features.

"I'd like to talk to ya for a few moments, if ya don't mind," said Radcliff, motioning as though he would like to come in.

"Oh, sure," said Roger, opening the door and already regretting it.

"Nice place," Radcliff said, taking the polite look around the living room. "Live here with your wife?"

"I live here alone." Roger noted the surprise the revelation customarily brought. A typical bachelor pad this was not. Roger's house was immaculate.

"Well, I'm impressed," said Radcliff, his eyebrows reaching well up into his lengthy forehead. Then his face instantly became pinched, and he looked sideways at Roger with almost slanted eyes. "You spend all your time takin' care a' this place all by yourself," he said, not a question, but almost an accusation.

"A maid," said Roger flatly. "Twice a week. Now Mr. Radcliff, what can I do for you today?"

"Jerry. Please." He seemed to relax at the news of a maid.

"Okay. Jerry. What can I do you for?" Getting a little irritated, Roger mentally played his little game of matching people with a stereotype of the opposite sex. The woman falling for Jerry Radcliff would have to be an insecure romantic, a woman with no brains who craved complete domination.

"Maybe you've heard," said Radcliff, going back to his pinched-up-sideways glance when he saw Roger smiling.

"Sorry," said Roger, immediately conjuring up a quick lie. "I was just thinking about my cat and how I was about to give her a cold shower just before you got here."

Radcliff leaned back in his chair and folded his hands. His eyes were quite wide as he assessed Roger, who was correct in assuming this guy thought he was a fruit cake.

"Well," said Radcliff very carefully, "y'all are very lucky to even have a cat right now."

Roger sat further back on the couch, resting his chin in the palm of his left hand.

"Maybe you've heard. Maybe not," Radcliff continued. "No one woulda dreamed such a thing. At first, we thought it was the coyotes. Them damn things is all over the canyon. Dogs turnin' up missing. A few cats here and there.

"Now, I guess some of them just might have been grabbed by a coyote or two. But there was a mean-ass Doberman, and partner, I mean *mean,* just up and disappeared. Well, not exactly. We could see something big had been killed and drug off. We just figured it was old Brutus."

Radcliff shifted a little and his eyes trailed out the door. Roger was certain old Brutus had belonged to Jerry Radcliff. He also had an idea of what all this was leading up to.

"Then it happened," said Radcliff suddenly. "Charlie Blake was with his wife and boy out in the canyon behind their house, and damn if a fucking cougar didn't come right out of the brush and grab little Kenny. Right in broad daylight! The kid was only ten feet from both his parents, and they were right there behind their own yard!"

Radcliff was taking deep breaths and looking out the door again. He shook his head, his eyes staying fixed on an object out of Roger's line of vision.

"I read about it in the paper," said Roger quietly. "Even our paper had a big write-up about it."

Radcliff looked back at Roger and nodded upwards, asking a question.

"I work for the *Courier*," answered Roger.

"Oh, good Christ," said Radcliff. "A neyooz man."

"I sell advertising," said Roger, trying not to look offended but failing miserably. What the hell, he thought, I should be offended.

"Only thing worse than a newsman is an attorney," said Radcliff. "But just barely. And I mean, just barely. And that's rock bottom."

"Well, I don't work in the news department," said Roger, wondering why he was even pursuing this, and not throwing Radcliff out on his ear.

"Don't matter. All the same."

"Look, Mr. Radcliff," said Roger. "My lunch break is about up, and I have to get back to the office." He held his palms up, asking if there was anything else.

"Why I came by is," said Radcliff, oblivious to Roger's impatience, "we're gettin' us a group together to try and trap this damn thing or shoot it down."

"Here," said Roger. "Here's my card and I'll write my home number on it. Write down your number for me, and I'll be in touch."

Radcliff instantly handed Roger a scrap of paper, which already had a name, address, and phone number scribbled on it. Roger glanced down at the paper and wondered if this had been some kind of setup.

CHAPTER 7

Mahri and Melena had each taken a cautious step back, but both were too terrified to move any farther. Halina stood her ground, but Mahri knew this time the fight would be futile. Courage was wonderful, but Halina was gonna die. So too, probably, would she.

The puma took a step forward and Halina howled. Mahri felt the growl in her own throat as well, although it was not really voluntary. Mahri was on complete instinct control.

"Such a welcome," said the puma, her sexy voice making Mahri start to feel delirious. The huge cat stepped closer to the farries and crouched down all the way to her forepaws.

"We will not be your lunch, puma," said Halina calmly.

"I should hope not," laughed the cougar. "You little girls are taking me all wrong. If it was food I wanted, the three of you would have been swallowed an hour ago."

"And shall we believe you?" asked Halina. "In a Canyon struck by lack of prey?"

"Really, pretty ones, relax. I wish only to talk, and it is so rare to see the little farries about. I've always been amazed at how many colors you have, and how different you all look from each other. The cats of my line all look the same."

Mahri began to regain control of her system. She wanted to believe there was no danger, but her body still quaked all the way down to her extended claws. That incredible smell and the wild, sultry voice were beyond anything she had ever thought to comprehend. She knew Melena was feeling the same, but somehow Halina was unaffected by either the smell or the voice. Halina was even starting to sit down!

"You are not like them at all," the puma said to Halina. "I would say you belong out here in the Canyon more than with the men. Although I envy your ability to adapt. You line is wild, is is not?"

"Yes it is," said Halina. "At least, I believe it to be so. I have lived with a paladin as long as I can remember, yet I know how different I am from the other farries, and there are strange callings within me at times."

"I believe it to be so as well," said the puma. "And that is a compliment. I have never seen another of your kind, but you have the grace and beauty of a wildcat, like maybe a smaller lynx. And you have not the fear of your friends, who are still fluffed and unable to speak." She smiled very affectionately and looked at Mahri and Melena. "Oh forgive my rudeness, please," said the puma. "I am Sarena, of the line of Shoasha."

"I am Halina, and this is Mahri and Melena."

"Mahri. And look at her fur! It's so long and beautiful! Lady Farri blessed you well, dear one. She gave my line such short hair, to keep us from tangling in the brush. And only one color to hide us. But you, dear Mahri, have many colors of such long locks."

Sarena walked passed Halina to the other farries, both of whom still trembled slightly, although lowering their fur. "Look at you," she said to Melena. "A baby black panther! I've heard of our cousins abroad who are black as night, but none can match you, I would dare to say. Listen, dears, I won't bite. Relax here like your friend, Halina."

And Mahri *was* beginning to relax. She eyed the cougar carefully, noticing her calm, how she gave off none of the early-warning signals one associated with a strike. She also noted the tone of Sarena's voice. It was sincere, not condescending, nor did it hold any malice. Sarena just appeared to be a really nice cat. Make that a really nice *mountain lion*.

Suddenly Sarena turned and Mahri was struck with a huge tongue, raking across her side. She jumped sideways, her best strike airborne with lightning speed, fully clawed. Nothing. The huge cat was out of the way before the blow was halfway there.

Sarena literally roared with laughter. "Just checking out how you taste, little kitten," she laughed, giving Mahri a wink. All three farries were on their feet, but none knew what to say or do. All Sarena had done was give Mahri a harmless lick.

"I should have warned you, kitten," said Sarena. "But I was afraid you might refuse. I wanted merely to see how it would feel to groom such locks as yours. It must be quite a chore every day!"

"I get by," choked Mahri, speaking for the first time, completely out of breath. Quite unnerving to be groomed by a tongue half the size of your entire body.

Sarena went flat on the ground and rolled over on her back.

"Okay, dears, you win," she giggled. "Just make it painless."

This finally brought laughter to the farries. They all exchanged looks and somehow knew everything was fine. Sarena was smiling, and purring with a louder rumble than Mahri thought possible, even from a puma.

"This part of the Canyon is certainly peculiar," said Sarena to the sky. "I'm here only two days and I see such strange things, capped off by three wandering farries."

"Two days?" asked Halina, suddenly becoming more alert.

Sarena rolled over to her stomach. "Yes. Just two days."

"I came here a week ago on my own," said Halina. "I did not see you then, nor did I speak with anyone who had. But there were certainly rumors of your presence."

Sarena's face fell instantly from humor. She looked hard at Halina, and then to the ground. "No," she said, "you heard nothing of me. I've moved many miles in search of this home, and have been here since the day before yesterday. This is my third day.

"But lo, the rumors. I know of them and I heard them too. Terrible things. Atrocities of unspeakable horror. And so it was when I arrived here. I found it to be true."

She was quiet and motionless for a few moments, thoughtful. Mahri could sense a wisdom about Sarena, a wisdom besting even Halina, who was the smartest animal she had ever known.

"You have met in your lives," said Sarena, "farries worthy of your affection because they are good. There are others you avoid, because they are not so. They can be bad enough to make life miserable for you and others like you. But on the true scale of life, and I know this sounds cold, your bad farries are insignificant.

"As with you sweet kitten farries, there are good pumas and bad pumas. But unlike our little cousins, when a puma is bad, it is very significant. Alas it is so. When I arrived here, it was a bad puma who had stricken terror in the land." Sarena jumped up and began to pace with a frenzy. The news forthcoming, if to be delivered at all, was obviously very upsetting to the cougar.

"Kill, kill, kill!" said Sarena, gritting her teeth. "That's all I heard, and was shocked to find it so. Sasho was his name and he killed for no reason. Oh, he killed for food, which is justifiable and necessary in the cycles of life. But it's so! He killed for power. Or something. I just don't know. He may have the beginnings of the insanity disease, and if this is so, Lady Farri, it is very bad indeed."

She stopped pacing and threw herself on the ground, and Mahri thought the cougar was about to cry.

"Very bad," continued Sarena, regaining her composure. "It might be too terrible as it is. The biggest horror I heard was from our cousins, a pair of lynxes. It was they who told of Sasho's attack on a man."

The farries all became wide-eyed, and wondered if it was a paladin of a farri they knew. Then they began to realize the implications.

"It was not an adult man," said Sarena, "but a little one. A little one, which is worse. And right in front of his parents, so they *know* it was a puma. The adult male beat Sasho off with a stick or else the young man would also be dead.

"I fear the worst. I have no love for men. But nor do I hold hate. They are there and so are we, and therefore we must each find a place to live. I have never encountered a man, so I have no grudge. I do fear them, though, and I fear how they might strike back not just at the bad cougar, but possibly at any predator they may see. Sadly, it is their way."

"Where's Sasho now?" asked Halina.

"I don't know," said Sarena. "But for a time, I believe he is gone. It was with the two lynxes I confronted him. His eyes were wild, and I fear he will never love me, yet he dared not confront me. Alone, I am a formidable opponent for any puma, and together with our cousins, Sasho knew he was no match. So he fled, and is gone. Where? How long? I have no answers. Had you met him today, instead of me . . . Well, you know the answer to that, now."

Mahri was starting to feel edgy again, and Halina did not look happy at all. Mahri, for the first time, was wondering why they had come into the Canyon. Halina had never really been clear. She had just said there would be answers. Well yes, but to what?

"We came to the Canyon today, seeking help," said Halina, as if reading Mahri's thoughts.

"You came *here* looking for help?" asked Sarena. "Lady Farri save us! The day gets stranger yet!"

"I had even hoped to get word of you," said Halina, "although I didn't know you were here. I think we may have been looking for Sasho."

"Sasho!" cried Mahri. "You would lead us to a mad mountain lion?"

"I did not know our danger," said Halina sadly. "I wanted to find someone who could help us, and I was hoping, betting on running into someone like Sarena. Luck is with us today."

"So it's a service you seek?" Sarena laughed. "And how may a puma help farries?" She looked skyward and shook her head. "The day gets weirder, Lady Farri."

"We came for news of a pack of krahstas in the Canyon," said Halina. "One of them has attacked our group already, and we fear others may follow if food gets thin in the Canyon." She looked at Sarena hopefully and added, "We were also looking for someone to help keep them away."

"Oh, Lady Farri, now I have heard everything! And I am such a young puma too!" Sarena laughed and laughed and shook her head in amazement. "Fight off a pack of krahstas for a group of farries who live in the man settlement!" She turned over onto her back and rolled in the dirt. An accidental swing of the tail caught Melena on the side and knocked her complètely over, causing the cougar to laugh even more.

"You three kittens need to go back now," said Sarena finally, becoming serious all of a sudden. "It will be too hot to travel, soon, and you don't want to be caught in the Canyon in the evening."

The three farries were stunned at the quick change in Sarena. Mahri looked at Halina and could never recall the mistress ever looking dejected before. And Mahri knew that she too looked the same way.

"Really, you must go now," said Sarena, giving them a warm smile. "I'll have a little chat with your krahsta friends. I'll suggest they find a new haunt, and leave my dear farries in peace.

"In fact," she added as an afterthought, "I'll bring along my new friends, those two lynxes who live on the other hill. My presence alone would be enough to shake up the krahstas, but with the other two, why, we'll just scare the fur right off of them. You will see no more krahstas."

CHAPTER 8

It was one of those client calls Roger got frequently. Nothing to buy or sell; no layout schedules to discuss. Just a checkup call to see if all was well and running smoothly. These were usually the best, because all Roger had to do was be nice; the client just wanted reassurance.

But Roger was preoccupied today. He fingered the card on his desk, the one given him by Jerry Radcliff only an hour earlier. Roger finished the courtesy call and looked harder at the card. Putting both elbows on his desk, he put his chin in his palms and looked up at the wall.

Roger's great success in selling ads was based upon how well he could read the client. There were things unseen and unsaid that Roger picked up, a gift that left even his closest friends baffled. They often chided him about having ESP.

Whatever it was, it was always there, and it always left him with a definite feeling. He looked back at the card and decided something was very wrong. It wasn't the arrogance, or lack of tact, or anything he could really put a finger on. In fact, all of those traits were normal in his business. Salesmen and agents were the most obnoxious people in the world, and yet he never had a feeling like this.

He picked up the phone and called the newsroom's in-house number. "City desk," came the woman's voice on the other end.

"I'd like to speak to the most gorgeous girl in the world," said Roger, his tone serious.

"You'll have to be more specific," said the woman. "I don't know who you're talking about."

"Why you, of course," said Roger, sounding exasperated.

"Goon!" shouted the woman, and then broke into laughter. It was Laura Kay, the city editor, and Roger's only friend in the news department. "Hi, you. Whaddaya want now?"

"The same as always," said Roger. "Just to spend every waking moment with you."

"Yeah, right. You say that to all the girls."

"So what?" said Roger seriously. "You know I only mean it with you."

Laura answered with a raspberry, and then another laugh.

"I was wondering if you could find something out for me," said Roger.

"Uh-huh. Who is she?"

"Jerry Radcliff," said Roger.

"Who?"

"This guy dropped by my place a little while ago," said Roger. "Says he wants to get a hunting party together to track down the cougar by my house."

"The one who attacked the little boy?" asked Laura.

"Yeah."

"Great! Let me know when it is. We'll send a reporter and photographer. Can you find out for me by tomorrow?"

"Okay. About this guy, though. Jerry Radcliff. He gave me the creeps. He apparently lives up the street from me, at 3412. I'd just like to know if he's for real before I get involved with a bunch of rednecks carrying rifles."

"Jerry?"

"Radcliff. R-A-D-C-L-I-F-F."

"Does he own the house he lives in?" asked Laura.

"I have no idea. But I'm sure he does. Most people do in my neighborhood."

"What am I checking for?"

"I don't know. Maybe nothing."

"Well, anything for you, babe," said Laura.

"Sure. You say that to all the guys."

"That's true. Gotta run. Bye."

The line clicked and Roger held the phone by his ear for several moments more, gritting his teeth all the while. He set the phone back down and smiled sadly, shaking his head. Once again, for the millionth time, he silently wished Laura Kay really would do anything for him.

CHAPTER 9

Halina was usually the last of the farries to leave the Den for a date. The local toms were often intimidated by her strength and wisdom, and would ask her to mate only when all other queens were gone. This was not too upsetting, since Halina understood the macho factor involved with toms who wanted weak mates. But it never really mattered, because there were always more than enough dates for her entire group, including herself.

Things were beginning to change.

It might have been the expulsion of Coron, but Mahri had her doubts. After all, Sleron, the sleazy friend of Coron, had shown up two of the three nights since the big showdown.

Mahri thought about the heat, and then quickly ruled it out. If *she* was still willing, the toms, who were usually twice as frisky as any queen, should be too.

Then, sadly, she thought about the farries who were grouping together as her foes. The jealous ones who did not like scarred queens stealing healthy toms. It was only three days since the first whispers, but three days was a long time for cats, who by nature acted quickly.

Fewer toms were showing up each night. And Halina was being asked for first, rather than last. Even Sharlo, Mahri's favorite, arrived early and asked for the mistress. When pressed by the other girls, she would neither elaborate nor speculate.

When Sharde arrived and asked for Mahri, her spirits lifted and they strolled off together. Sharde was a slender Siamese with a light brown face and rich blue eyes. Mahri thought he was attractive enough because he was generally playful and clean. As far as appearance, though, she was never sure if Siamese were good looking or not. She always thought they all tended to look the same.

"So quiet tonight, Sharde," said Mahri. "Are you nervous? Or is something wrong at home?"

The two farries walked along the sidewalk away from the Canyon, and Sharde stopped and sat down. He looked around for a few moments and then looked at Mahri.

"Well, I needed to talk to Halina tonight," he said, "but she was already gone. These are strange days."

"Yes. Strange indeed." Mahri tried to hold back the smile, remembering how strange it was for Sarena the cougar. By order of Halina, they had not mentioned the incident to anyone.

"You know," said Sharde, "I'd be real careful if I were you. There are farries around here who are openly threatening to harm your group. They're even threatening the toms who come over to mate with you."

"I've been hearing that for almost a week," said Mahri. "So far, though, I haven't seen a thing."

"I'll bet the number of toms who come to see you is getting less," said Sharde.

Mahri did not answer. She was frozen, sensing the presence of another farri. Sharde too stood up and looked around. Then Mahri got the smell. It was female, but she couldn't place it.

Suddenly there was a farri on each side of them, and one behind. Mahri and Sharde turned instantly and took a step back from the three farries, all female. Mahri had never seen any of them before.

"So, Sharde!" said the one on the left. "You mate with the trash cats." The loathing poured from her voice.

"I came only to warn them of you," said Sharde. "I thought they might give up if I told them the truth."

Mahri surveyed the odds. Three queens against herself and a tom who was trying to weasel out of even knowing her. She could not make it back to the Den, because it was on the other side of the three enemies. And even getting there would prove useless if the other farries had all gotten dates by now.

"You're being warned, all right," the middle farri was saying. "Both of you. But you in particular, trash cat," she said to Mahri. "We will hurt you all if you continue to defy Lady Farri and mate with the changes scar."

"Did Lady Farri tell you personally it was wrong for us to mate?" asked Mahri, starting to get angry and show it. The fur was rising all over.

"How dare you even question the Lady!" said the middle farri.

"I'm not, you stupid queen," said Mahri. "I'm questioning you. Since when does Lady Farri confide in the likes of you as to what's right and what's wrong? You're so . . ."

It was almost too late. Barks from the oncoming German shepherd scattered the group of farries. Mahri, seeing the immense and noisy kriba going directly for Sharde, turned hard and bolted for home. Sharde would make it up a tree and distract the monster, she was sure.

But still she felt pursuit. She dared not look back, so fast was she running, but she knew it was soft feet behind her, not the noisy and clumsy clatter of the kriba. It would be one of the three queens. She hoped it was only one.

Mahri ran hard, passing the last two houses before her own. When she got to the porch, she would turn and fight, and, she hoped, have a chance. She did. It was one queen, fluffy like herself, yet fairly unkempt.

On her home turf now, Mahri had the advantage. Even if things started going awry, enough noise would bring out one of her paladins, and the battle would be over. She hoped.

The other farri was fur-fluffed and growling, yet did not advance. Mahri's position on her own porch was a possible deterrent, but she sensed her opponent was not really geared to fight. The odds were no longer in her favor.

"Will I hear more threats now," said Mahri confidently, not asking a question.

"Beware, young farri," said the queen. "Our numbers grow every day, and your numbers will lessen. We will not stand by while Lady Farri is disgraced."

Mahri looked over the other cat, who stood fast on the

lawn and had still not moved. She wondered what Halina would say in a situation like this, and did her best to imitate the mistress.

"The only disgrace here is your jealousy," said Mahri. "And your attempts to speak for the Great Queen of our line. Leave here, or face a fight like you could never imagine."

The other farri hissed and took a step forward. Mahri, having felt confident and pleased with her performance, began to tense up and shifted her weight. Suddenly the door behind her opened up and a paladin voice boomed out.

"Blazer!"

Mahri watched the other cat scamper away. Confident the intruder was gone, she turned to the door and headed in for dinner.

Sandra was in the living room waiting with open arms. It was okay. Mahri's nerves were on edge and a little comforting was certainly in order. The young girl lifted Mahri and gave her a big hug, then put her back on the floor and began patting her back. Mahri responded by rubbing her head against the girl's arm.

"C'mon, sweetie pie," said Mommy. "Let's let the kitty have supper."

"Okay, Mommy. C'mon, Blazer!"

The sound of the package tearing open brought the cat to the kitchen in a hurry. Mommy was pouring Tender Vittles into the bowl while Daddy made a quick glance from behind the newspaper.

"Damn cat does nothing but eat and shit," grumbled Daddy, burying his face back in the paper.

Mommy ignored the remark and set the bowl down in its usual place, giving the cat a long stroke across her back. She loved Blazer, especially for how well the cat dealt with Sandra. She was sweet-tempered and affectionate, and patient beyond belief. An awkward three-year-old was by no means a master at handling a pet, but Blazer would purr off the rough handling and come back for more.

"Good kitty," she said. "Don't listen to that old grouch."

Mahri knew the "good kitty" had something to do with food, because Mommy said it every evening when she put down the dinner. Everything else sounded like the normal paladin talk, which could mean just about anything.

She looked at the food and sat down next to it for a moment. She was still a little shaky after the run-in with the three angry farries, and the standoff at the door after an attack by a German shepherd. All of this robbed her of whatever gift she might have gotten from Sharde, in addition to losing a mate for the night.

She finally started to relax and decided to just wait a minute or two before eating. She stood up and walked back toward the living room, where she would play with Sandra a little longer.

"Goddamn finicky cat," mumbled Daddy.

Melena did not fare as well as Mahri. Sharm was her date when they were approached by two other farries, and he vanished before Melena even knew what was happening. She stood alone, facing a huge tom and a nasty-looking queen.

"You must leave here, and leave us alone," said Melena, also trying to sound like Halina. Unfortunately, the words were cracked and the fear was written all over her face.

"We only want you group to halt," said the queen. "We really think you'll be better off away from them. Really! Listen to me. You're scared now, and trying to sound like who you're not. I can see you're a sweet farri, not a trash cat. Leave those others, before you get hurt!"

Melena looked back and forth between the two. The queen sounded so reasonable, she was almost convinced to leave the Den behind and follow them away. They had not been threatening, just sincere. But something was quite strange about the whole thing. Why had her date vanished so quickly?

"C'mon, sweetie," said the tom. "I think Lady Farri will really be pleased with you if you step up and away from those trash cats back there."

Melena thought about all of the other farries in the

Den. She thought about Halina and Mahri, both of whom had more class than any other farri she had ever heard of. And who could possibly match the integrity of Halina? And he dares call them "trash cats"?

The rage level peaked instantly, and the fear was gone. Melena struck at the tom and connected between his ears with her right claws. The follow-up bite to the shoulder was less effective, but enough to send her stunned victim scowling backward.

When the big tom looked back up, it was clear the damage was minimal. Melena knew she would not do as well with the damage about to happen to her. The tom was twice her size, and would have no problem ripping her to shreds. But only if he could get to Melena before his furious mate did.

Of all the farries in the group, only Halina had an undisturbed evening. She had not seen or heard any of the trouble with her girls, yet she somehow knew things were amiss.

Sharlo was lying on his belly and looking out over the Canyon from the roof they were on. Halina liked the view from this house next to the dead end, so she came here often with dates. Plus, it was always nice to mate under star-licked skies, especially in summer.

But tonight there was no mating. She had asked Sharlo to drop by early for talks, and now she sat beside him and listened for news.

Unknown to most of the girls in Halina's group, Sharlo was a very brilliant farri. He spoke little but knew much about matters of the world. His wisdom had even impressed Halina, who was usually credited with being the most knowledgeable of all the farries.

"It is as you feared," said Sharlo. At Halina's request, he had been on a spying mission.

"Coron," said Halina simply.

"Coron," answered Sharlo. "He is behind the group harassing your farries. They were a little jealous, I would say, but they would never have thought or cared to do anything about it. So Coron seeks revenge. He wants to humiliate you as you did to him. Only worse."

"These other farries are so insecure," said Halina sadly. "They're just unhappy with their lives and themselves. It only takes one deceiving tom like Coron to show up, invoking the name of Lady Farri, and all of a sudden these mixed-up farries are united in a cause."

"Yes," said Sharlo. "A very dangerous cause. And tomorrow they plan to gather all of their numbers and attack the Den outright. They want to scatter the group every night until you give up. They know not to face you directly, but your girls cannot withstand their numbers. They will get hurt."

Halina sat motionless, taking in Sharlo's words and observations. The group could not defend itself against an all-out attack by a large group of farries. But as Sharlo had said, Halina would have no problem in such an attack; her girls were the worry.

"All this, and tomorrow a full moon," said Halina, looking skyward.

"Do you think the krahstas will show up?"

"I think not," said Halina, and then jolted upright and looked across the Canyon. Sharlo was struck when he glanced up by Halina's expression, the look of a farri about to make the final, lethal pounce on her prey.

"What is it?" he asked, wondering if she saw something in the Canyon.

"Oh, nothing," Halina beamed. "Just some wild ideas."

CHAPTER 10

Progress at last. Dahrkron was finally beginning to rally the support of other krahstas in his efforts to draw the pack out of the Canyon. There was so much food to be had in the man settlement.

There was also power at stake. Dahrkron knew success was imperative if he was to become pack ruler. It was a good time for a move; the group was hungry, tired, and irritable.

Tonight's debate had gone well. Three of the others had loudly voiced their support of following him into the settlement. They too had seen the many farries who gathered at the edge of the Canyon every night without fail. Enough farries to possibly hide the ribs painfully beginning to show.

Dahrkron was getting tired of the feeling. The stomach, always nagging and making noise. The occasional morsel grabbed on a hunt only made it worse, the shock of intrusion causing terrible cramps. And then the real agony, when the stomach began to scream for more.

"I hope this is the right thing," said Trahna, nestling up to her mate.

"I hope so too," said Dahrkron. "I'm nervous about it for a lot of reasons. But I hate seeing you starve like this. All of us. Let's face it, Trahna, if we don't start eating well soon, we'll either have to move the pack far away, or starve. We're almost at the starving point now. We've gotta go after those farries."

"It's too bad you didn't catch one when you went on your own," said Trahna. "If you hadn't slipped on the hard road, you could have brought back a farri for proof. And dinner.'' She nuzzled Dahrkron affectionately. She had been with the pack on the night of Dahrkron's attack on the group of farries. He had told her the truth about slipping and falling in the street, and let her infer the rest. Getting beaten up by a farri was something a future pack leader did not share with anyone.

"The moon will be full tomorrow," said Dahrkron. "The pack will be wild and ready for anything. I will go to the settlement, and I think others will follow."

"I will," said Trahna, "and there will be others."

Dahrkron rested his head against Trahna. He would be with her forever, and he wanted the best for her. He wanted to be pack leader for her. For all of them, really, because the current leadership was so poor. He liked Trahkor, but thought the welfare of the pack was more important than foolish pride. And it was pride that had kept them away from the farries. Krahstas were supposed to hunt wild animals in the Canyon, not man pets.

"We'll each catch two farries," said Trahna confidently.

"Yes," said Dahrkron, hoping all the farries weren't as ferocious as the one he had encountered on his last trip. He didn't think they would be. That one had looked more wild than tame. And even so, it would be worth the try. It broke his heart to see Trahna so hungry, with him so helpless to do anything about it.

Suddenly and without warning they were on their feet. The smell alerted them first, but the feeling struck a half second later. Dahrkron's fur was beginning to rise, and he was certain he smelled lynx. But the feeling was so much stronger than the smell.

The entire pack was standing and going into automatic defense. An entire circle, flanks pointed inward, and voices barking with full velocity.

It was a lynx. It stepped out of the brush just to Dahrkron's left, and stood still. Then another, a female, over to his right. Confused, he let his bark trail off while the others howled, and wondered why a couple of lynxes would approach an entire pack of krahstas.

Dahrkron was about to shout at the others to shut up

when the group at his heels went into a yelping frenzy. Not wanting to turn his back on the lynxes, he took a quick glance over his shoulder to see the trouble. He had barely moved when the thunderous roar, so primitive and utterly terrifying, pierced every nerve in his body, sending him, along with the rest of the pack, involuntarily to the ground.

"Silence!"

It was immediate. The Canyon was hushed and still for miles. Dahrkron quaked from every limb. The lynxes had joined up with a *puma,* and now he and his pack were going to die. Food had gotten so desperate in the Canyon, the only food left was predators. Krahstas.

"Well, my dear krahstas," said the puma. "How are we doing on this eve of the full moon? Planning our hunts, are we?"

Dahrkron was so ashamed. He could not even speak, so desperately was he shaking. But none of them answered. The terror was absolute.

"Okay then, be rude and not answer," said the puma. "I came not to listen, anyway." The mountain lion gazed over the pack of krahstas, most of whom dared not return the look. Like the lynxes, however, she did not advance.

"I have only advice for my dear krahstas," said the puma finally. "Go where you like in the Canyon. It is your right. It is yours to roam and hunt. But I must warn you: the man settlement is out of your range. Do you understand?"

The puma paused for an answer, although she expected none. When silence was returned, she continued. "I have cousins and friends in the settlement," she said. "The little farries. They are my friends. Do you understand? The lynxes and I would be very upset if any trouble should befall the sweet little farries. Very upset.

"I'm hoping all of you will be good neighbors and respect my friends and relatives. They're so dear to me, you know. If any of them were to run into a bad situation, why, I would probably take it personally. Do you understand?"

The puma took the answer of no answer and together with the two lynxes slipped away into the night.

It was ten minutes before the pack began to relax enough to move. It was Trahkor who was first to speak, walking directly over to Dahrkron.

"Does Dahrkron the krahsta still wish to chase the farries?" he said sarcastically. "The friends and relatives of pumas and lynxes?"

"Friends!" growled Dahrkron. "You mean *dinners*. The big cats want their little cousins all to themselves."

CHAPTER 11

Mahri and Halina again braved the heat and the brush to call upon Sarena. The swelter was equal to their last trip, even though they left much earlier in the morning. They sat in the same place where they had encountered the puma a week earlier and watched the Canyon. This time there appeared to be more life than the last trip, despite the heat.

Unlike before, Halina was very up-front with Mahri about the reason for the trip. They were out for reminders and new requests, and hopefully a chance to live in peace for a while.

The two farries waited, but Sarena did not show, at least not for a long time. They sat through the heat of the day, knowing it would be foolish to try going back in the scorching sun. So they crouched in the shade, hiding with little luck from the merciless afternoon, and waited for cooler times.

Only moments after deciding to leave, they felt her. The prickly feeling all over, fur rising instantly, and the wild, exotic smell of ancient callings. Sarena stepped into the open.

"My dear little friends have survived the Canyon again!" she said with a warm laugh. She smelled different. Mahri detected fresh kill.

"Sarena, we have come for your help," said Halina bluntly.

"But I have given it!" said Sarena. "It was only last night I went with my friends the lynxes to visit the krahstas. I think we scared the fur right off of them. They should not bother my little friends. Or did they?"

"No, Sarena," said Halina. "We have seen no krahstas on the street. And I am truly thankful, and owe you much. I don't know how to repay someone as great as yourself."

"It was quite the pleasure," said Sarena. "Watching the krahstas shake was fun in itself. It also helps me out. I believe they will head farther east as a result, which gives me more room around here. They probably think I was threatening them because *I* wanted to eat the little farries. Ha! They are so blind and clumsy with their noisy packs. There are rabbits uncounted just down the gorge, and even a number of deer. It was just this morning I caught one unawares. I will eat well for a week!

"The krahstas know nothing of the area," she continued. "They run all night, far and wide, and find nothing. They know not where or how to look. I will eat well all summer, as will the lynxes."

She looked over the two farries, who still seemed a bit nervous. "And where is my friend the black panther?" she asked, referring to Melena.

"Her absence is part of our quest," said Halina. "She is injured badly. Her left ear was chewed by a huge tom, and she was scratched by two farries without mercy. Her paladin has taken her to the place of pain, where they do the magic to make wounds hurt more so they heal faster."

"Who did this?" demanded Sarena.

"It's the work of many," said Halina sadly. "There are farries who say it's wrong to mate if you have the changes scar, and all of the farries in my group—"

"The what scar?" asked Sarena.

"The changes scar," said Halina. "You know, when Lady Farri reaches into your stomach and pulls out your kitten box."

"I have never heard of such a thing," said Sarena. "I know of no pumas or lynxes who have a scar received from anything other than a fight. Where is this scar?"

"On our stomachs," said Mahri, finally calm enough to speak. She still found it impossible to relax around

Sarena, despite how friendly the big cat was. "The other farries say the Great Queen gave us the scar for a reason, and to mate when you have it is to go against her wishes."

"So you two can't have kittens?" asked Sarena.

"No," said Mahri.

"Our group still wishes to mate," said Halina, "even with the scar. There are jealous and misguided farries around who wish us to stop. Demand it. Tonight they plan a raid on our Den at the edge of the Canyon. Our numbers cannot match theirs, and there are toms in their group as well. We are but a few queens."

Halina and Mahri both went silent, giving Sarena some time to absorb their words. It was clear she found the world of farries perplexing.

"As I see it," the puma said finally, "a large group of your kind are going to attack your group tonight because you still want to mate, even though you have this scar. And the odds are not in your favor, so you are here to seek my help. Correct?"

"That is correct," said Halina cautiously.

"Chasing krahstas is not enough for my little friends," said Sarena. "Now they want me to chase other little cats. Lady Farri, will this ever end?" She laughed and looked skyward for a message from the Queen of Cats, and then turned back to Halina and Mahri.

"So what will you have a mountain lion do for you?" she asked.

After twelve years as a veterinarian, John Lowell was still amazed at how much damage could be done in a simple cat fight. He looked down at the pretty black cat, who crouched and shivered on his examination table.

"Will she be all right?" asked Mrs. Grant, who held on to the cat with both hands. John smiled inwardly, unable to decide which of his two patients needed more support. People often cared about the well-being of their pets before the welfare of themselves.

"She'll be a little sore for a while," said John, with his well-rehearsed calm and authority. "But I'm sure she'll be fine."

"Oh, Theseus, you've got me worried to death," Mrs. Grant said to the cat. "When will you learn to behave?"

The cat did not look as fine as John had said. Its right ear was badly chewed and might require a couple of stitches. The ear would not escape without permanent scars. The scratch marks on the cat's face looked messy, but were only superficial after close examination.

Apart from the emotional state of Mrs. Grant, the cat's left front paw was John's biggest concern. As far as the assailant was concerned, Little Miss Theseus had quite an enemy. The paw had been bitten very hard, and was swollen to twice its normal size. It looked like an infection could be starting to set in.

"It looks like I'm going to have to keep this young lady here in the office for a few hours," said John. "I'm going to have to put a stitch in her ear."

"Oh Theseus," whimpered Mrs. Grant. "You know, I try to keep her in as much as I can. But she gets so restless . . . nasty, I should say. She can throw such a tantrum. I have to let her out for the sake of my furniture."

John nodded. God had made cats social animals, and to be social, they had to go outside. John wondered why cats craved the contact of their peers so much, when it often led to injury. In a strange way, it reminded him of humans.

"I'm going to give you some pills for Theseus to take," said John. "They're antibiotics. It's important for her to take them, because her right paw might become infected, otherwise."

"What if she won't eat them?" asked Mrs. Grant, terrified.

"She won't," said John. "They taste awful. So I'm going to show you how to give them to her."

John left Mrs. Grant to hold on to Theseus and walked into his supply room. He picked up a small bottle of kitty penicillin and walked back into the examination room.

"You have to be firm, gentle, and fast," he said.

He took hold of the cat's head with his right hand, careful to avoid touching the injured ear, and forced its mouth open. With his left hand, he dropped one of the tiny pills into its mouth, then forced it shut. The cat licked twice, then swallowed. John let go and glanced up at Mrs. Grant, who looked horrified. The cat simply looked pissed.

"I have to do that?" squeaked Mrs. Grant.

"Twice a day," said John. "And try to keep her inside for a few days, until she's better."

Roger pulled his car over to the curb about a block and a half away from his house. It was early evening, about two more hours of daylight. He had almost forgotten about dropping in on Radcliff to find out about the impending mountain lion hunt. He wondered if the police knew about all of these wild plans. The mere thought of tracking down an exotic, endangered animal made Roger's stomach turn.

Radcliff's home was the typical San Diego half-wood, half-stucco tract house. It was painted bright red with white trim and sat on the canyon side of the street. The front lawn seemed adequately cared for, but there were few bushes or any other evidence of landscaping. A full-sized Dodge pickup sat in the driveway.

When Roger reached the concrete path to the front door, he was startled to hear a door slam shut on the pickup. He saw Radcliff walking around from the other side with something in his arms.

"Hello," said Roger.

Radcliff froze. He had been completely unaware of Roger. When he saw it was Roger, his expression turned to relief, followed by irritation, but the first look Roger had seen was a combination of surprise and fear.

"How are y'all tonight?" Radcliff asked. He stepped out from behind the truck. Roger's eyes opened wide with disbelief when he saw what the man was carrying. Clasped with both hands, Radcliff was holding a huge rifle. To Roger, it looked like something big-time, like a weapon the marines might use in combat.

"Going hunting?" he asked. He felt stupid, but couldn't think of anything else to say.

"Gonna get me a mountain lion," said Radcliff, walking quickly toward his front door.

"When are you guys going out?" asked Roger. "A friend of mine and I might want to go."

"Don't know yet," said Radcliff, reaching his front door. "I'll let y'all know as soon as I can."

When he got the door unlocked, he quickly stepped inside and closed it behind him.

Halina and Mahri left the Canyon and were back at the Den nearly two hours before sunset. Syranosh was already there, along with Shona and Naffa. The three were surprised to see Halina and Mahri emerge from the sage beyond the dead end.

"I'll explain it all when the others get here," said Halina to their questioning eyes.

When Melena walked up, Mahri felt her heart sink to the ground. Melena's right ear was bandaged and her face was scratched in three different places. She walked with a painful limp, favoring her left front paw. Mahri could see how swollen it was.

The entire group was silent when Melena sat down next to Mahri in the long, dry grass. Mahri could see the pain in her friend's eyes, so she nuzzled closer to try to comfort her.

"They sounded nice for a while," Melena said finally. "They even had me going, until they started calling our group trash cats, and called Halina evil. I had to strike. It was the honor of our group and a warning to them all. We'll go out fighting. And can you believe it? They had the nerve to call *us* trash cats."

"Two of them against just you?" asked Mahri.

"Yes," said Melena. "A big tom and an ugly queen. I can see why she's upset with us. No self-respecting tom would touch an ugly bag like her."

"We saw Sarena today," said Mahri, trying to be cheerful.

"Sarena! Where?"

"Peace!" said Halina, walking to the middle of the group. "There are some things best left unspoken. But for now, I must tell the group of our danger, and our plans.

"You need not be told of the farries marching against

us. You have all experienced their hypocritical jealous wrath in some way. And tonight our biggest fears will unfold. They are massing together right now for an attack on our Den."

Halina's last remark was greeted with a barrage of concerns, all voicing a desire to leave the Den and head for the homes of their respective paladins. Only Mahri was silent.

"Peace again. Please," said Halina. "We have help unseen and unheard of before in this strip of our world. We have the power of fear unmatched by anything your paladins could ever conceive of. Our great hope."

"What power is this?" Syranosh sneered. "Unless it is the power of fifty toms, what good is it? We should all leave from here at once."

"I think not," said Halina. "We will stay and face our enemies. Do not be surprised to see Coron beside them. He wishes to gloat over our demise. He will fail.

"My warning to you all: do not be afraid! You will be, but do not show it. Do not run from here no matter what happens. You will smell and feel a terror beyond belief, but it will not hurt you. It will come up from the Canyon to help us, although it will probably not show itself to the street. The mere presence will be enough.

"I will demand that the assailants leave in the name of the Lady Farri. They will call me names, but then the name of Lady Farri will take shape."

CHAPTER 12

Roger wondered why Mrs. Grant always chose times like these to come over. Laura was on her way and he was nowhere near ready to go. Mrs. Grant wanted to talk about her cat. He continued to get ready while the old lady from next door rattled on.

"If you do see her, won't you please let me know right away," Mrs. Grant was saying. "I couldn't even close the door, she was so fast. Zoom! Right past me. Poor little thing with her bandages and all. She must have gotten a great big tomcat angry at her, I'd say. Poor little Theseus."

Much to Roger's relief, Laura's car pulled up in front of the house and the driver's-side door opened.

"Oh my,' said Mrs. Grant. "Am I keeping you from getting ready for your date? How rude of me."

"It's okay," Roger smiled, hoping she would leave.

"She's a pretty one, I'll say," said Mrs. Grant upon seeing Laura. "You be nice to her and behave yourself."

"You bet," said Roger.

"Keep an eye out for my little Theseus and let me know," said Mrs. Grant, and then she was out the door.

Roger was relieved to know the old lady would corner Laura in the driveway, giving him another minute to get ready. They had the good old dinner-and-a-movie routine lined up for the evening. Roger figured Laura couldn't find anyone else to go out with.

"Hi, you," Laura's voice came through the door.

"C'mon in, gorgeous," said Roger from his bedroom.

He wanted to look as good as possible before being seen by his date.

"Who was that?" asked Laura.

"Oh, just your competition," said Roger of Mrs. Grant.

"Go for it," said Laura.

"Still holding out for you," said Roger.

Laura stuck out her tongue and gave a very wet raspberry. "Aren't you ready yet?"

"No, ma'am," answered Roger. "Had to fight off Mrs. Grant. Did she have anything interesting to say?"

"She told me to be nice to you," said Laura. "Said you were a nice boy and worth my while."

"And?"

"And she said to look out for her kitty."

Roger walked into the living room and looked at Laura. There was always a momentary loss of breath when he saw her for the first time in a while. She was standing in the living room, holding De Lilah and scratching her behind the ears. Roger simply smiled and quickly looked down.

Laura Kay was a first for Roger. The first woman he had fallen for since his wife and daughter perished when a drunk driver jumped the curb and wiped them out on a sidewalk nearly two years ago. Roger's life was shattered; the driver spent three months in jail.

But Laura Kay was something else. She was Roger's idea of the perfect woman. Absolutely stunning, but not offensively so. Perfect brunette hair and green eyes, and the figure of an aerobics instructor. She was smart too; that was the most important part. She was well versed in anything you cared to talk about, yet without being a know-it-all. And she knew how to have fun. Roger had gone out with her many, many times, and had always had a blast.

There was only one problem to all of this: Laura was not interested. Oh, she loved Roger as a friend, but nothing more. He was always too afraid to just come out with it, and she never failed to laugh off his subtle hints. But deep down he knew the answer, even if he tried. All these months and still just a hug at the door when they went out. No thanks.

"Hi, you," she said again when she saw Roger.

"Was De Lilah inside?" Roger asked.

"No," said Laura. "She followed me in. In fact, she came running from across the street when she saw me. I told you she likes me."

"Obviously," said Roger, slightly jealous. "She never lets anyone hold her this long."

"Good kitty," said Laura as she rubbed the cat's chin. "Oh, by the way, I got the rundown on your friend Jerry Radcliff."

"Oh good," said Roger, relieved to know there was something else to talk about when they finished discussing the cat.

"He works for the state," she said. "He's a narcotics officer for the state of California."

"A what?" asked Roger, surprised. Then he thought about his earlier encounter at Radcliff's house and nodded. "I guess it makes sense. When I dropped by after work to ask him about the mountain lion hunt, he was carrying one hell of a rifle. Looked like one of those huge automatics they used in Vietnam."

Laura flinched. She gave Roger a hard, puzzled look, then looked up as if lost in thought.

"Is something wrong?" he asked.

"He had an M-16?" Laura asked.

"I don't know what it was called," said Roger. "It may have been something else. But it was definitely a high-caliber rifle with a large clip. Maybe it was part of a bust he was in on."

"I talked to someone from his office," said Laura coolly. "Someone who owes me some favors. Anyway, his department operates around the border. Drug smuggling. My friend told me Radcliff's job was just a figurehead thing. He doesn't do anything other than speak for the group."

"Nothing?" Roger asked.

"Nothing," said Laura. "He doesn't go out on operations, he doesn't get involved with investigations, and he doesn't even leave the office, except for lunch breaks.''

"How did he get a gig like that?" asked Roger, wondering why he even bothered to pursue the issue. His strange feeling about Jerry Radcliff had faded since he had seen him. He also felt there were better ways to spend time with Laura than discussing this bozo.

"Shit floats," said Laura, bending over and lightly setting De Lilah on the floor. "You should know by now. He's just a turd. The bottom line is, he's a white boy in a department working the border, and he'd never fit in down there. Especially since they work mostly heroin. No smuggler on earth's gonna sell dope to someone who looks life Radcliff.''

"You've seen him?" asked Roger.

"No," said Laura. "He's white. That's enough. Anyway, I think there's more, but my friend wouldn't say. He laughed when I asked about him. The guy must be quite a character."

"Yes," said Roger. "Quite."

"I'm just wondering," said Laura, "if what my friend tells me is true, and I have no reason to doubt him, what would Radcliff be doing with an automatic rifle at his house? Did he say anything to you about it?"

"He said it might come in handy when they were tracking down the mountain lion," said Roger.

Laura rolled her eyes, then shook her head. Roger didn't think it was a big deal and wondered why Laura was so concerned.

"And by the way, he didn't know when they would be going out after it," said Roger. "He seemed awfully rushed about something. He obviously wanted to get the gun inside without it being seen by too many people."

"Can't imagine why," said Laura sarcastically. "This whole thing seems weird. I don't think I like the idea of some crazy cowboy shooting at mountain lions with an automatic rifle within city limits."

"I'm not too fond of it, either," said Roger.

"Well, should we go?" asked Laura, after a long pause.

"Yes, ma'am," said Roger, startled by Laura's sudden desire to change the subject.

"This is my kind of night," said Laura. "A full moon and high tide both at the same time."

"I hope I'm safe with you," Roger laughed.

When the doorbell rang, Roger and Laura looked at each other with knowing exasperation. Mrs. Grant would have to be dealt with again. In silent agreement, they walked to the door together, planning to tell the old lady they were late.

"How are y'all tonight?" It was Jerry Radcliff.

"Pretty good, Mr. Radcliff," said Roger, casually informing Laura of the identity of the visitor. "We're just on our way out. What can we do for ya?"

Radcliff seemed either pleased or relieved to see Roger with a woman. He beamed his huge toothy smile and tipped his hat to Laura. "Evening, miss," he said. "Jerry Radcliff. I'm your boyfriend's neighbor."

"Don't say that too loud," said Laura, not taking the bait. "My husband might hear."

"Oh my," Radcliff laughed. "Don't tell me such things!"

"Just kidding," Laura smiled. "I'm not married. My name's Laura Kay."

Roger opened the screen door and waited for Laura to step out. He hoped Radcliff would get the hint. He hoped Laura would get the hint as well. She seemed awfully interested in talking to Mr. Radcliff. Before Laura could get through the door, De Lilah bolted between her feet and bounded across the lawn. Roger just rolled his eyes.

"Sorry about being so rushed with you earlier," said Radcliff, stepping back to let Roger and Laura out. "I was in quite a hurry. Anyway, just wanted to update you on the cougar situation."

"It didn't attack again?" asked Roger.

"No, no. But tomorrow morning, being it's Saturday, we're getting the guys together to hunt the old lion down."

The sky was fiercely red in the west, guaranteeing another scorcher the next day. Mahri watched the sun fade slowly into the dark horizon of the Canyon and wondered if she would see sun again if their maneuvers failed.

To the east, the full moon was already well above the mountains. The krahstas would be about. Had Sarena really scared them off? They were reputed to be crazy beyond reason when the moon was full. Would the threats of a puma be enough to detour such primitive instincts?

Mahri looked around the group of farries. They were nervous, as was she. Even Halina was pacing. Not one tom had shown up requesting a date, and that was bad. Only Sharlo made an appearance, speaking privately to Halina and then sitting watchful, facing the street. He had not even looked at Mahri.

This was the night, thought Mahri. They would wait until darkness, and then they would come. Misguided and angry farries. The darkness would hide them from the paladins, who were commonly known to be blind at night, when the fighting instincts of farries were at their greatest. For this they waited.

Mahri began to scratch nervously at the long, dead grass surrounding the Den. She could not relax, no matter how many deep breaths she took. She wondered how many of the others there would be to face the girls of the Den. Probably far too many, she thought sadly.

The sun was gone for nearly a half hour when Mahri first saw movement in the street. Half a block away, there were too many farries to count. They were four times the size of Halina's group, and they were spreading out to form an umbrella around their victims. There was no chance for an escape now.

The attackers approached calmly and without hurry. Halina knew the attacking farries wouldn't dare go into the sage at night, so she had her girls form a straight line with their tails to the Canyon. Mahri stood between Melena and Sharlo, who stood farthest to the left of the group.

"Be calm and alert," said Halina. "Stay close to the Canyon and do not run, no matter what."

The invasion force stopped just five feet from the line of Halina's girls. The two sides stood silent for several moments, no one moving.

Mahri looked over the faces of the others. They seemed as nervous as she, and almost more afraid, despite their superior number.

Mahri felt the fur start to rise. She saw the faces of male farries who had been to their Den to mate many times. Even last night they had been here, bringing fresh kill for reward. And now they stood against her, in the name of Lady Farri. She opened her mouth to bare her teeth, giving a silent hiss. She felt, rather than saw, the other girls in her group doing the same.

"Who speaks for you?" asked Halina, stepping forward.

"I am Fahlo," said the tom closest to the center of the larger group.

"And I am Narshi," said the queen standing at his side. "We are here to demand a stop to these disrespectful and disgraceful acts."

"Namely?" said Halina.

"Namely," said Fahlo, "mating after being struck with the changes scar. And making toms bring you a reward for something which is their privilege."

"Is it?" asked Halina. "Then why do they feel so compelled to do it? And how is it you know of our dealings here, Fahlo? Have I not seen you here looking for dates?"

"You are all disrespectful to Lady Farri!" Narshi cut in.

"And did Lady Farri tell you this personally?" asked Halina. "It seems disrespectful to put words in her mouth. And if what we do is disrespectful, then so too are you who have come here regularly. Listen! You are being misled!"

While Halina debated with Fahlo and Narshi, Mahri detected movement behind the main group of the attackers. Only one farri, and it was white. It moved in her direction, crouching behind the others in its group. Mahri knew its identity without seeing. It had to be Coron. Her fur stood even higher.

"And who is this tom?" Narshi was saying, looking at Sharlo. "Why doesn't *he* speak for the group?"

"The dealings of our Den are none of your concern,"

said Halina. "Now leave here before we show you whose side Lady Farri is *really* on."

"How dare you!" hissed Narshi.

Halina's throaty screech surprised even Mahri. It was wild and ancient, shaking both friend and foe alike. Both Narshi and Fahlo stepped back, wincing at its fierceness. But not even the cry of Halina would prepare them for what would follow.

Halina leaped forward, her claws scoring the faces of her two opponents before they could move. She bounced off them and had her teeth sunk into the shoulder of another, sending all farries on both sides into the clash.

Mahri was instantly overwhelmed. Three of the enemies were around her in a flash, with two others closing. With a quick fake, she swung around and scratched hard at the nose of the only tom, but her exposed sides were quickly seized by the teeth of the two queens. She jerked back, both elbows folding in and crashing to the ground. She tried to roll over to her back, but the queens had guessed her move and held tight to their grips.

The teeth in her skin sent waves of fire searing through her sides. She tried desperately to stand, but was held by the pain of movement. When the expected blow by the tom she had scratched didn't come, she looked up, hoping Sharlo had chased him off. But the hope died faster than it had dared to rise. It was Coron who she saw when she was able to glance up.

"So, pretty trash cat," said Coron casually. "Is your snooty little mistress going to save you this time? Guess again."

The hatred was all over Mahri's face, but before she could speak, the terror struck.

Suddenly she was free. The two queens let go instantly and stood straight up with backs arched. Coron too was poised for attack, completely ignoring Mahri.

The sounds of battle were over. The hush was immediate and overwhelming. Not a single farri moved.

Mahri knew the feeling and then she knew the smell. And suddenly out of the silent Canyon erupted a roar of horrifying magnitude, causing every nerve in her body to scream and sending every farri on the street to the ground.

Then once again, the deadliest roar known in the wilds
of North America: puma.

Coron was the first to run, not even waiting for the
monster to show itself. Halina's group kept still, as per
her orders. Most of the enemy farries remained motionless as well, too frightened to move. But when the huge
puma stepped out of the sage and into the street, the
result was a maddening retreat.

In every direction the farries ran. The hysterical panic
spread tenfold when the puma roared again, sending several farries up trees instead of trying to run it out.

Mahri stood right where she had been when Coron was
about to strike. So too did most of Halina's other girls,
although two of them had been overcome by the terror
and had bolted. Mahri was very surprised to see the lion
walk so boldly into the street. Canyon animals were usually nervous around man settlements.

Mahri thought Sarena looked strange in the darkness.
She was walking toward Mahri and Sharlo when suddenly the voice of thunder rang out from down the street.
Mahri sensed something whiz by, and saw the pavement
splinter when it hit. Then another bang, and the sickening
sound of an impact with flesh.

The wail was instantaneous and heartbreaking. It was
Sarena.

The huge cat fell to her side and cried with agony. Her
face was wrinkled tight with misery as she clumsily bit
at the air, trying to chase away the pain. It was her right
shoulder; a gaping hole spouting with blood.

Mahri wanted desperately to help but ran anyway when
Halina screamed to do so. There was nothing any of them
could do. Mahri went straight for the same tree she had
climbed the night of the krahsta. She was halfway up
when another shot came, and the sad, tormented cries of
Sarena were stopped forever.

CHAPTER 13

Roger was still in shock. A night already unbelievable was starting to turn into a circus. He sat on the trunk of his T-bird and watched the bright lights of television cameras flood the area of the dead cougar. Laura was down there somewhere getting the story for the *Courier,* and he sat safely three houses away. Alone with a wrecked evening.

All of the neighbors were out. Even people from several blocks away were milling around. Roger had heard Laura and other people from the news department talk about the sightseers who always showed up at accidents and fires. They called these people VIs, or village idiots, but Roger never really understood it until now. Tonight there was a very high VI factor.

"Excuse me, sir?" broke into Roger's thoughts.

"Huh?"

"Hi. Do you live around here?" asked a short, petite woman in her early thirties with a very high voice.

"Yes, right there," said Roger, pointing up the driveway.

"Did you see what happened?" asked the woman.

"Well, yeah," said Roger. "I saw the whole thing. I was talking to the guy who shot it just before it happened."

"Great! Can we talk to you? My name's Rosemary Ogden from 'Eyewitness News.' "

"I guess so," said Roger, shrugging his shoulders. "We were just—"

"Don't go anywhere. I'll be right back," said Rosemary, and stepped away quickly.

Roger watched her flag down a TV photographer and start walking in his direction. He started to have doubts about the whole thing, but he knew Laura would be pissed if he turned the media down. She was always ranting about people who saw things but wouldn't talk or be quoted.

"C'mon, I need to get this sound pop," Rosemary was saying to the grudging photographer. He was easily twenty years her senior, with silver hair and a voice as low as Rosemary's was high.

"I need to get these shots," he was saying, sounding genuinely concerned. "They're gonna move the cougar in a minute."

"But I need to get this bite before the guy leaves," she said, pulling the photographer's sleeve.

"Okay, but make it quick."

"Hi again," she said to Roger.

The light ripped straight through to the core of Roger's eyes. Accustomed to the dark, he had to put up his hand momentarily to ward off the unexpected intrusion.

"Sorry," said Rosemary. "Anyway, you saw what happened?" She stuck a microphone in Roger's face.

"Yeah. I was just about to go to a movie with my friend when Jerry Radcliff shows up and says he wants to talk about getting a hunting party together for tomorrow to go after the cougar. No sooner had he finished his sentence than we heard this thing start roaring."

"You heard it roar?" asked Rosemary.

"Yeah. A total of three times."

"Then what happened?"

"We all ran into the street to see what was going on," said Roger. "And there it was. The moon was so bright you could see it just as clear as day. There was something else there too. Something smaller, but I was paying more attention to the cougar.

"Next thing ya know: bang! Scared the you know what out of me. Radcliff had a pistol out and was firing at the cougar. Three shots. The first one missed completely. Then he hit it and wounded it. The last shot finished it off."

"Did you know he had a gun?" asked the reporter.

"No. Well, he's a cop, so I guess he carries one."

"Then what happened?"

"We walked over and checked it out. Then we called the local cops and Animal Reg. They're gonna check it for rabies."

"You live right here next to the canyon. Do you feel safer now?"

Before Roger could answer, the photographer grabbed the mike and began to hustle back to the cougar. The County Animal Regulation people were beginning to move the dead cat.

"Oh well," said Rosemary. "Anyway, you did very good. Really."

"Thanks. What time's this gonna be on?" asked Roger, not knowing what else to say. The spots on his eyes from the wicked camera light and the sudden return to darkness left him hopelessly blind.

"Tonight at eleven," said Rosemary. "Is the guy still here who actually did the shooting?"

"Um, yeah. That's him over there with the cowboy hat," said Roger, finally able to detect Radcliff's outline in the distant light.

"And his name is?" asked Rosemary.

"Jerry Radcliff."

"Do you think he'll talk to me?"

"I think you can count on it," said Roger.

"Thank you," said Rosemary, and was gone.

Roger watched her beeline over to where Radcliff was talking with the San Diego police sergeant. The Animal Regulation truck pulled away with the cougar and Rosemary had the light on Radcliff within seconds. The photographers and reporters from the other two local stations joined in as well.

"What an arrogant ass," said Laura, walking up to Roger. "You were right. There's something strange about that guy."

"Why? Just because he's gonna be on TV?" asked Roger defensively.

"No," said Laura. "I'd expect him to talk to the press. That's his job. It didn't even bug me that he shot the cougar, although it scared the shit out of me. It's just something about him."

"I know," said Roger. "Well, let's try and check him out some more."

"I plan on it," said Laura.

"Oh, by the way," said Roger casually. "I'm gonna be on TV."

The tragedy was complete. Mahri watched the paladins gather around Sarena with their lights and cars, and what little hope there might have been vanished. Sarena was dead.

There were many of the paladins wandering about, so she stayed hidden in the safety of the tree. The man who killed Sarena might have seen Mahri standing right beside the puma, and might want to kill her too. For what, she did not know.

The man who killed Sarena. She couldn't believe it. A creature so strong it struck fear throughout the wilds. Big enough to bring down full-grown deer. Sweet enough to be Sarena, the mountain lion who just gave her life for a bunch of little farries. Did the man make a mistake? She didn't think so.

What she did know was that everything was over. Halina would be as deeply upset as she was, and neither would want to continue the group. The other farries would want to disband as well, as they should since no other toms would dare come by again. They had upset Lady Farri.

It must be true. Why else would the Lady destroy everything they had accomplished over several months in one night? And why kill their dear friend Sarena just for helping out?

Mahri shifted uneasily on the branch and then felt the gashes from both sides. The wounds from farri teeth had been momentarily forgotten, so deep was the pain of loss. She watched two men lift Sarena and drop her into the back of a truck.

Roger lounged on the couch with Tammy and waited for the eleven o'clock news. When Laura left to put together a story for the *Courier*, he had called Tammy. He couldn't witness his moment of glory alone.

"Do they know if this is the one who bit the little

boy?'' she asked, watching the last few minutes of the prime-time soap.

"I'm sure it must be," said Roger. "Mountain lions aren't exactly common around here." He looked at Tammy and then ran his fingers across her hair. She was starting to grow on him even though she sometimes asked dumb questions.

"I'm glad they got it," she said. "I was starting to worry about you living around here. And I didn't really like coming over, which says a lot. I like it here, believe me, but I was scared."

"Well, it's gone now, so there's nothing to be afraid of," said Roger.

"Except you," Tammy smiled. "You're still a beast."

"Yeah, but I don't bite as hard as cougars do."

"Since when?"

The headline tease at the top of the newscast mentioned the cougar first, followed by a homicide in Southeast San Diego, and the scooter craze in Mission Beach. Then came the commercials.

After the show open, the anchor read a brief intro about the cougar and then tossed to the story by Rosemary Ogden. The story started with a couple of file pictures of the little boy who had been attacked and the reporter giving a little bit of the history. Then it went to the scenes from tonight, with shots of the dead cougar.

Ogden quickly summed up the events that had led to the shooting and then went to an interview with Jerry Radcliff. Seeming somber and more controlled than usual, Radcliff talked about how bright the night was.

"There it was, big as thunder," he said. "I grabbed my service revolver and fired before it had a chance to do any harm out on the street. There was no telling if any kids were out, and I didn't want the darn thing coming after me."

Two more lines about the concern for rabies were followed by an interview with the officer from Animal Regulation. More pictures of the cougar being loaded up, and then Rosemary Ogden was on camera in front of the truck.

"Officials here say that they can't be positive if this is the same cougar that attacked a little boy just a week ago.

But, they say, the chances of another mountain lion being this close to houses is very unlikely. Rosemary Ogden, 'Eyewitness News.' ''

The show went back to the anchor, who started on the next story. Roger looked at Tammy and gave a disappointed shrug. His interview had found its way to the infamous edit-room floor.

On the evening of the third day after the death of Sarena, Mahri began to walk toward Halina's Den. The feeling she had was strange. She had not seen another farri since the horror of the other night, yet somehow she knew Halina would be there.

The walk, the length of a block and a half, was easier than she thought it would be. The vet had dealt with the gash on her right side with four stitches. And although the wound on her other side was not stitched, it somehow hurt even more. Cat bites were a serious thing.

When Mahri reached the Den, she was not surprised to see four other farries there. They had all felt the calling, and the need to talk it out.

Melena was the first farri to greet Mahri. The pretty black cat's ear had a new bandage on it, replacing the one torn off in the terrible fight. Her other ear was not bandaged but might well have been, it was so badly scratched up. There were even more scratches about her face and head. Mahri walked up to her and the two friends silently touched noses.

Syranosh was the same, scratched and chewed with a puffy left eye. She also bore stitches.

Farinna had a bandage on her forehead and several whiskers were damaged. The night had been a disaster for just about every farri involved on both sides.

Mahri watched Halina step out of the Den and was struck with instant sorrow. Halina limped heavily, favoring her left hind leg. She also had a gash behind one ear and a number of broken whiskers.

The farries sat in silence, waiting for the others to arrive. When all but two had arrived, Halina stepped up to the spot where she usually addressed the group. The two no-shows were the ones who had run when Sarena appeared the other night. They were not expected to make it.

"How much sadder can a meeting between friends be," said Halina, not really asking a question. "We have failed," she continued. "No. I have failed. I've failed all of us, and as a result, we've lost a true friend." She turned around and silently looked out at the Canyon for quite some time.

"Although I did not physically kill Sarena, I feel responsible for her death. She came here on my request." Halina turned back around toward the others, yet kept her head down. "I can only apologize to you, because I can't apologize to her. How sad it is to have many things to tell someone, but you can't because they're gone. I have never felt like this before.

"We have paid for my foolishness, dearest friends. We might all be dead right now if Sarena had not shown up to lose her own life. Look at us! We're all chewed up and scratched and battered." She again turned around and looked at the Canyon.

"Halina, it isn't your fault," said Melena. "You couldn't have stopped all those farries by yourself. Sarena was helping us out. You couldn't have known about the man with the gun."

"But it didn't need to happen at all!" said Halina. "Don't you see? I had to be so cavalier about the whole thing; I had to set up this great show of strength and cunning. All I really needed to do was send you all home. Obviously those other cats were right. Lady Farri doesn't want us doing this. If I had paid attention, all of this could have been avoided."

"But Halina, we were all behind you," said Mahri. "I even went with you to ask for Sarena's help. We couldn't just pack up and disband the group."

"No?" asked Halina. "Well, look what happened. We're all ripped to shreds, and we've lost a truly good friend. And now we're about to do what would have averted the whole mess. You're all very dear to me and I will love you always. But now, for our own good and the will of Lady Farri, we must part company forever."

Leader
of the Pack

CHAPTER 14

The neutral wash of twilight was Dahrkron's favorite hour. It somehow made a krahsta invisible, leaving the Canyon dangerously vulnerable to their prowls, for few animals in the brush possessed such an acute sense of smell.

Dahrkron was very pleased with the way things were going. Each night, more members of the pack chose to follow him instead of Trahkor. It would only be days before the entire group was behind him, demanding the death of his soon-to-be predecessor. In the world of krahstas, failure was bad news.

Trahkor had failed. He was still chasing the ghosts of rabbits long gone from the eastern side of the mountain, leading fewer and fewer starving followers in the pack. But Dahrkron's followers were finding a new, plentiful life near the dead end of the manroad.

Tonight, his group was heading for the territory now vacated by a dead puma. Rumor of the great beast's demise had raced throughout the Canyon as quickly as the sounds of the gunshots that killed her. Man's deadly thunder never went off so close to one of their own settlements, but the entire population of the Canyon thought a mountain lion might bring an exception.

Dahrkron loped next to Trahna but was out of place when the first rabbit of the night bolted the other way. Droanna snagged the prey immediately, and the catch was promptly eaten.

"We'll get one," said Trahna confidently to Dahrkron.

"Of course, my love," said Dahrkron. He loped close

enough to give his mate an affectionate nudge. "But I'm glad Droanna got that one," he said sincerely. He wanted all of his followers to return with full bellies, and it was only a few more strides before he flushed a rabbit of his own. Trahna successfully predicted the escape route of the terrified creature and blocked off the nearest outlet of the sage. When the rabbit cut back, Dahrkron was there.

"This is a good one!" said Dahrkron triumphantly. "I can feel the fat already."

Trahna walked over and helped her mate pull the cottontail apart. The entrails were the delicacy, and normally saved for the male, but Dahrkron let her have this one. He felt confident enough about the numbers of rabbits near the man settlement.

Droanna carefully approached the two while they ate. It was always wise to show intent within the pack, and Droanna wanted them both to know she wasn't after their meal.

"Mine was the best one of the season so far," said Droanna.

"There haven't been too many to compare with," said Dahrkron, shaking his head.

"Well, true," said Droanna. "But I've noticed before how much better the prey tastes if it lives close to man."

"Yes," said Trahna, "we've noticed too. That's why we're planning to raid the farries who live near the edge of the Canyon."

"Trahna!" yelped Dahrkron angrily.

"Oh, don't get so huffy," said Droanna. "You think we don't know? Whispers have passed through the pack since we heard about the puma's death. I figured it would be soon."

"We're not quite sure yet," said Dahrkron, confiding in his sister. "The farries suddenly vanished from their Den. I'm hoping they'll show up again before too long."

"Don't worry about it," said Droanna. "There's plenty of bunnies around here. We'll be fine for months."

"Whispers through the pack?" questioned Dahrkron. "Which pack? It seems like there's two now."

"I would say there's only one pack, brother. Trahkor has only a few remaining loyal and they'll eventually have to follow their bellies. And everyone wants only one pack anyway.''

Dahrkron sat silently in thought. He let Trahna finish his last few bites of the rabbit while he looked around and absorbed the newest darkness.

Scary as it was, the time was now. The rest of the pack would insist on it. Dahrkron would have to face Trahkor in a battle for the pack. A battle destined to leave one of them dead.

Dahrkron realized how sad it all was. He did not fear Trahkor: the old krahsta wouldn't have a chance against the stronger and more agile Dahrkron. Fear for his personal safety was unimportant. It was a matter of respect, and how much Dahrkron had for the old leader. The others in the pack would certainly understand the takeover, but he wasn't sure if he was ready for such things.

It was not long before the entire group had eaten and wished to return to deeper parts of the Canyon. Being close to the manroad still made some of the krahstas a little nervous, although Dahrkron hoped their fear would lessen in time. He himself had no problem with the road, or the men, as a matter of fact. Everyone knew the story of men and how they lost their vision when the sun went down. Never mind the fate of the puma and how she had died after dark.

No, Dahrkron was not afraid. At least he tried to believe so. He paired up with Trahna and sent the others back to the Canyon. He wanted to get a closer look at the dead end where the farries gathered. He hoped that they were still there after all this time and that the tough little bitchy female he had run into would soon find her way into his belly. Soon, but not tonight.

The two krahstas took a position in the sage on the small hill near the dead end. Sitting motionless for several minutes, they watched the road for any movement.

It was well lit. The streetlight blasted every corner of the block, with light bouncing off the houses. It would be impossible to miss movement under such conditions. But there was none. The farries were someplace else tonight.

''I wonder if the old story about men is true,'' said

Trahna, sitting comfortably with Dahrkron. "You know, the one about them being blind at night. They sure go to a lot of trouble to make those bright lights. I wonder how they do it."

"I think the story's true," said Dahrkron, "to an extent."

"Like how?" asked Trahna.

"Well, you know how it goes. Lord Krahsta went to the Creator to complain about men. Well, I'm sure he did. So did his great cousin, Lord Kriba, as did the lords and ladies of several other animals."

"I thought the Creator and Lord of All Things took Lord Krahsta's word alone," said Trahna.

"I've heard the tale from many creatures, and all tell it as their own lord or lady. But I think they're all wrong, as are the krahstas.

"Lord Krahsta and his cousin Lord Kriba went to the Great Creator and told Him how the man was so intrusive. Animals could not mate at night without the man showing up to watch. Even when they hid, the man would come snooping around, because he could smell them and hear them mating. And since he could see so well at night, he would eventually find them, and watch."

"Why?" asked Trahna, shaking her head in disgust.

"That's still unknown," said Dahrkron. "Some say it's because the man's brain never rests, and so he thinks too much. Even when mating, he thinks, and abuses the sacredness of the act instead of naturally enjoying how wonderful it is.

"Others say it's because the man mates all the time. Even when the females are out of season. They get bored with it too fast. They forget the Creator wishes for all of us to mate only at certain times and for certain reasons.

"I believe both of these answers. The man acquired an obsession with watching other animals, because they seemed so happy when mating, while the man was so sad. He watched and studied their technique, hoping to find an answer. But the foolish man, with all his wisdom, was too blind to look into their hearts."

"So Lord Krahsta complained," said Trahna.

"Yes," said Dahrkron. "They all did. But the Creator

couldn't believe the man would do such a thing. After all, men lock themselves up into their houses so no one can see them mate. Not even their own kind. The Creator assumed the men would respect other animals' privacy, as they demanded for themselves.

"The Lord of All Things told Lord Krahsta to make sure. So Lord Krahsta and Lord Kriba went away sad, for they knew of no way to prove it to the Creator. But then they saw Lady Farri going to the Lord, so they followed quietly and hid while she talked to Him.

"The Great Lady told the same story to the Lord, and the Lord was shocked. Lady Farri was always His favorite, and if she told it, it must be so. So he put a curse on the man and his ancestors. 'When the sun goes down,' said the Lord, 'all of My children will be free to mate in peace. For when the sun goes down, the man will become blind! Never again will he bother my children in the privacy of night!'

"And now they need to make lights to see anything. That's why they flood their streets and fill their houses with it."

"I also heard the curse affected their noses too," said Trahna.

"Yes I'm sure it did," said Dahrkron. "I've seen them in broad daylight. Their scent was strong enough to make me gag. But it was clear they couldn't smell me. I was close enough, but they didn't notice. I sure noticed them, though. The female must have been in season, because she stank of some sickening sweet odor, and the male didn't seem to mind. In fact, he got pretty close to her. I'm glad you never smell like that."

Trahna gently nestled up against him. "So you think Lady Farri convinced the Lord to blind the man?" she asked finally.

"Yes," said Dahrkron, and he clamped his teeth with contempt.

"Why do you think Lady Farri is His favorite?"

"It's so obvious," said Dahrkron. "He gives them everything. The whole family, big and small. They're faster, stronger, smarter, and more agile than any other animal on earth. Ruthless too, when they want to be."

"No," Trahna disagreed.

"Yes. They can crush any opponent twice their size. A bobcat could easily kill anything in this Canyon, except a puma, which is the fiercest of all. Nothing could stop one of those monsters. You saw how our whole pack shuddered when one lousy cat walked up. One lousy cat. We wouldn't have had a chance."

"But she had two bobcats with her," said Trahna.

"No one paid attention to *them*," said Dahrkron. "And you know it. True, they would have made formidable foes, but the puma would have thrashed us. Even one of our huge cousins, the great wolves of the north, would have backed away."

Dahrkron began to pant; the topic of cats always upset him. He hated how an animal so graceful could be so powerful and dominant. It wasn't fair.

"Even the rotten little farries on the street are tough," he mumbled.

"What?"

"Oh, nothing," said Dahrkron quickly, trying to cover up his slip. "Those cats on the street. They're awfully small. I hope size isn't deceiving. If they're anything like their wild cousins . . ."

"I don't think we have to worry," Trahna smiled. "There isn't a farri anywhere who would even dare to fight it out with a krahsta, especially one as big and brave as you."

CHAPTER 15

Another sales pitch. Roger was glad it was over. The guy was going to buy a good-sized ad to hock his goldfish, and Roger could care less. Goldfish might make good cat food, but otherwise had no purpose in life.

Cat food. De Lilah. Boy she'd been acting weirder than shit lately, he thought. He forgot completely about the ad and absently began to picture his cat. She had been staying in the yard, never going far from the house. And she wanted to remain inside whenever possible, which was also strange. Scottish wildcats preferred the great outdoors.

The phone rang and Roger was jarred back to reality. Single rings: an in-house call.

"This is Roger."

"Hi, you," came Laura's voice.

"Oh my, I was just dreaming about you." Roger grinned.

"Yeah, sure," said Laura. "You were probably dreaming about your stupid cat."

Roger frowned, and was glad visual phones were not yet universal.

"Sorry to wake you up," said Laura. "I know how rough you salespeople have it. Afternoon naps, and all. But I have some cougar news you might be interested in."

"Yeah?"

"It had rabies."

CHAPTER 16

Dahrkron returned to his group shortly after they had settled in for the night. Trahkor and his few remaining followers were still about, and Dahrkron was not surprised. They might be out all night chasing nonexistent prey.

Cuddling up close to Trahna, he rested his head on her forepaws and thought about how much easier it was to sleep with a full belly. Worries of the pack and other Canyon matters began to fade as he listened to the gurgling of Trahna's stomach and relaxed into a comfortable position.

Suddenly his fur began to rise and he was on his feet instantly. The warning sirens of his instincts blared, although the only new smell was of Trahkor and the group he returned with. But something was wrong. The entire pack was alert and standing, sensing trouble.

Trahkor walked straight through the nervous pack, directly to the face of Dahrkron. His panting was controlled and not weary, telling Dahrkron how briefly they had hunted. But his curiosity about the hunt vanished immediately when he met the startling gaze of Trahkor. The old leader's eyes screamed with hatred.

"Now is your time, Dahrkron," said Trahkor, breaking the desperate hush of the pack. "You have taken them all from me. The slink you are still, not even having the courage to fight for the pack."

"I've always admired you too much to want to fight you," said Dahrkron.

"Ah, he speaks of admiration." Trahkor laughed,

speaking to no one in particular. "Is this new? What kind of admiration is shown by embarrassing a pack leader? By cunningly deceiving his krahstas into following someone else? By being too cowardly to challenge for the right of leadership you so desperately covet?

"Well, I'm glad someone's got some admiration around here," Trahkor continued, "because I sure don't. I used to piss on dogs like you for breakfast."

"I'm sorry you won't be doing it anymore," said Dahrkron sadly.

Trahkor bared his teeth with a snarl, sending the entire pack backward. Dahrkron did not move. He alone could see the resignation in Trahkor's eyes. This was the leader's way of going out with dignity. All pack leaders eventually went down at the teeth of a young buck, and Trahkor wanted to lose the pack the same way. There was dignity in death. Anything else was disgraceful.

Disgraceful.

Dahrkron's mind flashed back to a run in with a certain farri a couple of months earlier and remembered disgrace. And questions too. Was Trahkor as easy a mark as he thought? He had never before heard of a krahsta losing to a farri. Would the pack leader turn out to be just as surprising?

Suddenly Trahkor darted forward, teeth bared and aiming high. Dahrkron lunged to the side, bending backward to get a quick nip at the leader's hindquarters as he passed. Trahkor turned and stood fast, snarling teeth and blazing, hateful eyes. Dahrkron secured good footing and scanned his opponent. He quickly took an inward sigh of relief. Trahkor was not a cat.

The remaining members of the pack began to form a circle around the two, and Dahrkron realized how quickly the loser would become an afterdinner treat. A scary thought, since Trahkor had obviously won many battles throughout his life, and Dahrkron had never fought anything except the farri a couple of months ago.

Trahkor moved again, faking high, and anticipating Dahrkron's response. Dahrkron tried his sidestep again, only to find the leader's teeth pulling a clump of fur from his forepaw. Dahrkron let out a tiny yelp, and instantly regretted it. All eyes in the pack went wide with alarm. They all expected Dahrkron to come out victorious, but none wanted a whiner for a pack leader. Trahkor had not yipped earlier when Dahrkron had grabbed his flank.

Trahkor's morale jumped immediately, and he soared forward for a strike. But Dahrkron was already there, meeting the leader halfway with jaws open, and the two krahstas clashed in midair. They met, teeth against teeth, the sound sickening as they collided.

His feet on the ground, Dahrkron felt Trahkor start to slide his face downward, but beat him to it. His head to the side, Dahrkron found the leader's throat and locked his jaws with all his strength. He held desperately, ignoring the screaming pain from his battered teeth. The warm blood poured into his mouth, and he heard Trahkor's last howl die before it ever left his belly. The old leader fell to his side and was gone.

CHAPTER 17

Only for the past few months had there been problems within the pack. The drought, the food supply, and Trahkor's inability to deal with it brought about his downfall. Prior to all of this, there were never complaints about his decisions or how he handled the internal structure of the pack. Trahkor had been loved and respected.

But now Trahkor was gone.

While the pack finished off the remainder of the fallen krahsta, Dahrkron and Trahna surprised everyone by stepping back and loping away together, leaving behind a group full of whispers.

Good leaders were always overrun by bad leaders, who would then be replaced by a good one. Full circle, always. The new ruler would always want to change everything, leaving nothing behind to remind the pack of how things used to be. Now they spoke in uncertain whispers, because, save for his lack of aggressiveness near the end, Trahkor had been a good and fair ruler.

"We'll be okay," said Droanna, trying to reassure herself and the others. They were all a bit concerned about the sudden departure of their new leader. Sudden and without comment. "He's always been nice and considerate. Be in peace."

"You say it easily," said Brezni, licking the last of his share of Trahkor from his face. "Dahrkron is your sibling, not ours. You know as do we how the leaders change their faces."

"And why isn't he here to let us know how he stands?" asked Traffni, who was one of the senior statesmen of the pack. He was beginning to rely more and more on the efforts of others for his food, having lost a step or two of his speed. "We need to know these things," he added, although speaking to no one in particular.

"I cannot answer for my brother," said Droanna, looking over the anxious faces. "In fact, I truly wish he were here to talk about it, and I'm just as surprised as all of you that he's gone. But both of you who spoke, and others who look at me questioning: didn't you all follow him on his hunts? You were there. You saw how he handled himself. And you chose to follow him instead of Trahkor."

"Not all of us," a voice rang from the sage outside the perimeter of the group. The brush rustled and a forgotten krahsta stepped forward and passed through the hushed group, standing at last before Droanna. It was Prushtah, the mate of Trahkor.

Confusion and fear swept over Droanna. She did not fear a challenge or an attack, but this was for the pack leader to handle and not her.

"Well, where is he?" asked Prushtah, seeming to read Droanna's thoughts. "Am I to be a second-class citizen now? Fed only what the pack doesn't want? Or am I to end up like my mate?" She motioned in the direction of the carcass of Trahkor, and then actually took a look at it for the first time. She had not taken part in the post-battle feast, so her first impression was the moonlight reflecting off the rib cage, licked clean by the pack. Prushtah closed her eyes quickly and turned her head away. The slightest whimper, not meant to be heard, slipped out.

Droanna immediately stepped forward and nestled her head against Prushtah's. They had been close friends for many seasons, and Droanna was ashamed at having forgotten about her in such a desperate time. The grief swept over them like the tide, and together they began to whimper unashamedly, and the rest of the pack walked away.

"They're going to be wondering about this," said Trahna softly. Neither of them had spoken since she and

Dahrkron had taken seats on their favorite secluded ledge in the Canyon.

"I have a lot to think about first," said Dahrkron. "I don't know whether to be happy or sad."

"It's natural to be both," said Trahna. "Trahkor was a good leader and a very nice krahsta. Grieve for him, but be happy too, because now the pack won't go hungry anymore. And no one was happy with the way things were split up. Now everyone knows who to follow."

"It was suicide, you know," said Dahrkron, looking out over the stars. "He wanted to die. I could see it in his eyes. He was losing the pack and it was humiliating. I wish things didn't have to be like this."

"Or how they must be," said Trahna, and Dahrkron turned to her, his look a question. "The tradition," she answered. "As leader you must throw out the old, and be your own leader. You must do nothing as he did. To do so would invite suspicion."

"But he was a good leader," said Dahrkron, shaking his head. "I want to be just like him, except more daring about the hunts. I'm going to try my best to be a good leader too."

"You must be tough, my love," Trahna said sincerely. "The others will expect it and they won't respect you otherwise."

"I can't be," said Dahrkron. "They'll be happy to get two fair leaders in a row. I think that's why they followed me to begin with. They were hoping I would take over and be as nice as when we hunted together."

"We must think of something then," said Trahna. She watched him anxiously paw at the rocky Canyon dirt and knew he could never accept being a tough or cruel leader. She loved him even more for it, yet feared the reaction of the pack. Tradition was tradition. But old ways could change with the right approach. After all, just the fact that they were discussing it was a huge breakthrough; leaders never confided important matters to their mates.

"I've got an idea," she said at last.

"Somehow I knew you would," said Dahrkron kindly.

* * *

The pack had grown quiet and calm as dawn began to ease its way into the Canyon. The songs of morning rang their usual harmony, with the annoying squawks of an upset mockingbird filling in the lead. All ears in the area were bothered enough to get the krahstas stirring a little. Few, if any had slept.

What little drowsiness there was within the group vanished instantly when Dahrkron and Trahna walked silently into their midst. The response was immediate. Everyone was on their feet and gathered around the two without a word. To Dahrkron it was a little bit ominous, though expected.

Dahrkron exchanged a brief glance with every member of the pack. The significance of his sister Droanna standing next to Prushtah was not lost on him. He stepped forward and gave her a slight bow.

"I am sorry, Prushtah," he said sincerely. "Trahkor was a great leader, and I will miss him."

"Yes," said Prushtah nervously. "Well. All things must pass. I hope it is for the best." She looked away quickly and then looked down. She was now just a single bitch in a pack with a new leader. He could have her killed if he wanted to, and half the pack suspected he just might.

"You will be treated well, as will everyone else," said Dahrkron.

All ears perked up at this announcement, although most still held strong doubt. Trahkor was the fair and just leader. Dahrkron would have to be different.

"There will be changes," Dahrkron said to the entire group, and everyone nodded, awaiting the grim news. "Changes in tradition mostly. And changes in style and technique."

Dahrkron could see the confusion and doubt start to appear on the faces of his pack. He liked it. Things just might work out.

"We will continue on the aggressive hunts those of you who followed me before are used to. We will work on being more organized in the way we approach our hunting areas. And we will hunt in areas where none of us have ever dared to venture before."

Another sea of questioning faces responded to this statement, and Dahrkron was pleased. He could also see a little apprehension in some of the older krahstas.

"Bold, courageous, and daring," Dahrkron continued. "Never again are we going to go hungry like we have this summer. If there's no prey in our normal hunting grounds, then we'll go elsewhere. We have to change with our environment. If it means going into another predator's territory and fighting it out, then that's what we'll do. If it means occasionally raiding the man settlement for a stray farri or kriba, then we'll do that too."

This caused quite a murmur throughout the pack.

"Be careful, Dahrkron. You know what happened to the puma." It was Khanval, Dahrkron's closest friend. The others in the group were happy to hear him speak, for Dahrkron would be less likely to turn so quickly on one he trusted.

"I believe the puma was killed because they were looking for the puma," said Dahrkron, having anticipated the subject of the cougar. "Besides, my friend, I didn't say we would do it for a regular source of food. Only if we become desperate, or if there is a great chance for an easy swoop with many kills. Don't worry; I fear the man too.

"But there is opportunity. I have seen it. Sometimes at night, at the very edge of the road where the Canyon ends, whole groups of farries get together and meet right out in the open. I have seen as many as fifteen on one night. Had the pack been with me, we could have had a wonderful feast!

"But like I said, only on rare occasions will we go there. And I don't think the men are paying attention now. They're happy now since the puma's dead."

"You mentioned fighting with other predators," said Brezni. "Do you think this is wise?"

"When you think about it," said Dahrkron, "we don't have to fight *anybody*. Let's say we find a great spot for food but there's a bobcat living in the area. We'll just hunt *him* down, surround him, and tell him to find someplace else. We won't attack him, or take any chances of getting any of us hurt. We'll just let him know there's one of him and thirteen of us, and he'd be much better off if he moved.''

The pack seemed to accept this well enough, and Dahrkron was glad. He specifically picked a lynx to use as his example, to plant a seed in their heads. He hated cats, and he wanted them to hate cats just as much as he did. He would make all cats the enemy, which they were anyway, but he would turn it into a cause. And they would all be satisfied things had really changed, while he continued to run things exactly how they had been. He would be a good and fair leader. He just wanted to prove that cats weren't superior after all. Never mind what would happen if they ran into *two* bobcats. He would deal with that dilemma when he had to.

CHAPTER 18

Everyone at the office thought they were a hot item. Everyone except the two people involved. Roger sat with Laura in the cafeteria, feasting on the fast food she had grabbed on her way in from a story. Roger noticed how the other employees no longer raised their eyebrows when they saw Laura and him together. Now it was just taken for granted. Amazing how these things worked.

Laura wanted to talk about Jerry Radcliff. But first she wanted to scarf down the huge chef salad she was working on. She would eat it all, Roger was certain. He also suspected Laura of being a closet Big Mac junkie, although she would never admit it. Health food all the way, she would say. She finished it all, and then gave the lunchroom crowd a quick glance.

"He's into something dirty, I think," said Laura. She paused and looked around again.

"How so?" asked Roger finally.

"I've heard too many bad things about him," she said. "I don't want to say much around here."

"That bad?" asked Roger.

"I don't know," said Laura. "It's not that, anyway. It's just something that would look good in the right places if things went well."

"I get it," said Roger. She was looking for a new job, and was up for one in another city. A good investigative piece would look great on the résumé right about now, even though Roger knew Laura didn't care about investigative stuff. She really didn't care about news, either, at least on this level. She hoped a larger paper would be more interesting.

"Staying out all night again?" asked Laura, answering Roger's yawn.

"You know I'd only stay out late if I was with you," he smiled.

Laura stuck out her tongue and gave a long, wet raspberry.

"I couldn't sleep last night," said Roger. "It sounds like a whole tribe of coyotes moved in down the block. The bastards howled all night."

"They know the cougar's gone," said Laura. "They're moving in on the territory."

"I liked it better with the cougar," said Roger. "At least it was quiet."

Laura smiled and checked out the crowd again. She leaned forward and lowered her voice.

"Radcliff is into something," she said. "I mean it. I don't know exactly what, yet. It might have something to do with the automatic rifle you caught him with. My friend downtown says there haven't been any busts where they've confiscated large weapons lately, and even if there were, Radcliff wouldn't have anything to do with it. And since the narcs don't use weapons like that, he certainly wouldn't have access to one."

"And?" asked Roger, raising his palms. He was afraid of where this might be leading.

"My contact was alarmed when I told him Radcliff had one," said Laura. "The cougar-hunting story didn't wash, even though he ended up killing one. With his service revolver, I might add. He obviously didn't need an automatic rifle. I'm still upset about the whole thing, even though the poor cougar did have rabies. It wasn't exactly something I wanted to watch."

"Me either," said Roger. "I've got a feeling all of this is leading to something."

"Would you go along with me sometime if I did some snooping?" asked Laura.

"Like how?" asked Roger.

"I don't know. Maybe follow him a little. I can find out where he goes and who he sees. We can just happen to be at a few places when he's there. Again, I don't know yet. We'll see." She looked at Roger with eyebrows up, quizzing for an answer.

"I don't know," he said. "We'll see."

CHAPTER 19

Mahri was delighted to see Melena. In the weeks following the death of Sarena, contact with other farries had been nonexistent. It seemed most of the neighborhood was still hiding.

But Melena came to visit, and Mahri was glad. The two friends touched noses with a rush of warm feelings, followed by a quick stab of pain and loss. So much loss. A life-style they had come to know, if not necessarily love, with so much interaction with other farries. Life was so lonely now. The loss of many friends, and of course, the permanent loss of a big friend.

"Well, my dear Mahri, who would have thought so much could happen to us?" Melena said after a long, not unpleasant silence. Mahri did not speak but returned a sad, knowing smile.

"Maybe all of it was wrong," said Melena, "but it's such an empty feeling now. I've really missed you all this time. And I miss Halina so much, and how smart she was. She always knew the right thing to say in any situation. And I miss the toms too."

Her last words were said almost with a hush and a hidden smile. Mahri understood. The arrival of Melena and her soft voice brought back a flood of memories. Not just of the group and their dealings with toms, but the good times she had with Melena, prowling around and looking for trouble. Fantastic hunting trips, and scuffles with other farries. And Melena was such a sweetheart. She could talk them out of bad situations when things got a little rough.

"Just a couple of girls out having a fun time," she would say to the angry tom who was about to rip their lungs out for jumping him and stealing his catch. "We didn't want your food. We just wanted *you!*" She would give him her sweet and sultry look and the old tom would just melt right there. No problem.

"Yes, I miss the toms too," Mahri agreed with a smile. "Have you seen anyone else from the group?"

"Just in passing. No one has wanted to talk about anything, so, well, you know how it goes. I saw Syranosh across the street once, but she just pretended not to see me and went the other way. You know how she is. Maybe it's just as well.

"Oh, and I forgot! I saw Halina! She lives close to me, you know. Right next door and I never see her anymore. My dear, she looked so sad. Well, I guess she looked like all the rest of us. She said she likes to spend her time inside the house these days. Imagine. Halina inside! Oh Mahri, things are so sad."

Mahri lowered her head at the mention of Halina. How desperately she would like to see the mistress, just to talk things out. And maybe . . . Maybe. Well, maybe talk things back in.

"I know how you feel," said Melena, reading Mahri's thoughts. "There's a lot of things that need to be said. About the group. About what happened. And even about Sarena. We had a final meeting and that was it. Since then I've thought of about a million things to say to Halina and the group. But I feel like it's no use."

"Me too," said Mahri, surprised and happy to find another member of the group who agreed with everything she had felt since the breakup. "I've wanted to talk to Halina so much. And you. And everyone, really. Well, maybe not Syranosh," and both farries giggled.

"I mean it, though," Mahri continued. "It's funny, we haven't even said anything, really. But we both know what we want and what we've felt. I think we should go over to Halina's house and see if she's out."

"Okay," said Melena. "I don't think she'll be out, though. But let's try anyway. Who knows; we may roust up some trouble just like we used to."

"*You* were the one who used to get us into trouble," Mahri laughed. "I was the one who was always praying to Lady Farri for our safe escape."

"No, dear," said Melena, trying to keep a straight face. "It was you who started it all, with me finishing things up."

"Yeah, you almost finished us to death," said Mahri with a sideways glance.

Melena hissed, and the two friends laughed together.

The walk toward Halina's house was filled with talk of old times. They took their time, since finding the mistress would be by chance anyway. It was also still fairly hot in the Southern California summer. Unseasonably hot and dry, although it was better than the earlier days when they had walked through the Canyon to see Sarena.

Halina lived nearly a block away from Mahri, who resided farthest from the Den of all the farries in the group. Halina's house was only three doors down from the dead end at the edge of the Canyon where the girls had met every night. And where the boys met.

Mahri and Melena walked up to Halina's hedge. Normally the mistress would be under the hedge near the front door, keeping cool and covered. She had a thing about always having her outline broken by some kind of bush or wild surroundings. Some of the girls had thought it was a mild case of the spooks, but Mahri knew better. Mahri had noticed how smoothly Halina's tones and exotic stripes blended in with the scenery. And like Sarena, Mahri suspected wild lineage in Halina's blood. Keeping hidden was an instinct.

Halina was not home. At least she was not in the yard and did not answer Mahri's calls.

"She must be inside, dear," said Melena. "It's too bad we don't know the paladin's magic for opening doors, or we could drop in and pay a visit."

"Why don't we take a walk over to the Den," said Mahri. "Just for a look. Maybe we'll see someone else on the way."

"Are you sure?" asked Melena skeptically.

"I haven't been down here for so long," said Mahri. "Oh, come on. Maybe we can call a tom."

Melena laughed and agreed.

They stepped out to the sidewalk, and Mahri was surprised to see Syranosh standing in the yard across the street. Melena lived next door to Halina opposite the Canyon, and Syranosh lived two doors down from her. Syranosh was only the second cat Mahri had seen since the breakup of the group, and she motioned for Melena to follow her across the street.

"Go ahead," said Melena. "She doesn't like me much. Besides, I want to walk down to the Den on this side. I'll meet you down there in a few minutes."

"Syranosh doesn't like anyone much," Mahri smiled. "I understand. I'll see you over there."

Mahri turned and started across the street. Either Syranosh had not seen them yet, or she was choosing to ignore them. Mahri approached directly, but not threateningly. Syranosh was hunched down to her elbows and looking away.

"Hi sister!" Mahri beamed.

Syranosh turned her head around slowly, her face offering no expression. "Aren't you a little bit out of your neighborhood, girl?" she said with almost growl tones.

"Just dropping by to see old friends," said Mahri, slightly taken aback.

"Then go see them," said Syranosh, and turned her head away again.

Mahri backed slowly to the sidewalk, and then walked toward the Den. There was nothing more to say, and getting upset about it would not solve anything. She was about to turn around for a final look then decided against it. Syranosh wasn't worth it.

She followed the sidewalk along for the two more houses before the Canyon and the Den. She looked back across the street but did not see Melena anywhere. Had she found Halina? Mahri would know shortly. They might all be meeting at the Den. Wouldn't it be great? Together with her two favorite farries. Well, two of the three. Sharlo was pretty neat too.

Suddenly all senses went to alert. A tail, short and very bushy, was standing straight up from behind the other side of the curb. Mahri could not tell what animal was its owner, but from here it had "prey" written all over it. She crept forward the slightest bit and peered over to take a look.

Squirrel. Prey.

Mahri ducked back down and moved quickly along the sidewalk and then over to the curb above the squirrel in the gutter. It seemed to be looking intently at something, although Mahri had not dared expose herself long enough to find out what. Surprise would have to be everything.

She reached the point where progress was an inch at a time. Crouched as low as she could be, she reached the edge of the curb, from where she would have to make her move. She was mildly surprised she had gotten this far without the squirrel looking over the curb at least once.

Every nerve in her body twitching, she tensed and prepared to jump. She estimated two leaps between herself and the bushy, twitching tail. She leaned back, putting her weight on her hind legs, held her breath, and then sprang with all of her strength.

High and straight she flew, and was halfway through the first leap when she realized the peril. She leaned hard to her left to change her course, and only the element of surprise saved her life as she landed awkwardly and took one quick step to the side and froze. It was immediately clear why the squirrel had not ventured a glance over the curb, and just as clear who was now the center of attention.

Mahri stood at the edge of the gutter, motionless and hardly able to breath, face-to-face with a fully coiled rattlesnake.

It's eyes, stupid and cruel, bore down on her and she felt panic and dizziness sweep over her entire system. Mahri had never seen a snake before, but every instinct warning available was blaring full blast. This was trouble.

The snake seemed intent on just staring her down, yet she knew the slightest movement would be disaster. It did not matter, though, because the longer she returned the snake's gaze, the more impossible it was to move. The hypnotic effect had every muscle locked, and she understood why the squirrel still remained standing in the gutter, even though the snake's attention was now directed the other way.

The serpent raised a tail full of rattles directly behind his head and shook them with fury. The position of the snake enabled Mahri to see the rattles without taking her eyes from the snake's face, foiling the whole intent of the rattling.

The shiny, diamond-patterned reptile skin sparkled in the sun as the snake moved ever so slightly, further straining Mahri's concentration. Her head began to spin, and she tried desperately to fight it off while remaining still and not looking away from the enemy. The flashing sparkle even began to make her forget about the fangs, so long and fierce, and clearly deadly.

Desperation was setting in. Breathing was becoming forced and difficult, and she knew she had to move or die. Move *and* die probably, but at least there was a chance. Standing here left no option.

Her mind screamed at her body to jump fast and hard and be prepared to twist. No response. Somewhere the message got lost. Legs had not moved, feet were still in the same place, and her whole body was still within easy striking distance of those two gleaming and very deadly fangs. Or were they? Didn't it look like the snake was smiling?

The first thing she noticed out of the corner of her eye was the slightest movement by the squirrel. It was recovering from the hypnosis. It did not, however, move enough to distract the snake.

The next thing Mahri saw was movement behind the snake. It was black and it was coming from the same direction she had. Mahri dared not focus on whatever it was, but her mind held no doubt. It was Melena.

The black vanished and Mahri wanted to scream. Melena was stalking the squirrel, just as she had done. And although Melena must have seen her too, she obviously missed the snake.

Mahri knew she was going to die, and wanted to warn Melena and save her the same fate. A scream would end it all quickly, for the snake would surely strike. But a scream would also scare off Melena, and maybe even the squirrel could get away too. But just like the demand for action, the scream got lost somewhere before it reached her throat.

Suddenly the sky was dark and Mahri's gaze at the snake was broken for the first time as she looked up and saw Melena airborne and diving for the squirrel. But the attacker's look went from triumph to terror when she saw the snake far too late, and landed directly on its coiled back.

The response was immediate. The snake's fangs were in Melena's left flank before her entire weight had come full. The cry was far beyond the simple pain of the wound. It was the cry of ultimate sorrow, and the knowledge of death.

Melena bounded into the street and already her limp was almost a drag. The snake turned toward Melena in pursuit; Mahri saw the squirrel jump up to the sidewalk. The spell broken, Mahri ran wide of the snake, and then after Melena, who had finally reached the other sidewalk across the street. When Mahri reached her, she was on the lawn of the house nearest the Canyon. Her accelerated heart rate from the terror and ensuing sprint across the street pumped the venom through her body. She was already dragging both hind legs as she reached the shade of a low tree in the yard.

Melena's eyes were glazed and frantic, and she whimpered softly as she collapsed to her left side. Her face was broken with defeat, and she looked into Mahri's eyes with unspoken words louder and stronger than any she had ever voiced. A very dear friendship was about to end.

"Oh Melena!" Mahri cried. "Oh dear Farri, this should be me! Why couldn't I warn her?"

"Dearest Mahri," Melena whispered hoarsely, "snakes are evil things. I know of their ways and I know you could not speak, even if you knew I was there. I should have taken better care."

Mahri licked her dying friend's face gently, doing all she could for comfort. Melena panted roughly and rested her head on her paws.

"Fight it!" said Mahri suddenly. "Please don't let it take you!"

Melena was almost gone. Her eyelids fluttered, trying to stay open. Mahri could barely see her deep green eyes.

"It's okay, my love," said Melena. "The Lady is calling. I hear her now. We'll be together again. I promise. We'll . . . Never mind. Just remember me, dearest Mahri. Just remember."

CHAPTER 20

He hoped the phone would not ring tonight. Roger wanted a night without having to talk to anyone. A six-pack of Molson, maybe some Jack Daniel's a little later on, and the opening game of the San Diego Chargers preseason on TV. Roger was not sure who they were playing, although it mattered little in the preseason. Tryouts, really, until the real season started and then the Chargers would go at it again with the world's greatest offense and world's worst defense. At least it never got boring.

The cat was between his feet and rubbing hard against his ankles. Dinner time. She was being more subtle than the usual howls when her bowl was empty. Roger wondered if she was just bored.

The store had been out of the normal gourmet food she preferred, so Roger bought the real cheap stuff. Really cheap. Generic minced mackerel.

"You're gonna love this shit," Roger smiled, reaching for the can opener, and remembering how it was he, and not necessarily De Lilah, who liked the gourmet food better. The expensive stuff had the easy-open cans.

The can was only half open when the smell hit him. Generic minced mackerel was a real nostril burner, to say the least. He pulled off the top and reached for a fork, but found the fork unnecessary. The rich dark brown contents oozed into the bowl with a runny plop.

"You're gonna love this shit," repeated Roger. "Generic canned diarrhea." He put the bowl down and watched De Lilah walk up, cautiously sniffing. She walked around the bowl twice and then looked up at Roger.

"Yes, I expect you to eat it," he said, answering De Lilah's look of disgust.

De Lilah turned away from the bowl and pawed at the floor, making the motions of trying to bury it.

"Fuck you," said Roger, and walked into the den.

Roger stretched out on the couch and thought of work. Even the weekends were getting rough. The office was swamped with back-to-school-rush ads, and Roger was spending a sixth day at it once again. Another day of advertising agents and their obnoxious demands. Roger opened a beer.

It only took until the second play of the game before the cat was sitting on his stomach and blocking the view. She started to bathe but Roger picked her up and put her on the top part of the couch, only to have her back on his chest before the start of the next play. She crouched to her shoulders and looked him right in the eye.

"Is there something I can do you for?" Roger asked De Lilah. Her eyes were wide and direct, unusual for a cat who had been in the house all day. Lately she had remained lazy and did nothing but lie around. He thought about the night she came home all scratched up and wondered if that was the reason.

"You've got good food in there and you know it. People all over the world are starving and you won't eat mackerel." When the cat did not respond, he added, "I bet you just want me to miss the Chargers kill the Rams."

The doorbell rang and Roger groaned. It was avoidable, though. The car was in the garage and nobody knew he was home. And who ever came over without calling anyway? He just paid the paperboy last week. He scratched De Lilah's head and decided the problem would go away if he ignored it.

Whoever it was clearly knew he was home and was persistent. Roger mumbled a complaint and sat up, holding De Lilah in his lap. He picked her up and carried her to the front door and put her down on the old brown recliner. He gave a quick peek through the curtains and saw Mrs. Grant from next door. He ran his fingers through his hair with a sigh of defeat, and then opened the door, immediately giving the old lady his best salesman's smile.

"Hi, Mrs. Grant." Roger beamed, but was instantly taken aback by how upset she looked.

"Roger. How are you, son? Could you spare a few minutes?"

"Of course," said Roger, showing concern yet inwardly gritting his teeth. So much for a quiet evening. He opened the door to let her in, only to have her startled when she almost collided with De Lilah, who was bounding full speed for outside. Roger was actually glad to see her dash around the hedge and disappear.

"Oh my. You should keep her in, Roger," said Mrs. Grant gravely. "Twice my little Theseus got chewed up in fights. And then today—"

"Here, sit down," Roger offered, and hoped Mrs. Grant would not cry. Obviously bad news about Theseus was on the way.

"Thank you. I'm okay, really. It's been a long day."

She sat with her hands clasped on her lap and absently looked over Roger's cluttered living room. She looked quickly back to Roger, knowing he would be uncomfortable being caught with a messy house. He was usually so neat.

"Today Ben Conover from a few houses down called me," said Mrs. Grant. "You know Ben. He lives on this side, right on the edge of the canyon."

Roger nodded, although he didn't know and didn't really care who most of his neighbors were. Ben could have been anybody.

"He knew my Theseus," she went on. "He had taken her to the vet for me before, when I was out of town. Well, he called me today because there was a dead cat on his lawn and he thought it was my Theseus. There was no doubt, of course, but he just wanted to make sure.

"Anyway, he thought it was an awfully strange place for her to die, right there on his lawn. He noticed some blood on her left hind leg. Not a lot, so he asked me if she was in heat and of course she wasn't 'cause she'd been fixed. So Ben thought maybe some neighbor kid shot her with a pellet gun, and wanted me to take her to the vet to find out.

"Well, you know me. I was just too shook up to want to see my kitten anymore like that. But he was insistent about it because he's got a couple of dogs, you know, and he wanted to find out if kids were shooting guns at people's pets. So he took her in at his own cost just to find out.

"Poor little Theseus. What an awful death. She was bitten by a rattlesnake. Ugh. How awful."

"A rattlesnake?" asked Roger, truly alarmed. For some reason he could better have accepted the pellet gun theory. Mrs. Grant nodded and Roger looked across the room and out the screen door. "God, what else is gonna come out of the canyon this summer?"

The phone rang as if answering his question, and he stood up, excusing himself. He passed by the TV set and turned it down. It was the news reporter who had interviewed and not used him the night of the cougar death.

"Listen, I'm sorry we couldn't get to you," said Rosemary Ogden. "I wanted to use it but they cut us short because of all the other stuff going on that night."

"I guess that's the way it goes," said Roger.

"Anyway, we're doing a story tonight," said Ogden. "A follow-up story in the neighborhood. I don't know if you heard, but the cougar had rabies."

"I heard."

"Oh, good. Well, we're gonna be around tonight, asking people what they think about everything that's happened, and I was wondering if we could stop by and interview you again. You were so good last time."

Roger bit down hard to keep back the one-liner dying to surface after her last sentence. He simply laughed instead.

"What?" she asked about the laugh.

"Just use the interview from three weeks ago," said Roger. "It'll still work."

"The tape got erased," said Ogden. "I wrote 'save' on it, but it got lost anyway."

"I can't tonight. I'm going out," Roger lied.

"When? We can get there before you leave. Or maybe meet you somewhere."

"I don't think so. I'm late already."

"We'll only take five minutes," Ogden insisted.

"Sorry, gotta go."

Roger went back out to talk with Mrs. Grant. He had barely sat down when the phone rang again. He rolled his eyes and stood up, and was surprised to see Mrs. Grant stand as well.

"You're busy," she said. "I'll talk to you soon. Just be careful with little De Lilah, and keep her inside."

"Okay," said Roger as she stepped outside. "And I'm really sorry about Theseus."

"Thank you, dear. Take care."

Roger got to the phone on the fourth ring and then almost didn't answer it. He was certain it was Rosemary Ogden again.

"Hello," he said, sounding very irritated.

"Hello yourself," said Laura.

"Oh, hi. Sorry," said Roger. "I was expecting someone else. Remember the TV reporter who interviewed me the night Radcliff shot the cougar? She just called."

Silence on the other end.

"Hello?" said Roger.

"I'm here," said Laura. "Just thinking. What did she want?"

"My body, of course," Roger grinned, but got no response. "She wanted to interview me again. She's doing a follow-up on the cougar and the rabies."

"I saw her last night," said Laura. "She was at Friday's."

"And?" asked Roger.

"And she was with Jerry Radcliff."

"Really? That's interesting," said Roger, although he was more interested in who Laura was with, but would never ask.

"It is interesting," echoed Laura. "I don't think Radcliff is the type who would hang out in Friday's, so he was obviously there *with* her. And she was definitely there with him. She was hangin' all over him."

"I guess there's someone for everybody," said Roger.

"Guess so, but I think this is getting pretty weird. I still have more checking to do on Radcliff. Talk about weird. I'll tell you all about it later. I'm kinda on the run. Let's go out Monday night."

"Okay. Call me and we'll arrange it," said Roger. She never asked if he had other plans. She always said, "Let's go," and knew he would, other plans or not. And always Monday or Tuesday. Never on a weekend.

"See ya," she said, and was gone.

Back to the football game; the first quarter was already over. And the phone rang again. It was Tammy, who wanted to come over and watch the rest of the game with him.

CHAPTER 21

The night was unusually alive with sounds. The warm summer air was perfect for movement in the Canyon, and the failing moon gave necessary cover to all of the residents. Birds were awake and noisy despite the darkness, although nearly drowned out by the loud drone of insects. Rabbits and squirrels romped about, taking advantage of the break from the hot afternoons. The sage rustled gently in the calm, caressing breeze.

Coyotes were about.

A strange night for such predators. The end of the moon was the end of hunting in the dark hours. Raids were limited to the early hours, when the sun first licked the mountains in the east. Nights like these found coyotes sleeping, and the rest of the Canyon knew it.

"You don't have to go," Dahrkron had told the pack. "If you want to rest for the morning I understand. But I think we'll do well tonight and won't need to go out tomorrow."

"Krahstas don't hunt on nights like this, Dahrkron," said Brezni. "It's tradition to rest when the moon dies."

"You're right, old friend," said Dahrkron. "That's why we should strike now. No one will expect us. Remember when I told you we will break tradition? Now is one of those times."

The pack set out toward the man homes, but turned away shortly before reaching their newly claimed territory and headed south instead. Dahrkron ordered silence, although no one was up for any chatter or howling anyway.

Dahrkron stopped at the top of a ridge overlooking a small branch of the Canyon. There was very little brush along the edge where they stood, but the lower part was thick with sage and holly. They had never been in this part of the Canyon before, and the pack gathered around Dahrkron quietly. The sense of prey was on them, and the tradition of sleep was quickly forgotten. Everyone was wide-awake and ready to strike.

''We're going to move along the edge there for just a little bit,'' said Dahrkron, ''and then we'll spread out and go straight down the hill. Catch what you can, but no noise. Remember. No noise. We'll want to try this again if it works.''

The pack loped along the dirt and rocks on the ledge, stopping one at a time until the whole group was spread in equal distance. They all looked down the hill, remaining motionless until Dahrkron stepped forward. The chase was on.

The hill was steep but the krahstas moved well. Dahrkron was between Trahna and Prushtah, and he secretly hoped for a chance to chase something in the direction of the latter. He had discussed it privately with Trahna earlier in the afternoon, and they both agreed to keep her as happy as possible.

Three squirrels broke the instant Dahrkron hit the brush. He charged the center one, leaping a bush to intercept it before it reached a hole. The squirrel cut back to the right just as Dahrkron landed, and scooted right between his back paws. He turned to chase, seeing the hole and knowing escape was only a few strides away. He made a dive straight for the entrance and bit down hard and fast, hoping he wasn't too late.

The result was a squeal and a face full of claws. He had the squirrel by the tail, and it had turned on him quickly and was clawing and biting at his face. Dahrkron let go fast and bit at the squirrel's abdomen. One solid crunch, and the battle was over.

He held up the prize and was happy to see Prushtah holding one too. Trahna had not been so lucky with hers, but flushed another one before taking three more steps. And they were *everywhere*. Dahrkron saw every member of the pack holding a squirrel before he could even drop his catch to chase another. This valley was a great find.

It took only a few minutes for the majority of the squirrels to hide, but it was time enough. There was plenty to eat for the pack of Dahrkron the Leader, and any remaining doubt about the new boss passed with the breeze into the night.

The pack carried their kills back to the top of the ridge and feasted on squirrel. And every individual, including Prushtah, approached Dahrkron and congratulated him on his genius. He had won them over faster than any legend of any leader.

Most of the pack finished their meals and pranced around in small, playful circles. They nipped at each other and rolled in the dirt, acting like the young pups who still stayed back at the den with their mothers. Dahrkron watched and was glad to see how fast the morale had changed for the better.

"How do you think of these things?" Droanna asked her brother.

"Things?" asked Dahrkron, still watching the pack play.

"How did you know to come out here tonight? Everything you've done so far has worked out."

"Yes. Well, luck I guess. I like to take chances. Tradition is just like the pack. It sticks together, and you can't see outside of it. I broke away from the pack when Trahkor was leader so I could see what else was going on. We were going to follow him into starvation.

"Tradition is like that too. We've always followed it, without even taking a look elsewhere. Bad tradition can starve us just as easily as a bad leader. So I'm going to keep breaking away as long as it works. Plus, it keeps the pack alert. They never know what to expect."

"Take care in talking too much about this," warned Droanna. "Tradition is long, but memories can be short. Keeping the pack fed will do you no good if you bite the wrong tails."

"That's part of the plan, Droanna," said Dahrkron. "Keep them guessing enough so they don't realize just how few tails are being bitten. Tradition is strange enough for them to be angry if I treat them well. I just won't give them time to think about it."

"Okay, brother," said Droanna, "but just beware of who you say these things to."

Dahrkron looked over the happy group of playful krahstas and said, "I'm not worried about it yet."

When the pack began to relax and sit still, Dahrkron stood up and walked into the middle of the group. "I think we can head back now," he said. "But first, I'd like to walk down to the bottom of this gully and look around. We'll go along the bottom all the way over to the other end and then come up over there.

"We can probably leave our extra squirrels here until we get back," he said, looking at the food to be brought back for the mothers and their pups. "I didn't smell any predators around."

The pack walked casually back down the hill. They still saw squirrels, although no one gave chase. They would be back.

"Keep your eyes open for any signs of rabbits," said Dahrkron. "I didn't see any when we were down here, but there might be some along the bottom."

They walked along the center of an ancient, rock-bottom creek bed, dried forever except for the brief rainy season. They preferred the openness of the creek, even though the footing was sometimes shaky. Walking through the brush was asking for stray thorns and stickers of every kind.

The creek bed reached the point where the ledge at the top of the Canyon broke away, so the pack began to climb up to head back. The Canyon wall was far more level on this end, and it was an easier hike than where they had first come in. The brush was spaced enough for easy walking and good visibility, but still Dahrkron saw no signs of rabbits.

At the top of the ledge, Dahrkron said, "Let's step over to the other side, here, and take a look down over there."

The pack walked along the narrow, lower lip of the north side of the ledge. The ledge was only two feet above them, but they could see nothing on top of it. They could only see north, and could tell right away it was inaccessible from where they were. They went to the end of the path and then jumped back up.

They found themselves in the exact spot where they had left their squirrels, only to everyone's surprise, things had changed. One of the dead squirrels had moved. It was now hanging from the mouth of an equally startled lynx. The bobcat dropped the squirrel and looked around the pack.

"Why should I not be surprised at this?" said the lynx with disgust. "Who else but a pack of filthy krahstas would go through my territory and slaughter prey for no reason? Look at this, you butchers." The lynx looked down at the carcasses of over a dozen squirrels.

Dahrkron stepped forward and began to smile the slightest bit. Behind him, the pack began to fan out into a semicircle around the lynx, leaving his back to the slope of the Canyon.

"*Your* territory, puss?" asked Dahrkron. "I think not. This is our hunting ground now. You're welcome to leave." As they had practiced earlier in the week, the pack had left an opening for the lynx to escape without a fight. They would just make sure he understood how permanent his departure would be.

The lynx growled, fluffing up all areas of fur. "You will not just take my territory. My claim is sacred, and I will fight for it."

Dahrkron took a step forward, a signal for the pack to do the same. He could sense them all: tense, crouched, and ready to spring at his word. Their hot breath was an encouragement to go on.

"Last chance, puss," said Dahrkron. "Back out now, or be mauled. You cannot take our numbers. Leave here forever."

"You stinky dogs will all suffer for your mistake," said the lynx.

Dahrkron smiled with satisfaction and felt himself relax as the lynx took a step back. Suddenly the lynx was airborne, heading straight for Dahrkron. Ducking too late, Dahrkron felt the vicious front claws catch the top of his head. He reached up to bite but the cat was on top of him and using his back as a springboard. Rear claws stuck in Dahrkron's ribs, the lynx launched over the line of krahstas and was at full speed before they could react.

Trahna was the closest and she began the chase. The pack was in full pursuit behind her, howling and barking with each step. But strength in numbers only hindered the krahstas, who were no match for the graceful speed of the lynx. He was lost before they reached the end of the ledge.

The pack stopped and everyone turned to Dahrkron, who came up last. He was scratched and bleeding on the head and side, yet he smiled wide, brimming with excitement.

"Oh, it's worth it," he said to their questioning eyes. "Such a small price for so much. All of this territory is ours!"

CHAPTER 22

Mahri liked mornings the best. The sun rose on the front side of the house, enabling her to curl up on the porch and feel its fine, warm rays before they got too hot. A farri could ask for no more than a nice, cozy nap on the protective turf of her own paladin's front doorstep.

She was restless, but hoped to sleep anyway. She had been awake most of the night, going back and forth between Sweetie Pie's room and the parents'. It was three days, and still she could not shake the vision of Melena and the rattlesnake. She wanted desperately to talk to Halina, but was nervous about walking down near the Canyon again. Funny how things can change, she thought with a sigh. But today she would seek the mistress out.

The legs and tail twitched in an unusual fashion. Too tired to sleep. Her whole body shook a little with the feeling, and she stretched her front paws forward and hoped the sun would help her relax.

She heard it first, her ears turning slightly and then perking straight up. She opened her eyes and saw nothing moving, but then picked up the scent that brought her to her feet. Another farri.

Mahri stood with neutral posture, wanting to identify who it was before showing attack or friendship. She couldn't imagine a hostile farri approaching this deep into her territory, but most of her friends lived quite a ways distant. When Syranosh hopped onto the three-foot fence at the edge of the lawn, Mahri extended her tail straight out and fluffed for fight.

Syranosh looked at Mahri indifferently and jumped

down into the yard. She walked forward without anger or friendship—just Syranosh. Mahri stayed fluffed and opened her mouth to hiss.

"Okay, sister, you got me scared to death," said Syranosh, making light of Mahri's stance. She continued to walk forward and stopped right at the edge of the step where Mahri stood. "Drop the fur, dearest. We need to talk."

Mahri's response was a quick jab at the face of Syranosh, whose half step back took her out of reach. Mahri almost fell off the step.

"Once more: drop the fur, baby," said Syranosh, who still hadn't fluffed. "You don't want to fight it out with me. I'll rip your pretty little face right off."

This, unfortunately, was true. Mahri would have no chance in a battle with Syranosh, who, besides Halina, was stronger and faster than any female farri in the area. And mean on top of it all. Even the neighborhood toms were afraid of her, those fierce yellow eyes blazing when she was provoked.

"Melena might be alive if it wasn't for you!" cried Mahri, who remained fluffed and hoped she looked angry and not frustrated or sad. She wanted to rip the other cat's lungs out, but was helpless to do anything about it.

"And how's that, sister?" Syranosh said with impatience. "Should I have stepped in and bitten the snake's head off?"

Mahri's eyes narrowed with contempt. She thought back to the events leading up to Melena's death and knew Syranosh had nothing to do with it, even though she associated Syranosh with her friend's death. Mahri thought she and Melena would not have separated if they had not seen Syranosh, and might have spotted the snake from a safe distance. Mahri also felt guilty about Melena being bitten and not herself. She just wished Syranosh would act as if she cared.

"What do you want?" growled Mahri, an accusation.

"Halina wants to see us," Syranosh said simply. "Come to the Den tonight." She turned around and started to leave.

"Does she know about Melena?" Mahri asked quickly.

"Of course, dearest," said Syranosh, who stopped and turned around. "My Farri! It happened three days ago! You think Halina wouldn't know about something like that right away? You've been chasing your tail too much." She reached the top of the fence with an easy and graceful leap.

"Thanks for coming out here to tell me about tonight," said Mahri, the sarcasm dripping from her voice.

"No problem, sister. What are friends for?"

Mahri believed she was more nervous now than when she, Melena, and Halina had walked through the Canyon together. She walked lightly, trying to be silent but feeling like every step landed with a hard thump. Her eyes scanned every direction, her whiskers and ears alert, searching for any trouble, seen or unseen.

What used to be a routine stroll every evening now had Mahri edged with fear. She walked down her own street, heading for Halina's Den near the Canyon. Things were different now. There hadn't been any rattlesnakes in the old days, or large groups of angry farries for that matter. There were even some new kribas in the area, and for all of these, Mahri watched nervously.

But there would be no problems tonight. Only the girls from Halina's Den knew they were meeting. No angry, misled farries to cause problems. No rattlesnakes. Melena's terrible fall was probably an isolated incident (Mahri hoped desperately). After all, she had never even heard of snakes before. But still, there was always a chance, and her eyes raked the street and gutters just to make sure.

The only activity around was a young boy with a beach ball. It was almost as big as he was, and he kicked it, squealing vigorously and chasing after it with concentrated laughter. He never saw Mahri, nor would he have cared if he had.

When Mahri finally saw Halina, all trouble vanished. The fear, the nervousness, and even the sorrow melted away with the warmth of her smile. The setting sun threw an amber halo around her beautiful orange and brown coat, and was captured by eyes that looked like piercing fire.

"Well, dear Mahri, welcome back," Halina smiled.

"Halina!" Mahri welcomed the wave of warmth pouring through her. She went up to Halina, almost in a run, and the two friends touched noses. All of the other girls were there already, but Mahri only saw Halina.

The mistress looked good. Mahri thought she looked a little different, probably from not being outside too much recently. A little hard to put a paw on, really. She looked tired and at the same time refreshed. But gone was the look of defeat they had all seen on the Den's final night.

"It's good to see you, Mahri," Halina said after a long yet comfortable silence.

"It's wonderful to see you, Halina," said Mahri. "I've been trying to see you for so long. In fact, we were looking for you the day . . ." Her voice trailed off and she looked down.

"Yes, dear Mahri, there is much to talk about," said Halina. "I'm afraid not all is good, as you know. But some should be, I pray."

Mahri looked around at the other girls. There were two young farries she had never seen before, a slender white short hair with blue eyes and a black and white farri who looked a lot like Syranosh—who was there too. She was sitting slightly apart from the rest of the Den, bathing her front paws and ignoring the others. All of the other regulars were there too, except for Larsha, and of course Melena.

"Let's start by introducing two new friends," said Halina. "For those of you who don't know Sina and Jassa, they'll be joining us in the future should we decide to meet again. They had both been interested in our Den before we split up a while back, but they were both too young at the time. However, they are here now, and they are our friends. Make them feel welcome."

The black and white was Sina, and Mahri was delighted to see the young farri give a shy smile when her name was mentioned. Fortunately she only looked like Syranosh. Jassa, too, seemed rather pleasant in temperament.

"Not all of our numbers are here," said Halina sadly.

"Larsha spoke with me today and declined the invitation to join us for this reunion. As you know, she was chewed up pretty badly the night of our big folly. She still suffers pain, the poor dear, and I daresay I understand her desire to stay away. I think she wants to believe we were right, but of course she has her doubts. Maybe in time she will visit with us.

"And as most of you know by now, we suffered an even more serious loss," Halina continued, and then looked out toward the Canyon. "The wounds of Larsha, both physical and mental, will in time heal themselves. Unfortunately for all of us, the wounds of Melena will not. We lost her three days ago to the evil poison of a rattlesnake."

It was clear everyone had heard already. Most of the farries either looked down or looked at Mahri, but none looked surprised.

"Mahri, my love, would you please tell the tale if you're able?" asked Halina.

Mahri looked around the others and thought she would choke. She didn't want to remember any of it, let alone tell the Den about it. All of their eyes were on her, and suddenly she wanted to cry. But something kept telling her that to tell it all would actually help in some way. She needed to let it out and they needed to hear it. The telling would be tough.

"Well, go on and tell us about it, sister," said Syranosh, looking up from her bath.

"Be kind, Syranosh!" said Halina. "You too may need us all to listen someday." She looked at Mahri kindly. "Take your time, Mahri, and don't tell if it troubles you too much. But I believe you will find a great relief in sharing."

"Thanks, Halina," Mahri said. "You're right, you know. It will help. I'll do my best."

She told of how Melena had come over to see her, and of their decision to search for Halina. She left out the part about why they were looking for the mistress and continued on with the events leading up to the tragic end. She even left out the part about how rude Syranosh had been, although she would later look back and wonder why. Mahri still believed Syranosh's attitude had somehow contributed to Melena's death, but said nothing of this. Instead she mentioned that she had walked across the street to say hi and then gone on down the street.

When Mahri finished, the Den sat silent. A few of the farries had given out soft cries throughout the story, for Melena was dear to them all.

"This is truly a disturbing tale," said Halina. "After all of our other problems, there are still unspeakable terrors thrown against us. We must take this with grave consideration."

Halina took a moment to look into the eyes of every farri individually. Mahri gave them all a quick glance to try to see what Halina searched for. It wasn't until their eyes met that she knew; and she instantly knew none of the others understood.

"This is the most complete description of Melena's fall that we have heard," said Halina. "Of course, only you were there, Mahri, and only you can tell what really occurred, which I believe you truly have. And yet your eyes say the tale is not complete. No matter. There are always words better left unsaid. Yet I must ask you the purpose of your attempt to seek me out."

"We missed you, Halina," said Mahri quickly. "Of course we did. We missed all of you." With the exception of Syranosh, she thought.

"There is more, my love," said Halina. "It's best we all know now. It's been in the back of all our minds, or none would have shown up tonight."

Mahri looked around the Den nervously. All eyes were on her, and she could see the looks were beginning to hold realization.

"We . . . I, anyway, felt empty," said Mahri. "I think Melena did too. There was so much more to be said about our Den and what we used to do here."

To her surprise, Mahri saw the other girls begin to fidget and look away. She and Melena had not been alone. "We wanted to talk about maybe starting over."

This statement brought responses from all. The entire Den began to speak at once, and Mahri could see a general uncertainty.

"Peace, loves!" said Halina. "We will all have a chance to speak. I think our friend Mahri has finally put words to the feelings in all of our hearts. But this has become so complicated in every way. Oh yes, very complicated."

"So why don't we just do it?" asked Syranosh, who finally looked interested. She had not seemed to pay much attention to Mahri's tale of Melena and the snake.

"So many omens, love," said Halina. "So many omens. Bad omens at that. When you consider all of the occurrences in our past, it becomes very scary. Even for me."

This brought a sudden hush to the group as everyone sank into their own thoughts. Hearing Halina admit to being afraid was a first.

"We don't have to worry about those other farries attacking us again," said Syranosh. "They saw us call up a puma out of the Canyon. And they know it was a fluke she got shot. They believe we can call up another one at will. And the more I think about it, the more I think we can."

"We?" hissed Mahri. "Where were you when *we* were in the Canyon asking Sarena to help us out. You never even met her. How dare you say such things, as if Sarena was just something we could make appear with magic. She was our friend!"

"Calm down, sister," said Syranosh.

"You . . ."

"Stop! Both of you," said Halina. "We will never be able to face our adversaries if we cannot even face ourselves. Mahri and I have both lost a tremendous friend, Syranosh, and so naturally we are sensitive about off-the-paw comments about her. I can't make a puma magically appear any more than I could make another Syranosh appear. Only the Creator of All Things can do such a trick. So please be respectful when you speak of lost friends."

Syranosh crouched to her forepaws and sulked at the reprimand. Mahri thought it was too light, and wanted to rip Syranosh's lungs out.

"On the other hand," said Halina, "there is some wisdom in your words. We cannot, as I said, create another puma. We know this, but no one else knows. They saw us bring one out of the Canyon on demand, and truly her death was a fluke. At least I hope so. This is something else we'll need to discuss. But the other farries saw us call a puma and then stand our ground. I would be nervous if I was them.''

"Nervous of what, though?" asked Farinna. "They won. They broke us up. They know we won't do anything since we don't even meet anymore.''

Halina looked out past the Canyon into the sunset. The other farries joined her in brief, silent thought. Another day forever gone.

"Don't we?" asked Halina finally. "True, we have not. Yet here we are, all together, even though we have not called out for toms. We are here and it will be known. Large groups of farries cannot go unnoticed for very long."

"They can't gather enough to face us tonight on such short time," said Mahri.

"No, we need not fear them tonight," said Halina. "We need only fear ourselves and the decisions we make." Again she looked around the Den with questioning eyes.

"Let us see who of us would like the Den to be as it was, with nightly meetings and callings of toms," said Halina. "I believe we have said enough for some action. I will ask all of you who are not interested to walk away and go on with your lives. There will be no questions and no bitter feelings with those who wish to stay. You can only be admired for the courage it would take to leave, equal to the courage it would take to stay. And if enough of you go, then certainly so must all of the others. The Den has safety only in numbers."

"Should we do it this way?" asked Mahri. "Or should we just plan to meet tomorrow night? Then those who choose not to be a part can just not show up. It might save embarrassment for everyone."

Words of agreement were echoed throughout the Den. Halina looked around and then paced several steps back and forth without speaking. The Den had learned long ago to accept this as her sign of hard thinking, and not to interrupt. Halina stopped midstride, and then looked back at Mahri.

"There is wisdom in your words, dear Mahri," she said. "I was troubled about a small group showing up here, and then having to face a large group of Coron's follies. They might show up if they hear we will meet again, and we must be prepared.

"Yet in the end it does not matter how large our group is, for ultimately, each girl must go out on her own with her toms. So even as a group we are divided. Those willing to run those risks will meet here tomorrow, and I will be one of those. Maybe the only one, but still I will try. We will think of ways to protect ourselves. The mass we fought was brought together by a fool. I believe we can be more clever than the farries who will follow such a fool."

Mahri twitched uneasily, and thought about how disastrous it would be to run into Coron and his gang of farries. She knew Coron alone could rip her up badly. There was more to this decision than loyalty to Halina. Someone could get hurt.

"It is so much to think about," continued Halina. "It will be wise for all of us to ponder it overnight before making a choice. I say now I will be here, but tomorrow the sun may rise differently and shine light I have not seen. So heed my council tonight, if you will, but follow only the words of your own hearts."

In silent agreement, the Den stood up to go home. They walked as a group for as long as possible, both for protection and a show of unity, until the block ended and they had to go separate ways. Halina passed her house to remain with the group and then turned to walk back.

Mahri watched them all go in their different directions. She loved them all, she guessed. Even Syranosh. She wondered if she would ever see them all again. Certainly some would never return to the Den. She knew she would see Halina there tomorrow. If no one else showed, at least the two of them would. Mahri didn't need all night to think about it; she wanted to mate again and she wanted to be with Halina.

CHAPTER 23

If they hadn't taken Laura's car, Roger would not have gone. It took all the nerve he could muster as it was. Secretly following around law enforcement officers was far from what he had envisioned when Laura called and said she wanted to go out with him that night.

But here they were, parked just a few houses down from Jerry Radcliff's house. Only a few houses from Roger's house. And true, it was a Tuesday night, but Roger believed there were far better things he could be doing than sitting in Laura's little RX-7, quietly listening to the stereo with the windows up to keep out the mosquitoes.

"Like what?" asked Laura. "What else would you be doing?"

"Anything," said Roger. "I could be feeding the cat. She gets hungry too, ya know. Speaking of which, I'm starved. I haven't eaten since lunch. How long are we gonna sit here?"

"Until he goes somewhere, goon," answered Laura.

"But what if he doesn't?" asked Roger.

"Then I'll buy you dinner. Let's just wait another half an hour."

Roger snorted and rolled his eyes. He didn't really mind. He liked being with Laura regardless of the circumstances. Tonight would be wonderful as long as Radcliff stayed home. Wonderful, yet sad. He was starting to think more and more about Tammy.

"How about if I just go up to the door and see if he's going out?" Roger suggested. "I'll ask him if he's interested in shooting some coyotes. That's legitimate enough. The bastards haven't stopped howling for the past week.''

Laura reached over and squeezed his knee. ''Just sit tight, dude.''

They sat quietly for several minutes, listening to the stereo. Roger thought about how the evening would probably progress. Radcliff would stay home and Roger would go to dinner with Laura. They would talk and have a good time, and then Laura would take him home. They might go somewhere and dance a little first, but the end result would still be the same. But for some reason, this didn't seem to bother him anymore.

For some reason. Yes, some reason could be spelled out in one word if he dared to think about it. One word spelled Tammy. She was regularly sneaking into his thoughts these days, and this made Roger nervous.

Was it the way she looked at him? Her eyelids would lower slightly with the most sensuous come-on look he had ever seen. Not a cheap ''Let's fuck,'' but a deep and overall ''I want every bit of you.'' She would take and caress his hand, slightly changing the pressure with her movements in a fiercely erotic way. Could rubbing someone's hand be erotic? And her lashes would flutter all the while over her great blue eyes, and she would part her lips just enough to be noticed. Tammy usually did all of this in public places and Roger wanted to scream.

Roger smiled inwardly, thinking about how Tammy had casually begun to lobby for more of his time. She was turning out to be quite a smart girl, far smarter than he had imagined when they first met. She wanted to see him often but respected his need for free time, and never asked what he did on nights when they were not together. Laura never asked either, but Roger knew it was because she didn't give a shit. Tammy did.

''What?''

''There he is,'' repeated Laura. ''Were you asleep, or what?''

''Just thinking about work,'' Roger lied.

''Shhh. He's getting into his truck.''

Radcliff had a black Dodge pickup. ''Not no foreign

crap for me," he had told Roger. "I need a big, built in U.S.A. model."

The taillights went on and the truck rolled ahead. Radcliff pulled out into the street and turned toward the main streets. Laura carefully started forward the same way.

It was all Roger could do to keep from laughing at her style. Every detective story she had ever seen on TV was being reviewed and followed as the gospel of how to tail a suspect.

"We need to fake him out," Laura said. "We'll stay back for a while, then catch up. We need to change lanes too."

"I'm sure he's not even paying attention," said Roger. "Besides, it's dark. All he'll see is headlights anyway."

"We need to be careful, goon," she said. "If he's into as much shit as I think he is, he's gonna be watching for people following."

"Maybe. But I think the way you're driving is going to attract more attention than just staying back and driving normal."

"Quiet! I'm trying to concentrate."

It wasn't long before they were driving out into part of the famous California freeway system. Interstate 805 south, and cruising at the normal sixty-two miles per hour on the bridge over Mission Valley. Roger always remembered the story about how there was enough concrete in this bridge to pave a sidewalk from San Diego to San Francisco. A real engineering marvel, considering the normal ineptitude of the California Department of Transportation.

The stayed on 805, heading south through National City and Chula Vista, two of the smaller cities in San Diego County. Laura eventually gave up the hide-and-seek tactics and followed at a safe distance. There was plenty of traffic to blend in with, and she began to border on carelessness. But it seemed to work out all right: Radcliff showed no sign of awareness.

Twenty-five minutes after they had left Radcliff's house, they were passing through San Ysidro, and the destination was now clear. Only two more miles to the border. Jerry Radcliff, a California narcotics officer, was going into Mexico.

"I wasn't ready for this," said Laura. She pulled over to the far left lane, the last-chance U-turn before leaving the United States.

Roger watched Radcliff's truck sail through Mexican customs, which was, of course, a joke. Like all of the other southbound traffic, the truck never even came close to a full stop. The Mexican officer waved him through without so much as a long glance. Getting into Mexico was quite easy.

"Son of a bitch!" said Laura. "What's he doing down there? Damn!"

"Why didn't you follow him?" asked Roger.

"I'm too afraid to drive down there. Next time we'll take your car and you can drive."

"Yeah, sure," Roger laughed, but was surprised to see how serious she was.

"We're gonna find out what the fucker's doing."

"Oh," said Roger, taken aback by the sudden profanity.

"He's up to his redneck ass in something," said Laura. "And I wanna know what."

"I can tell." Roger's face twitched slightly.

When she looked over, she saw how nervous he was, and she smiled. "Let's go eat," she said. "It's on me. Where do you wanna go?"

"Somewhere with a view," said Roger. "And room service."

CHAPTER 24

Mahri thought she should be surprised, but wasn't, really. It was clear by all their faces that everyone had planned to show up right from the start. Every farri who was at the last meeting was here today, all looking happy and relieved.

Halina looked vibrant and beautiful as usual. They all did. The final glow of sunset put a warm highlight of sparkle around them all, and Mahri thought they had never looked better as a group. There would be no problem attracting toms tonight.

"Well, Mahri," said Halina, "will your sweet voice do its magic tonight? It hasn't forgotten how to call, has it? After all, it's always been you who has driven the toms crazy."

"I will try, Halina," said Mahri. "It's been a long time, but I think I can do it."

"I'm sure you can, love," said Halina with a smile. "We'll all try, at least those of us who remember how."

For Mahri, the delivery of a good, solid call was pure ecstasy. She felt it start from her helplessly outstretched claws all the way up her spine with a wild and ancient tingle. The fur on her back would always rise slightly, not with anger, but a rush of warmth. And this was just from the call. With any luck, the real fun would come soon.

Mahri had warmed up earlier in the afternoon. No serious calls or cries, but merely a few more words with Sweetie Pie than usual. The little girl loved it when she talked, even though Mahri knew the young paladin couldn't understand a word of the common tongue. For as smart as the paladins were supposed to be, they were surprisingly ignorant about something as simple as communication.

The air began to fill with rusty and forgotten calls. The girls in the Den were doing their best, only the sounds were not encouraging. Halina looked hopefully at Mahri, who had not yet started her calls. Taking a deep breath, Mahri closed her eyes and felt the sensation begin. It came low at first, a borderline growl. But soon it began to narrow and take the shape of a smooth and clear demand for passion. Her cheeks were on fire and her eyes misted. She had only begun. The air in her lungs was long expired but the roar began to magnify.

The other farries in the Den stepped back in disbelief, smiling nonetheless. Any tom not responding to that call would have to be dead. Mahri reached for breath and then let out another one, even better. This one seemed to be experienced by the entire Den. Even Syranosh was smiling.

"We're in debt to you, dearest Mahri," said Halina. "As usual, you come through with your sweet song. Sometimes I wonder if you even have the changes scar at all. You sound better than most farries who don't have it."

Mahri blushed and smiled self-consciously.

"The toms will show up tonight," Farinna smiled. "Very nice call, Mahri." The rest of the Den echoed this sentiment, and Mahri was pleased. It looked like things might go well after all.

No one in the Den was surprised when Sharlo arrived first. They were all very happy to see him, for he had always been the Den's nicest and favorite customer. And everyone remembered the fateful night when he had stood side by side with them and helped fight Coron's mob. Mahri wasn't the only girl in the Den who was madly in love with Sharlo.

Mahri suffered a brief loss of breath at the sight of Sharlo. A more handsome tom she had never met, and tonight he looked stunning, surpassing even her fondest memories. He would later tell of the hours his paladin had spent grooming him for a show earlier in the day. He liked the way so many paladins would spend time admiring and petting him, and wondered why they always left a blue ribbon on his kennel but on none of the others.

"Good evening, dear ladies," said Sharlo.

"Hi Sharlo!" responded the entire Den almost in unison.

"I've missed you all," he said. "I'm glad you've decided to come back."

"And we've missed you, dearest Sharlo," said Halina. "Welcome, as always, to our Den. You are a lucky tom tonight. You have first pick of all these lovely farries."

Mahri felt herself flush and hoped desperately to be chosen. She sensed similar feelings throughout the Den, and hoped she wasn't as obvious as the rest.

"I want them all!" said Sharlo. "You know that, Halina. It's so unfair to make me choose one!"

"And unfair to make me choose for you," Halina laughed. "Yet I can see it is best to do so in this case. Better for me to hurt the ladies' feelings than for you to. Please take Mahri tonight, and have a wonderful time."

"I will. Thank you, Halina."

Mahri was elated, and stepped away, leaving the disappointment of the others behind her. She lightly touched noses with Sharlo and felt a sudden rush of lightheadedness. Sharlo's smile was warm and affectionate when he motioned for her to follow. They started walking down the street away from the Canyon and passed by two toms who were headed for the Den and some action.

"Nice to see you girls back," said the tom with yellow and white stripes.

"Nice to be back," Mahri beamed. "Have fun tonight."

"Of course we will," the black tom answered.

Sharlo walked beside Mahri with his good posture and charismatic arch. After his few words to Halina before leaving, he became silent with Mahri as the two farries walked toward his house.

"How did you know?" asked Mahri.

"Know what, dear?" replied Sharlo.

"You knew we'd be meeting tonight. You had to, or else you wouldn't have been so close by and ready to go."

"Of course I knew," said Sharlo. "Halina told me yesterday. She said you'd be there. . . ."

"Yesterday?" asked Mahri. "When yesterday?"

"Afternoon. She said you'd all be there and I could have my pick if I got there early enough."

"But we hadn't decided to meet yet," said Mahri. "We didn't know until tonight we'd all be there. We hadn't even discussed it yet when she told you. How did she know?"

"I'm just telling you what she told me," said Sharlo. "Even though I promised her I wouldn't. But I want to always be honest with you. Really, she told me yesterday."

"She knew," said Mahri, completely amazed. "Somehow she knew."

"I'm not surprised. Halina knows many things. Things we don't even see or hear, she knows about. I guess she knows her Den well enough to see how loyal you all are, and how much you missed meeting with the toms. You did miss it, didn't you?"

"Of course I did!" said Mahri. "I especially missed seeing you!"

"You know, dearest Mahri," said Sharlo, "you don't have to be at the Den to see me. I can visit you anytime. And I'd even prefer to see you away from the Den. That way I won't have to deal with the other farries and their jealousy."

"I'd like that, I don't like their jealousy, either, although they really don't mean it. I'm jealous too, whenever you go with someone else. But I'd like you to come over to my house sometime before I go to the Den. But then I'd be thinking about you all night!"

"Well, I think about you all night anyway," said Sharlo. "I think about you all the time. I think about your beautiful face and pretty, long whiskers. I think about your nice, fluffy coat. And you know what else I think about?"

CHAPTER 25

"**R**umors on the wind," said Halina. "Rumors about many things which need clearing up."

"And you think we should go back into the Canyon for answers?" asked Mahri doubtfully. She had felt no desire to venture past the dead end since the tragedy of Sarena's death. Not only were there sad memories in the sage, but there was an underlying feeling of even greater danger than before. On her first trip into the Canyon, she had been blind with curiosity and ignorant of what to fear. The next visits were made with the false hope that Sarena would always be there to protect them. Now there was no Sarena, only the cold reality of rattlesnakes.

"Okay, my dear Mahri," said Halina kindly. "I can see it in your eyes. I don't wish to go into the Canyon either, yet I fear it is a must. I will go alone then. Stay here and be at peace."

Mahri was amazed at how much influence the words of Halina had over her. She could no more let her mistress face the Canyon alone than she could let Coron have his way with her. And Halina knew this.

"Okay," said Mahri reluctantly. "You know I'll follow you. What are we looking for this time?"

"I wish I could say," said Halina. "But I honestly don't know. Something is amiss in the Canyon, and I feel I must know what it is. I think it somehow affects us, but I need to see and hear more before I can decide if this is so. Shall we take Farinna or Syranosh along?" she asked. "Or maybe one of the others. How about one of the new girls?"

"Let's go alone, Halina," said Mahri. "We have so much to talk about, and I don't think I'm up to having Syranosh around."

"Okay, love," Halina smiled.

They walked out into the street toward the dead end. They passed by the Den and made their way into the sage along the edge of the pavement. The day was mild compared to the swelter of their previous trips into the Canyon. A slight breeze from the Pacific brought a comfortable sway to the sage.

"How did it go with Sharlo last night?" asked Halina.

Mahri could not see her face but knew the mistress wore a smile. "Wonderful, as usual," she said. "Why did you tell him we were meeting?"

"I knew he'd want to visit," said Halina, still smiling. "And I knew all the girls would want to see him. Didn't you?"

"Of course," said Mahri. "You know he's our favorite. My favorite."

"And you're his favorite too." Halina stopped beside a huge rock and sat down. They had no planned destination. "He asked me about you. He wanted me to arrange it so he could be with you last night. He's missed you."

"Yes, he told me all about it. I didn't know whether to believe him or not. I guess I did a little."

"Believe it a lot, dear," Halina smiled. "He really loves you. I guess this would be bad for me to say . . . well, not bad, really. Only bad for the Den, I suppose . . ."

Suddenly the two farries were in a shadow and the air was filled with a terrifying scream. Mahri crouched low instinctively, but was surprised to see Halina leap. Halina's claws went skyward, and her growl was followed by a deafening screech. She came back down hard, and watched several feathers float harmlessly to the ground. On top of the rock beside them sat a very angry hawk.

"So feisty today, aren't we, Halina," said the hawk. "I thought a little scare might be fun."

"Fun, Mr. Treep, is not being carried off by a hungry

bird," answered Halina. "You had more than just a scare in mind, I think."

"You farries are so amusing," said Treep. "Do you think the whole world cares enough to be your enemy? Or wants you for dinner? You've obviously never tasted cat before."

"But clearly you have," said Halina. "And neither of us cares to remind you of the taste."

"Ah yes. And who is your lovely friend? Have you not always come here alone before?"

"This is Mahri," said Halina. "She is one of my Den. She has been with me on earlier trips to the Canyon. You, no doubt, were delivering your scare tactics to less fortunates about."

"Halina. Halina," Treep said, shaking his head. "Why do you talk to your friends so? Haven't we helped each other in the past? You only come out here when you need help, so they say."

Halina relaxed a little and sat down beside the huge stone. Mahri was still fluffed and very nervous, despite Halina's calm. Hawks were predators, and one had nearly taken her away for lunch.

"I do need help," said Halina. "Information, really."

"That's all you ever want," said Treep. "I must put a price on all this talk, sometime. Chatting with you is so wearisome."

"I think you can be rewarded soon," said Halina. "But I can't say when or how yet. You must first tell me more tales of the wild. I need to know the movements of the Canyon. And you, Treep, see all."

"That I do, Halina," Treep smiled. "More than I could ever dare say. What specifically do you wish to know about?"

"Krahstas, lynxes, and pumas," said Halina flatly.

"Always the bad guys," Treep laughed. "They are all my enemies, you know. They steal my food when they can.

"Anyway, the krahstas are bad news. They have spread out and moved into areas previously unknown to them. And they are bold, attacking lynxes and moving danger-ously close to the man settlement. I believe they will brave the road soon. Their new leader seems to fear nothing.''

"New leader?" asked Halina.

"His name is Dahrkron," said Treep. "His pack supports him completely, for he is brave and cunning, and keeps them well fed in these thin times. His name is feared throughout the Canyon, by prey and predator alike. As I said, he has led the krahstas against a lynx more than once, and this is unheard of in this Canyon. Krahstas and lynxes usually avoid each other."

"So why does Dahrkron go after them?" asked Mahri, finally relaxed enough to speak.

"To steal their territory for its prey," said Treep. "Lynxes are usually smarter than krahstas and have the best hunting grounds. Dahrkron understands this and lets the lynxes settle long enough to spy on their land and then force them out. A treacherous demon, this Dahrkron. His pack loves him."

"And what about the lynxes?" asked Halina. "Why do they put up with this?"

"There are only three in this whole area," said Treep. "Two are mates, and the other is not on friendly terms. Dahrkron never goes after the mates when they're together, and lately they've not split up very much. Together they could give the krahsta pack some real problems, and Dahrkron knows it. Alone, a lynx is no match for a pack of krahstas and will always flee without a fight. It's on this that Dahrkron depends, and it boosts the morale of his pack to chase off a lynx. Dahrkron seems to have made cats the pack's main enemy."

"Just what we needed to hear," said Halina. "I feared as much. He has all the lynxes in the Canyon upset. What about pumas?" Halina, Mahri noticed, had run it all together and made the last question seem offhand.

"One has died this summer," said Treep, looking away. Mahri thought he was trying to hide something, an expression or look in the eyes. "But you knew about it already. Yes, Halina, you saw it, if I recall. Other pumas I don't know about. They hunt mostly deer, so they are no concern of mine."

"So there are other pumas about?" asked Mahri.

"I can't say," said Treep. "They are no concern to me, so if I happen upon one, I do not notice, really. And I forget about it within moments because I'm usually up hunting for food at the time. I only pay notice to krahstas and lynxes, for they are my foes. Anything else is not worth my bother to investigate. Pumas usually don't come this close to man settlements, anyway."

"I see," said Halina. "Anything else you can tell us?"

"Only that it is time for me to hunt for lunch," said Treep. "And as always, you have exhausted my wind-pipes, Halina. I expect to see you again, with the promised payment for my time."

"I made no promise, Treep," said Halina. "But you may receive reward yet. I'll be in touch."

The great bird made a quick crouch and was instantly skyward, barely visible in the bright sun. Mahri examined one of Treep's fallen feathers and then followed Halina back into the brush. They walked along a narrow path at some length without speaking, each farri lost in thought.

"You were hoping to meet another puma," said Mahri. They stopped beside a small cactus and looked over the unfriendly spines. Halina stared indifferently at the plant and didn't answer, appearing lost in thought.

"If that's what you were looking for, then we should go back to the Den," said Mahri. "The hawk said there weren't any around. And we got the news you wanted." Mahri was still edgy about the near miss with the great bird. She had never before feared anything from the sky, and she wanted to leave the Canyon now. But much to her displeasure, Halina's face remained unchanged; the hint not taken.

"Hawks cannot be trusted," Halina said at last. "They do not lie, yet they do not always deliver what is real. They speak in truths and half-truths, and leave out what could be a dangerous amount. It is to their advantage, for their friends are few, and only among their own kind. Farries, along with everyone else, are their foes."

"Then what did Treep leave out?" asked Mahri. She wondered how Halina became so skilled at knowing other animals. "He said a lot about the krahstas and lynxes."

"He did," said Halina. "And I believe him. While Treep does not love me, we share a mutual respect for each other. About krahstas he gave us a critical warning: they are near and they are getting bold enough to dare the man settlement. And they have the lynxes in the Canyon running scared. This could work to our advantage."

"How?" asked Mahri. "And why would Treep warn us if we're his enemy? And what—"

"So many questions, dearest Mahri," Halina laughed. "I don't have all the answers. Not yet, anyway. Treep would warn us about krahstas because they are not only his enemies, but his rivals. They compete for food here in the Canyon. We don't. Treep doesn't want us to become food for the krahstas. Not because he cares about us, but because he would rather see the krahstas go hungry."

"What about pumas?" asked Mahri. "Do you think he's seen any?"

"If there are any around, Treep has seen them," answered Halina. "Treep sees all in the Canyon. Nothing can pass through without his knowledge. And despite his indifference, he is very concerned about the movements of pumas. All animals in the Canyon have to be. But has he seen any recently? I can't say for certain. We shall see what we shall see."

CHAPTER 26

Roger hated calls like these. Her name was Suzanne and Roger had gone out with her for about a month during the spring. Uneventful enough for Roger to have forgotten about her as soon as the next one had come along, and now she was on the phone a few months later talking about love.

"You wouldn't even recognize it if it walked up and slapped you in the face," said Suzanne.

"Probably not," agreed Roger. He wished she would hang up.

"I don't think you're like that," she said. "Not at all. I think you're a warm and sensitive person. I could tell by how gentle and caring you were when we were together."

"Listen, I just don't think this will work out. . . ."

"Why don't you give it a try?" Suzanne demanded. "Love will find a way."

Roger rolled his eyes and then smiled. It was the case they always pleaded after he went on to greener pastures. He had her on this one.

"No, love will not find a way," said Roger. "You see, I happen to believe love is blind. And how in the world can something blind find the way anywhere? It can't."

"Good-bye, Roger," she said, and hung up.

Mercifully, it ended. Roger was glad, but still did not want to put the phone down. He was afraid Laura might call, and the thought was unsettling. Tonight if she called, he would say no. Tonight if she called, he would say he had other plans. Tonight if she called, it would be the first time he had not dropped everything and come running. He hoped.

Roger had a date with Tammy, and he really wanted to see her. A peaceful night with those sparkling eyes would be just fine. Enough with these wild-goose chases after cougar-killing narcs.

The proper attire chosen, Roger dressed and then sat on the couch to relax. He had a good half hour to kill before he needed to leave to pick up Tammy. He was just about to stretch out when he saw the cat trot into the living room and approach him with a friendly "tails up" greeting.

De Lilah rubbed her side against Roger's leg, and he bent over with a brush. She stood perfectly still, her purr box roaring with supreme ecstasy while Roger groomed her coat. He scratched her head with his left hand, using his right to work the brush. He felt a twinge of guilt for not having spent much quality time with De Lilah the past couple of weeks. He switched hands with the brush and worked her sides and stomach even more vigorously. She leaned heavily against him.

Again Roger thought about her strange behavior of late. He knew the neglect had a lot to do with it, but something else seemed to be bothering her as well. If only cats could talk . . .

Roger stood up to get the vacuum cleaner. De Lilah stayed right between his feet the whole way, anticipating what was to come. De Lilah was the only cat Roger had ever heard of who enjoyed being vacuumed. He turned on the small, hand-held device and ran it all over the cat's back and sides. De Lilah's expression made Roger believe she probably enjoyed this even more than sex; that is, if she still had sex after being fixed. Roger continued to vacuum for about five minutes. It worked mutually for the two: De Lilah got her thrills and Roger got a cat who shed less.

When it was time to go, Roger opened the door and let De Lilah out for the night. Roger took one step out and then heard the phone ring. Fearing it might be Tammy calling to say she would be late, he stepped back inside and walked across the living room. He stopped halfway and then turned away. Deciding it was probably Laura, he walked outside and left the phone unanswered.

The evening had gone very well. Tammy looked beautiful; her nicely done blond hair falling about the shoulders of her low-cut, lavender dress. Roger and Tammy had enjoyed a lovely candlelight dinner at a romantic restaurant overlooking Mission Bay, and Tammy's enormous blue eyes had taunted him with mischievous innocence all night.

Without so much as a word, they had driven straight back to Roger's house after dinner. Tammy had caressed his right hand the entire drive, with only the slightest hints of sexy gestures as she massaged.

Roger led her into the bedroom, but did not turn on the light. The soft, indirect glow from a living-room lamp around the corner cast a warm, golden glow on their faces. With one motion, Roger kissed her, and slipped her dress to the floor. Beneath it, she wore only panties. Roger put his arms around her shoulders as he leaned to his right, and together they fell to the bed.

Tammy giggled as she helped Roger with his shirt. He kissed her hard while holding his breath. She felt so unbelievable when she was pressed against him. She tossed his pants off the side of the bed.

Roger rolled on top, kissing her furiously. He held her close with both arms while she grabbed frantically at his hair. He wanted to kiss her all over, but she reached down and squeezed his bottom, suggesting something else. Suddenly Roger felt something large and furry between his thighs. He jumped up and looked over his shoulder. It was the cat.

"De Lilah," Roger groaned. He reached over and picked her up with his left hand. It was very awkward to move her from the position he was in, as well as heavy. He had to roll over then toss her to the floor. "Get lost."

"She's just jealous," Tammy giggled.

"She should be," said Roger. "You're very beautiful."

Tammy smiled, and Roger nestled into a position beside her. He began to kiss her cheek, moving slightly in the direction of her ear.

He felt the cat jump back onto the bed. Tammy started to laugh, but Roger only sighed. He began to ponder laws regarding cruelty to animals. He continued to look at Tammy and felt the bed move as the cat walked toward the back of his head. When she reached his shoulders, she jumped over Roger and landed on the pillow right between their faces. They both jerked their heads back as De Lilah sat down instantly and began to groom her right forepaw.

Tammy went into stitches of laughter. Roger rolled over onto his back and looked at the ceiling. He put his hand over his forehead and closed his eyes. After a few moments he looked back toward Tammy, who was still laughing, but couldn't see her through the cat.

Pushing himself to his knees, he picked up De Lilah and rolled off the bed. He walked over to the door and unceremoniously tossed De Lilah into the living room. He closed the door, locking out both the cat and the light.

"Miserable bitch," Roger muttered, but Tammy continued to laugh.

"Where were you last night?"

Roger looked into the receiver and shook his head. No "Hello, how are you, good to hear your voice." He pushed aside the continuity sheet he was working on.

"Who is this?" he demanded, knowing Laura's voice and manner quite well but wanting to aggravate her nonetheless.

"Just one of your many women, goon," said Laura. "I called you last night but you were out sleazing around, again."

"So?"

"So, I saw your friend Radcliff at Friday's again."

"Did you follow him there?"

"No. It was a pleasant surprise. Very pleasant. And guess who your friend was with again?"

"Besides you?" asked Roger, knowing the answer.

"Oh, I don't know. A dead mountain lion?"

"Rosemary Ogden," said Laura. "And they were just as cozy as the last time I saw them. I think this is weird."

"And?" said Roger, not wanting to sound impatient. He no longer cared about Jerry Radcliff, and his feelings for Laura were not at an all-time high either.

"And I think we need to check this out more," said Laura.

Roger didn't answer. Why did *we* need to check it out? he wondered.

"It was a learning venture last time," said Laura. "This time we know what to expect and we'll be better prepared."

"For what?" asked Roger.

"To go into Mexico, goon!" said Laura. "We'll follow him all the way this time. If that's where he goes."

"I don't know if I'm really up for this." Roger felt himself weakening.

"Come on. I'll pick you up tonight at six-thirty. We'll have dinner afterward. Just think, we'll be alone together."

"Of course," Roger said in defeat.

CHAPTER 27

The sun had nearly an hour's worth of strength left, and the krahstas waited. Hunting had gone very well since Dahrkron's decision to chase off lynxes and go for their territory. The krahstas' status and influence in the Canyon was stronger than at any time in pack memory or legend. They walked unopposed wherever they went.

"We must discuss where the manroad and the Canyon meet," said Dahrkron. The pack sat attentively around the leader and awaited tonight's plan of attack.

"The farries have been spotted again," he continued. "As before, they've started to meet right at the edge of the Canyon each night. A quick raid in the early evening might prove to be quite a benefit."

"I thought we weren't going to risk the manroad unless things became desperate," said Kreni. "The Canyon is providing us well at the moment."

True testament of Dahrkron's leadership was hearing a female speak out in open debate. Although they had been suppressed throughout the history of the pack, Dahrkron had encouraged them to share their ideas with the others, to astounding success. It hadn't been easy. Timid females and traditional males found the notion difficult to accept. But in time, with the voicing of many remarkable ideas by the females, the plan had become part of life. And the females were turning out to be more clever than the males.

"The Canyon does provide well right now," said Dahrkron. "And it looks like it will continue to do so for quite a while. It will remain constant if we stray for one night. I fear the farries on the road will not. They may vanish like they did before. It seems too easy a kill to just pass up.''

''Nothing is too easy on the road, my leader,'' said Brezni. ''Let's not take lightly the fate of the puma, even though it is your belief the men were hunting her.''

''I agree,'' said Khanval. ''It was your council, Dahrkron, to keep to the Canyon as long as it provided. I think we should leave the farries for winter when food will become thin again. Of course, I will follow you to the road if you wish. You know I can always be counted on.''

Dahrkron knew. He knew they would all follow him, but unhappily. It was the wrong time. If the pack was hungry, things would be different. But for now, they were content to stay in the shelter of the Canyon, where they wielded so much power. There were too many unknowns and uncertainties on the road.

''Your concerns are just,'' said Dahrkron. ''Just as they were when we started our attacks on the lynx and other predators. There are risks in all of our moves of late, and we seem to be thriving on them. Keep all of this in mind, for one day we *will* raid the little farries. But for now, we'll keep to the sage.''

Dahrkron could see relief in the eyes of many pack members. He made a mental note to remember who they were. He would be sure to aim more anticat rhetoric in their direction soon. It had worked on nearly a third of the pack, and he believed it would be only a short time before the ideas were accepted completely. Dahrkron wondered if he should be worried since only the slowest learners and least intelligent of the pack had caught on so far.

Dahrkron gave instructions for another night in the Canyon. He soon forgot about the farries and the road as he talked about another raid on what the pack called the valley of squirrels. While he talked, he thought about another idea that had been floating around for some time. Something about deer.

When the pack began to lope off for the hunt, Dahrkron and Trahna fell behind slightly.

"They may never brave the road," said Trahna. "Maybe we should slip off without them a couple times and feast for ourselves."

"We'll only have one chance," said Dahrkron. "After our first appearance they'll find some other place to meet. The pack will come along. It'll just take a little time."

"The farries weren't scared off after you went after them before," said Trahna.

"True, but there was only one of me," said Dahrkron, wishing she had not remembered. "Maybe you're right, but I don't want to take a chance. And anyway, it's not just a meal I'm after. I've tasted farri before, and they're not very good. It's just a good opportunity for the pack to wipe out a large number of cats with one quick raid. I feel like it's our duty to rid the world of as many of these filthy things as we can. Lord Krahsta would think so, I'm sure."

CHAPTER 28

Sharlo approached the Den early, hoping for his choice of the girls. He was happy to see Mahri sitting next to the tall grass at the edge of the Den and walked toward her with a smile. Mahri stood eagerly and began to step forward.

"Mahri is taken already tonight, dear Sharlo," said Halina.

Mahri was stunned. Sharlo too was taken aback and stopped awkwardly while looking at the mistress.

"Well, I guess it's understandable," he stammered. "If I may, I'll go with Farinna tonight then."

"Please do," said Halina. "And have fun, dears."

Lustful eyes followed the two farries as they stepped away from the Den and walked down the street. A slight twinge of jealousy had begun to work its way into the Den. If Sharlo was going to have a favorite, the group was glad it was Mahri. But it didn't keep the rest of them from wanting his teeth gripping their fur occasionally.

Other toms arrived and two asked for Mahri. Both were turned down by Halina. Mahri sat on the grass and began to sulk. She couldn't understand what Halina was doing, yet dared not question the mistress in front of the others. She watched in silence as the last of her favorite toms walked off with Syranosh. There was no one else left.

"Who am I being saved for?" Mahri asked at last when Syranosh and Malon were gone.

"You are being saved, dearest Mahri, for me!" said Halina.

Mahri looked puzzled for a moment, but then realized

Halina would not have kept her back if it wasn't important.

"Well, not me exactly, love," said Halina. "You're going to meet someone new tonight. Dori is her name."

"Dori? What kind of name is that? We've never had anyone by such a strange name visit the Den before. Is she new around here? Is she going to join the Den?"

"Dori has been around for many years," said Halina. "She has seen you many times, although I doubt if you have seen her. She is quite shy for someone of her strength and wisdom. You see, Dori is an owl."

"An owl?" Mahri had heard about them but had never seen one. They were predators who were a lot like farries in the way they hunted. They were not to be feared though, as hawks were, unless you were still a kitten. A full-grown farri was of no interest, since owls liked smaller prey like rats, mice, and an occasional rabbit.

"She is a dear friend, although I woke her up by mistake this afternoon," said Halina. "Like ourselves, owls prefer the dark. But despite my rudeness, Dori has agreed to meet with me later, and I thought you might like to go along."

"Of course," said Mahri. She was anxious to see if the similarities between owls and farries was as great as she had heard. And although she had never even seen one, she was not surprised to learn Halina had not only seen one, but befriended it, too.

"Sharlo will survive without you for one night," Halina smiled.

Mahri smiled back but then felt a slight jealous pang. Sharlo was out there mating with Farinna.

"Come, dear Mahri, let's go look for Dori," said Halina. "And maybe we'll find some catches of our own tonight, instead of depending on the toms. The food my paladin has been bringing home is of a particularly foul variety of late."

The Canyon was no place for farries at night. Halina seemed to be calm enough as they walked through the brush, but Mahri was nothing short of terrified. She had seen krahstas come out of the Canyon at night. Then again, when she had seen the puma and hawk, it had been in the daytime. She decided the Canyon was no place for farries at any time.

Mercifully, Dori's tree was close to the road.

"This is where she was and where she said to meet," said Halina. "She is probably out on a hunt. I suggest we stay close to the tree so we can climb quickly if there are krahstas about. I have no wish to face a pack of those foul beasts on their own turf at night."

Mahri needed no further encouragement. She wondered why they didn't just climb the holly tree now and not have to worry about it. The tree was not very big by street standards; the top branches would barely be out of a jumping krahsta's reach. It was little more than a large bush, and to Mahri it didn't look quite big enough, but she would gladly take to the thin branches in the event of trouble. She wished Dori had chosen a taller tree, although there were few in the dry, Southern California sage.

Another warm summer night, but Mahri felt a chill coming on. She reached her claws from the base of the tree.

"No dear," said Halina. "Dori has not met you and would be quite upset to find a strange farri in her tree. Be at peace, love. She will return soon. Then we will climb up and join her at her beckon."

The night sounds of the Canyon seemed to creep in on Mahri while they waited. There were sounds real and possibly imagined, not heard on their previous trips abroad. But then, those trips had been made during daylight.

After several minutes, Mahri cautiously began to relax. Halina was calm, yet alert. They sat with their backs to the tree, facing slightly different directions to watch for unfriendly visitors.

"There are elements of the paladin conditions for which I am still at a loss," said Halina. Mahri gave her a quick, sideways glance, wondering how Halina could discuss paladins under such bizarre circumstances.

"How so?" asked Mahri.

"Last night, my paladin brought home a female he has mated with frequently," said Halina. "The recent questions regarding the business of our Den has pulled constantly at my heart, and I believed a closer examination of the paladins would ease our concerns and reaffirm our beliefs.''

Mahri gave up her task of sentry and stared directly at Halina. Such an admission of doubt from the mistress was quite unusual.

''I thought there might be something we were missing, because of how differently they mated,'' said Halina. ''As you know, they usually mate face-to-face. It is rare, but I have seen Roger and a female mate as we do, although Roger does not bite the female's neck to hold on.''

Mahri nodded. On one occasion, she had seen Mommy and Daddy do the same.

''Last night, it looked as though they were about to begin face-to-face,'' continued Halina. ''I jumped onto the bed to see if such a position was possible with farries.''

''Is it?'' Mahri asked hopefully. The idea of something new seemed quite exciting.

''I don't know,'' said Halina. ''Roger asked me to get off the bed before I could observe. You might try it, my love, the next time you're with a tom.''

Mahri wondered what Sharlo would think if she suggested mating like humans. It would be nice to see his face as they mated, even for such a short period of time. She knew human mating lasted much longer than farries'.

''I also had questions about why the paladins press their faces together when they mate,'' said Halina. ''I went back up onto the bed to see if they did it simply because of their position, or if there was more involved. Again, the effort was fruitless, I'm afraid. Roger asked me to leave the room.''

With no screeching, flapping, or sounds of any kind, Dori landed. The great horned owl scanned the territory with a remarkably flexible neck, then looked down at the two farries.

''Farri Halina, you look well tonight,'' she said with what Mahri believed to be a smile. It was hard to determine the expressions of unfamiliar animals, especially those with beaks.

"Dearest Dori," answered Halina. "And I must say your beauty is exceptional tonight, as always."

"Oh, Farri Halina you flatter so," said Dori with a giggle. "It is the way of someone great, and only hours after seeing me at my worst do you say such sweetness."

"My dear Dori, you are beautiful even when you are awakened in the hour of the sun's strongest presence," said Halina.

Dori answered with another giggle.

Mahri was fascinated by the large bird. Beautiful was an understatement, but no other word could come to mind. The great owl *did* resemble farries in certain ways. The tufts of feathers starting from above her eyes and sticking out on the sides of her head gave the appearance of pointed ears, making the outline of her head the same shape as a farri's. The face was flat and she had a beak instead of lips, but the features were similar in an odd sort of way. And although Dori was covered with feathers, she was colored remarkably like Halina, complete with striking yellow eyes.

"Your farri friend is quite a pretty thing too," said Dori, turning her attention to Mahri. "Is she the one you spoke of, Farri Halina, and what kind of fur is that?"

Mahri did not know if she or Halina was supposed to answer, or what question to deal with first. Dori's rapid speech was quite confusing.

"This is Mahri," answered Halina. "And indeed, she is the one I spoke of. She is one from my Den, and together we have braved the Canyon in the past. Although I daresay, never at night. As for her fur, she might best answer herself."

Mahri was used to questions and comments about her coat but had no idea what the owl wanted to know.

"Do you hide well with it and do thorns get tangled?" asked Dori.

"There aren't many thorns to get into where we live," said Mahri, finally understanding. "I live in a house, although sometimes we go for romps in the Canyon. Things do get caught in it, and it can be tough to get out. But my paladins brush me every day, which makes it a lot easier. And there isn't much to hide from on the streets.''

The talk of paladins and houses and brushes left Dori as confused as Mahri had been. But the owl dismissed it as farri talk and then looked back to Halina.

''Two mice tonight, Farri Halina,'' said Dori. ''You simply must hunt with me again soon, and won't we have fun like before?''

''Is it safe to hunt with you, dearest Dori?'' asked Halina.

''It is if you can fly, my friend,'' said Dori, and her voice became hushed. ''You are wise to be so close to the tree, and you should climb up right now. Have I been rude, Farri Halina? Please come up where it is safer.''

Halina jumped up first, followed by Mahri. The tree was not big enough to make the climb any effort at all, and the two farries were instantly perched next to the owl.

''Will you tell us about krahstas?'' asked Halina.

''There is so much to tell about krahstas,'' said Dori. ''In fact, there is not much else to talk about in these strange days.''

''We heard they were chasing lynxes,'' said Mahri.

''Peace!'' said Halina. ''Let Dori tell us what she has seen.''

Mahri flinched slightly at the reprimand, and then crouched low onto her branch.

''I have seen krahstas,'' said Dori. ''I saw them to-night. I left my hunt early to warn you, but they ran off, and they're so nasty. Two of them were here, watching for you on the street. They have seen you gather and know of your numbers and still they watch.

''It is Krahsta Dahrkron or I am blind,'' she continued. ''He is the pack leader, but they do not follow him to the edge of the road where he and Krahsta Trahna watch the farries. They watch more and more these days, and chase you they may soon yet.''

''It is as I feared,'' said Halina. ''They will wait for the rest of the pack to get hungry enough, and then they'll strike.''

''That may be a while, and do you know how much

food they've been finding? As Farri Mahri said they have attacked lynxes and other krahstas. Krahsta Dahrkron is a demon, did you know? He is. He rules the pack with what many in the Canyon believe are cold teeth and threatening eyes. I don't believe it and I saw them all follow him with such admiration and love. They *love* him. And all the Canyon is in fear. A demon more cunning and dangerous than the legendary foes of the great lords and ladies, and how does he rule the entire Canyon?

"Beware farries, for I believe he will lead his pack to you soon. Grow wings! Or find a new home. Stay in the homes of your men if you can for a while, and the rest may forget, but not he. If they forget, they will not follow. But I believe he is dangerously obsessed with the destruction of cats. All cats, and who will be next? There are those with power in the Canyon who would let him be, but who will be next? Cats have no friends in the world, but who will be next? I hope this demon will be stopped, but I know not how or by whom."

Dori became silent and turned her head around to look across the Canyon. She turned back to the farries but said nothing. The moonlight kissed her eyes, and in them Mahri could see fear.

"Are there any pumas about?" asked Halina after quite a silence.

"Pumas are rarely so close to the man," said Dori. "One was lost, but they are best not spoken of at night, don't you know?"

"Of course I know," said Halina. "But I hoped you might tell me anyway, so I'll know whether to hunt with you or not." She smiled and looked kindly at the owl. The two clearly had been friends for many seasons.

"Your worries are with krahstas, Farri Halina," said Dori. "Beware! And brave the Canyon no more without emergency. There is little I can help you with anyway and I must hunt now. Farewell, Farri Mahri, and take good care of the mistress!"

Dori spread her wings and was airborne before the farries could speak. They both gave a quick scout over the Canyon from Dori's tree and then climbed down into the brush.

The walk back to the street was brisk and without sound. Both farries were on extreme alert for the scent of krahsta or any other stray beast. Mahri also watched the ground for snakes, although she had no way of knowing how unlikely it was for a rattler to be out after dark.

The feeling struck suddenly and without warning, followed by the sickening and fearful scent. Krahstas were very close. Halina sprang instantly toward the last of the holly trees near the edge of the sage, with Mahri following right at her tail. Hiding was impossible, if the farries could smell the krahstas, then so the opposite had been true for quite some time. They were very close.

The path ended abruptly. A barrier of brush stood between the farries and the tree. Halina guessed left and darted off to find a break, but Mahri chose to go to the right. A split target was harder to catch, and there was as good a chance for an opening as the other way.

Mahri could hear them now. How loud they rumbled in the sage. It was amazing they could sneak up on anything! Mahri fought through the unfamiliar turf, concentrating on the search for a break in the sage wall, and lost her footing while trying to cut to the left. She fell hard and actually rolled to the edge of a huge cactus. She allowed a quick sigh of thanks for the fall, else she would have run full force into the wicked spines. The relief was snapped instantly, however, as one of the krahstas bounded through the sage toward her.

What to do? It was too late to run. She bolted around the cactus and crawled underneath in hopes of Lady Farri's luck. If krahsta's night vision was only half as bad as the dogs on the street . . .

The yelp was shrill and the ensuing howl deafening. Yet somehow Mahri had feared worse. The pain in the cries was too obvious to be terrifying, even though Mahri stood less than five feet from a full-grown krahsta. It had turned its back on her and was pawing at its face. She moved instantly and dove through the break in the sage and raced for the holly tree.

Dahrkron's mood changed in less time than it took to exhale a breath at panting speed. The crazy luck of loping around with Trahna and finding two farries in the Canyon. They waited for the farries to walk right into them, taking advantage of the smaller animals' limited smelling ability at long range. Then the chase: Trahna following the scent of one and he closing on the scent of the other.

He had planned it so well too. He had anticipated the course of the prey, heading straight for the holly tree. He leaped over the wall of sage too high for a farri to clear, and cut straight through to meet the farri at its destination. It worked so well. He was there in time and happily waited while the dirty little thing ran directly to him. And now this.

Trahna was crying horribly on the other side of the thicket. An evil farri had done something treacherous, and this was bad. He now stood face-to-face with the other farri, and this was worse. He was standing within easy reach of the same farri who had ripped his face up and humiliated him earlier in the summer.

"You're in my territory now, little one," said Dahrkron, trying to sound convincing. He was convincing, to himself anyway. He heard the cries of Trahna and became furious instead of depressed.

"You will let me pass," said the farri. She stood calm and passive, yet wildly fluffed, just as before.

Dahrkron could stand it no more. He tensed to strike but was hit with the claws before he moved. He turned quickly and bit hard, finding some hair but no substance. The gash across the corner of his eye was bad.

Not again. This couldn't be happening again. This time was worse, he thought. Trahna's cries were down to a whimper, and she would soon see him ripped up too, if things continued. This was bad. A pack leader could not be chewed up by a farri in front of his mate and expect to survive. This was very bad. He looked back at the farri.

"What are you doing in the Canyon, little one?" he asked. He was now more interested in information than in fighting, although he was sure his pride would force him into another clash.

"You will let me pass," said the farri, "or I will hurt you worse than before. You may not survive this time."

Dahrkron felt a growl starting to rise, but stopped short of attacking when he heard movement in the brush behind him. He turned quickly and was stunned to see another farri walk out. Even more stunning was the feeling of teeth and claws in his flank. He had forgotten about the first one.

Dahrkron reeled hard and growled, biting only air. He turned back toward the new farri, hoping for an easier match, but was startled numb by a screech in the sky. It was an owl; claws extended, and diving straight for him! Dahrkron jumped hard to his right, but still felt the talons graze his hide, followed by yet another bite from the first farri. This was too much.

Not even looking back, he bounded toward the thicket and jumped over the same way he came. He reached the path on the other side and then searched for the whimpering Trahna.

Following for one more silent dive, the owl sank its weapons in Dahrkron's right ear. Caught off guard, he yelped and bit upward, coming away empty again. His ear was not so lucky. The owl had tried to carry it away! Owls never attacked krahstas. Dahrkron put his head down and hoped the strangest night of his life was only a nightmare.

Nerves rattled but otherwise unharmed, Halina and Mahri crashed through the edge of the brush and ran into the street. Slowing to a trot, they approached the Den and sat on the grass near the curb. Mahri was still trembling out of control. Halina groomed her paws as if nothing had happened.

"How do you stand up to them?" Mahri asked finally. It had been several minutes before she was able to speak.

"I don't know," said Halina. "They strike no fear in me, at least when they are alone. Fortunately only the one followed me, for which I am in your debt. You know, he was the same one who rushed the street earlier this summer."

"He must have been surprised to see you!" Mahri laughed.

"Yes. Disappointed to say the least. But I must ask

you what you did to the other krahsta. It sounded so hurt. Was it Dori who helped you out?''

"No," said Mahri. "It was an accident, really. I fell down, and then crawled under a cactus plant. I knew the krahsta hadn't seen me yet. It was following my scent. I hoped it was running too fast to notice, and counted on how bad the kribas around here see at night. I got lucky.''

"So the krahsta ran into the cactus?'' Halina laughed.

"Yes. Took it right in the face and both front paws. I don't think it ever did see me.''

"Maybe not, but the other one certainly did," said Halina. "You must be more careful, my love. He might have gotten you if Dori had not dropped in. I am now in her debt too. Why didn't you run back to the street when you had the chance?''

"I couldn't just leave you, Halina," said Mahri.

"Dearest Mahri, by now you must know I can look after myself. And if not, what would you have done? Oh, what a fool I am. I'm sorry. I didn't mean to hurt your feelings. I love you for caring enough to come back. So many others would just run without even thinking about it. But in the Canyon, this is what we must do.

"If we are to venture into the Canyon, we must assume its responsibility. Only the wild can live in the Canyon, and wild we are not. But we can be for short times, if we are wise. While we live in protected houses with paladins who feed us, animals of the Canyon live only to survive. Everything eaten is hunted and killed, not put in a bowl by a paladin. Not ending up in another animal's belly is the way to survive, which means running away from trouble even if your dearest friends are in it worse.''

"I guess I understand," said Mahri. "I just couldn't leave you to face a krahsta alone after hearing what Dori had to say. What if it had been Dahrkron, the pack leader? Didn't Dori call him a demon? He might have been too much for you.''

"Possibly," said Halina. "But then again, dearest Mahri, what could you have done about it? What if I was already dead by the time you had gotten there?''

"I think it would take more than one lousy krahsta to do in Halina," Mahri beamed.

''But maybe it only takes one, dear. And how do you know it wasn't the pack leader? He is a very large krahsta.''

''Dori called him a demon,'' said Mahri. ''Wouldn't being a demon make him really different? What is a demon anyway?''

''Dori was only talking,'' Halina smiled. ''She was comparing the pack leader to a demon. At least that's what I hope. If he truly is, then we would have no hope against such a foe. But by his very existence, I believe he cannot be one.'' She looked out toward the Canyon and then the other way down the street. There was no movement anywhere. All of the Den farries had mated and gone home.

''A demon, dearest Mahri, is a sad and cursed soul,'' said Halina. ''Sad and cursed, and one to be feared. They possess a fiercely jealous hatred for those who live and breathe on the earth, for they no longer can. Nor can their kin, for they have none.

''There are many kinds of animals, as you know. There are some who live in other parts of the world who we will never see, yet somehow I know they are there. There are also animals who are not there, but used to be. The entire family of their kind has died off and no longer walks the lands of this world. The word for this is extinct. Unfortunately, and fortunately, there are many animals who have become extinct since the Creator gave life to the world. There is legend of some of these animals being as large as houses, with teeth bigger than our paladins.''

Mahri breathed a sigh of astonishment. She could not imagine an animal larger than the paladins, let alone as big as a house. She believed those animals to fit into the category of ''fortunately'' extinct.

''The Creator expected these animals to live forever,'' continued Halina. ''That was His intent. Why create a life only to have it die? In some cases it was not their fault, but in most cases it was. Not necessarily the animals themselves, but the lords and ladies of their kind. So the Creator called upon the lords of the extinct and demanded answers. Many offered feeble excuses and others cast blame, but none gave the real truth of how they failed to recognize changes in the world and make adjustments with their lines.

"The end result was that the Creator was furious with the lords and ladies. First for letting their races die, and second for not answering for it. The results were horrifying." Halina looked out to the Canyon again, and then up to the trees lining the street. What she searched for, Mahri dared not guess, knowing it would be something she would prefer not to see.

"In the end," said Halina, "the Creator cast out the Lords of the Dead, and banished them forever from His haven. They continued to possess their spiritual power, but they no longer wished to use it in the proper way. There was no one left of their kind living on the earth, so they decided to use their powers against those still living, who they blamed for the deaths of their kind, and ultimately for their banishment."

"So they bother animals who are still living?" asked Mahri.

"Sadly it is so," said Halina. "Not only did they destroy their own charges, but they wish to destroy others who still live. It is their great jealousy. And they succeed. More animals vanish every day from the world, and the demons, as they are called, are very happy to have their numbers grow with each one. Still to this day, the Lords of the Dead are banished to the dark world outside the Creator's haven. It is my belief they wish to have all of the world's animals extinct, leaving the Creator to either live alone or take them all back. Or maybe in their foolishness, they wish to overthrow Him."

"So it's the Lords of the Dead who are called demons?" asked Mahri. "What about the animals of their lines? Are they demons too?"

"No, dearest," said Halina. "Those animals were not to blame for the deaths of their lines. They are in peace. It is their lords who are to blame, and it is they who have been punished and haunt the earth as demons."

"So how could the leader of the krahstas be a demon?" asked Mahri. "What was his name? Dahrkron?"

"He could be a demon posing as a krahsta," said Halina. "I think this is what Dori suspects. And by his actions, he may very well be. He seems to be intent on going after many types of cats. Even the big ones, which is unusual for krahstas. And if half the rumors in the Canyon are true, the whole area is terrified of his pack. This is also unusual. True, a pack of krahstas is a serious threat, but the tactics of this particular pack borders on the bizarre. Demon or not, their leader has quite an innovative imagination.

"What could also be the case is that Dahrkron is not a demon at all. It could be someone else in the pack who has the leader's ear. This could be an even more effective way to hide identity and still achieve the desired purposes. And of course, there may be no demon at all in the pack. It could just be Dori's fears getting the best of her. Of course, it is very strange for a pack of krahstas to upset an owl. Or a hawk, now that I think about it. Treep wasn't too pleased with the strange aggressions of the pack."

"The story of the demons is so sad," said Mahri. "It's hard to believe they would want to destroy other animals, especially after seeing their own kind perish. I don't see how they could kill off all the other animals on earth anyway. Do you? The paladins would never let them kill us off. Or the kribas. Then the demons would have to kill off all the paladins too, and that will never happen. The paladins are too smart to let all the life in the world be destroyed. Aren't they?"

CHAPTER 29

In a way, Mahri was not surprised to see Sharlo waiting outside her house the morning after the visit with Dori. She was glad to see him, although curious as to his intentions. Sharlo never visited Halina's girls away from the Den.

Mahri stepped out onto the porch and stretched, letting Sharlo gaze at the full glamour of her coat. The morning sun was at just the right angle to enhance the dazzling colors, and she was glad for the extra time she had spent grooming that morning.

"How was your evening with Farinna?" Mahri asked innocently.

"Farinna is a nice farri," answered Sharlo. "Of course, I would rather have spent it with you. Who were you being saved for?"

"For a strange and scary evening," Mahri said. "Everything from meeting an owl to being chased by krahstas." She shook her head and then giggled.

"Chased by krahstas?" asked Sharlo. "Did they rush the street again?"

"No, sweetheart," said Mahri. She recapped the evening for Sharlo, starting with the walk through the Canyon and ending with their escape. She left out the discussion of demons, still upset about the idea of extinction.

"This is all so strange," said Sharlo. He had paced nervously throughout the entire tale, then sat down close to Mahri.

"Why did you come here?" asked Mahri. "Not that I

mind. I love seeing you. It's just so unusual for you to come here. Or do you secretly visit the homes of the other girls?''

"No, dear Mahri," said Sharlo defensively. "This is rare indeed. I have things I wish to discuss with you, though Lady Farri knows, I probably shouldn't.''

Mahri's eyes brightened and she lost all of her breath. Forgotten was the trip to the Canyon and the krahstas and owls. This could be the moment she'd longed for, the moment when Sharlo told her he never wished to mate with the others anymore, and wanted only her. How he wanted her to leave the Den and see only him. And she would do it too, wouldn't she? Certainly she would. The Den was only a means of finding toms to mate with. What if there was one who would mate with her all the time? What if . . .

"I need to talk to you about Halina," said Sharlo.

"Ha-Halina?" Mahri stuttered. She was stunned. Sharlo looked preoccupied. There was no affection in his face.

"I have discussed it with her, but to no avail," said Sharlo. "Maybe she will listen to you. You, after all, are her favorite."

"Discuss what?" asked Mahri, trying not to sound as crushed as she felt. She wanted to bite herself for being so foolish. Sharlo had shown no interest in romance tonight.

"She seems to be going about this all wrong," said Sharlo. "I don't know what she expects to find in the Canyon, and it worries me that she drags you along too."

"I follow Halina because I want to," said Mahri. "And what are you talking about, anyway?"

"The other farries are starting to gather again," said Sharlo. "The ones who attacked the Den that terrible night. They have not the numbers as before, for many fear Halina's ties to the Canyon and how she called up a puma the last time."

"But Halina can't do it again," said Mahri. "And anyway, looking for pumas is not why we go into the Canyon.''

"The other farries don't know that," said Sharlo. "To

be quite honest, Halina is a very strange farri, and most of the others wouldn't be surprised if she could call ten pumas to the street. The other farries have their spies, and they have seen you two go into the Canyon more than once. They saw it before too, and then they saw the results. They don't know there aren't any other pumas out there.''

"We only go into the Canyon for news of the krahstas,'' said Mahri. "We've talked to an owl and a hawk, and they've said nothing about pumas. Only krahstas.''

"If Halina was truly worried about the krahstas, she would move the Den,'' said Sharlo simply.

"We've talked about it when we've met,'' said Mahri. "No one wants to move. Especially Halina. I think she needs to be close to the Canyon for some reason. Sarena once said she thought Halina was wild, and I believe it.''

"Maybe,'' said Sharlo. "I don't know. I only know how concerned I am about you and the others. I love Halina dearly. A braver farri I have never met. Nor are there any wiser than she. I am concerned, that's all.''

"So what do you wish me to say to Halina?'' asked Mahri.

"I don't know, I guess,'' said Sharlo. "She knows about the others. She knows their numbers will grow, and Coron has a lot to do with it. It is surprising how many toms have been showing up at the Den and how quickly they decided to come back. Even the threats of Coron are no match for the ancient needs.''

"Coron has been threatening toms?'' asked Mahri.

"Of course,'' said Sharlo. "He threatens the toms and sparks jealousy among the queens. Why else would they bother? He makes them believe it's a moral cause. Since when have farries been known for their morals?''

"You got me, dear Sharlo,'' said Mahri. "So what is all this leading to?''

"Tell Halina to find another answer,'' said Sharlo. "Please, Mahri, stay away from the Canyon. You know how deadly it can be. I think if you can chase off Coron, you'll have no more problems.''

Mahri thought about "chasing off Coron.'' Killing Coron was what Sharlo really meant. There was no other way to get rid of such a beast. And how would you go about it? Halina could stand up to Coron and win a fight, but he could always run away, or make enough racket to attract the paladins, who would chase them both off. It would take a group effort, and someone was likely to get hurt. And that was if Halina agreed to all of this. If not . . .

"I don't know," said Mahri. "I'll talk to her. Will you help out if we decide to go after Coron?"

"Of course," said Sharlo. "Anything to spend more time with you."

"Let's go see if we can find Halina," said Mahri. "We'll discuss it right away."

"I think you should talk to her alone," said Sharlo. "Or maybe bring it up before the Den. I don't know how your group works, or how the politics are set up. Do what you feel is best. Make sure she knows how important it is to get rid of Coron. Bye, dearest. I'll see you tonight."

Sharlo turned and walked away. Mahri thought about how strange the conversation had turned out. She had gone from indulging romantic dreams to discussing murder, although there was no such word or concept in the language of farries. Survival of the fittest was a fact of life in the Canyon, but farries lived on the street side, where Nature's calls were not quite as volatile. She had never heard of a fight to the death between farries. It was too easy to get out of it. And a strategically planned group assault on a single farri was beyond her imagination.

Mahri walked into the street and headed south toward the Den. It was a fine summer morning, warm and clear, with the heat wave decidedly broken. A delicate wind out of the west caressed the trees with only the slightest humidity, and large numbers of birds cluttered the air with endless racket. But Mahri noticed none of these things. Her mind raced with too many worries, and she walked along the street nearly blind with thought.

Halina was in the street near the Den and called out to Mahri. The mistress was stretched out with Sina and Jassa, relaxing in the early sun. Mahri was surprised to see Halina so out in the open with no bushes or high grass to break her outline. Halina was especially prone to hide during the daylight hours, and Mahri was reminded with a smile of the great cat-family bane: none could resist a nice warm nap in the sun.

The idea appealed to Mahri as well, and she trotted toward the others with the friendly approach of tail skyward.

"Dearest Mahri, you are so beautiful this morning," said Halina.

"How do you get your fur so shiny?" asked Jassa, the gray shorthair who was arguably the least attractive of Halina's girls, yet most playful and fun to tease. "I try grooming as often as I see you do, but I get nowhere."

"Mahri is truly in Lady Farri's favor," Sina smiled. "As she should be. If you weren't so mean and rotten, Jassa, you might some day turn as pretty too."

"If mean and rotten determined looks," said Jassa, "then Syranosh would certainly look like a possum."

All four of the farries laughed. Even Halina beamed with unusual good humor, and all of Mahri's earlier worries melted away in the sun. She began to stretch out with the others when a slight movement in the tall grass by the Den caught her attention. She stood back up and assumed the stalk position.

"Go get it, pretty one," said Jassa. "It's a foolish mouse in the cathouse, and you need the practice. Being the toms' favorite's made you lazy."

"Hush!" whispered Mahri. She took several steps toward the Den while the other farries watched with amusement. She had no idea what was moving in the grass, but a stray Canyon mouse was a hopeful guess. She could flush it into the street and they could all chase it around for a while.

Mahri had the advantage. She ducked behind the several large clumps of dried grass surrounding the prey, who had now moved into an opening. Mahri could not see it yet, but was very familiar with the small, flat section of dirt on the other side of her blind. When the sounds of moving grass stopped, she knew it was in the open. Without hesitation, she leaped over the grass for the attack.

The terror struck the instant she cleared the grass. It

was a rattlesnake. She landed within inches of its tail and
lived only because it was caught unaware. Her momentum carried her for another bound over its back as it instinctively struck at the original point of impact. It
whipped around with amazing speed and poised in a coil
ready to strike again before Mahri had any chance to
escape.

Halina was on her feet and racing toward the grass.
She stopped just at the edge, where she could see Mahri
frozen in a staring match with the snake. Jassa and Sina
joined the mistress a moment later.

Mahri couldn't believe this was happening again. Face-
to-face with another rattlesnake. The same rattlesnake,
as far as she could tell. The same stupid eyes and the
same cruel fangs. The sparkling pattern of skin was already making her dizzy.

"We've got to distract it," Halina was saying, but
Mahri could barely hear her. It sounded like she was on
the other side of a wall, or lifetime. "Mahri, be ready to
run!"

Didn't Halina understand? thought Mahri. You can't
run from this. I can barely breathe. How could I ever
run? My eyes are getting fuzzy. Run Halina! I wish I
could open my mouth!

Suddenly a shadow and a piercing screech brought
Mahri to her elbows. She half opened her eyes, fearing
the snake had struck her and this is what it sounded like
to die. A scream so violent had to proceed from a soul
being torn away from the body.

The snake was gone. Sina and Jassa looked as stunned
as Mahri felt. Only Halina's face betrayed what had happened. Halina was looking skyward.

Mahri followed Halina's gaze and saw Treep, the majestic hawk of the Canyon, sitting on top of a telephone
pole. Hanging from the clutches of his fierce claws was
a very limp and very dead rattlesnake.

CHAPTER 30

Dahrkron had no way of getting all of the cactus spines out of Trahna's nose and lips. She had pawed at them the second she was jabbed, forcing the needles deeper into the most tender part of her face. She had whimpered continuously throughout the night.

The cut below Dahrkron's eye was not too bad, and he had forgotten about it, anyway. The cries of his mate would always hurt far deeper than any farri wounds. They would pay dearly for this offense. It wasn't just him this time. No one would live after injuring Trahna.

The pack had suffered right along with Dahrkron. It was a long night with little rest, because Trahna was well loved by everyone and her cries affected them too.

"This is not the first time this has happened," said Dahrkron to the weary pack. The questioning eyes were unanimous, even from the ailing Trahna.

"I said nothing of it before," said Dahrkron angrily. "Maybe I should have. But what aspiring pack leader would dare reveal a defeat by a farri? No one among us would! Well, it happened to me."

The shock was vocalized in the form of a loud gasp from everyone in the pack. They had just heard their leader admit to losing a fight to a farri.

"I even fooled myself into believing a lie, but now we must all face the truth. There is at least one farri on the street who had no trouble ripping my face up. Twice!"

The pack was too stunned to do anything but sit in unmoving silence. Such an admission could mean death to a leader.

"I'm telling you this for a reason," continued Dahrk-ron. "As you know, since becoming leader I have strongly campaigned against cats of all kinds. It was to prepare you all mentally for what we might be up against someday. At first I could only guess and did so because of my wounded pride. But after the treachery of last night I can feel certain. The leader of the farries on the street is a demon."

CHAPTER 31

"Twice we have faced evil rattlesnakes," Halina said, addressing the Den when all farries had arrived. "Mahri was there both times, and she believes it to be the same snake. Fortunately, we will have to face it no more."

Halina told of how the snake had found its way into the Den, and how the episode ended with Treep diving in for an early lunch. Most of the farries were stunned to learn of Halina's association with a hawk. Although Halina had nothing to do with Treep's sudden arrival at the right time, the mere fact of her knowing the hawk's name made most of the girls believe otherwise. Especially when she began to speak of Treep as a friend and possible ally in the future.

"I should not speak openly of this before I consult my friends with wings," said Halina, "but I believe it's best to share our hopes with the entire Den." She looked at Mahri and gave a warm smile.

"In less than one cycle of the sun and moon, Mahri and I saw two different birds come to our aid," said Halina. "One was intentionally trying to help, the other, I fear, had self-interest at heart. No matter. The results were the same. Mahri and I are both alive."

The questioning eyes were answered with a recounting of how Dori had swooped down to chase off a krahsta, another amazing story. Halina had also befriended an owl. The surprise was in the confirmation, since most in the Den suspected Halina's dealings in the Canyon. She was usually just secretive about it.

"I believe Dori will help us out of friendship, and Treep will help us for a price," said Halina.

"Help us, Halina?" asked Syranosh. "I'm just wondering a little bit here, and I suppose others wonder too. What do we need help for?"

"Dear Syranosh, do you not talk with your dates?" asked Halina. "Or are you too busy being selfish to learn?" The second question brought a sudden hush to the group. They had never heard Halina insult one of her Den before. Things were changing.

"You speak of wild trips in the Canyon and strange dealings with winged predators," said Syranosh. "Tell us why, Mistress, and then we'll judge who's being selfish."

"It's the other farries, Syranosh," said Halina. "The ones who attacked here on the night of Sarena's death. They are regrouping, and I fear another attack is imminent."

"And trips to the Canyon will solve this?" asked Syranosh. A true battle of wills was taking place, and the other farries sat silent. No one ever challenged Halina like this.

"Dear Syranosh, we must be as strong as we can," said Halina. "Having allies in the sky is a true benefit. Who would expect it? The krahstas certainly didn't. And, dear Farri, they're about too!

"There's quite a lot of unsettling news from the Canyon. The krahstas are striking terror into previously unmolested areas. The two we saw last night were very close to the road. I am certain they were sent there as spies, to watch our movements."

Syranosh was about to interrupt with a sarcastic remark, but Mahri spoke first.

"I fear the krahstas more than the other farries," said Mahri. "Wouldn't a simple solution be to move the Den away from the Canyon? If we met down the block, the krahstas would never come after us." She bit down and silently let the air out of her lungs with relief. Sharlo's first suggestion was out in the open, yet she found herself hating the idea even as it left her mouth. She suddenly realized how much she loved the Den, and no place else could ever be the same.

"There are many fears in the world besides krahstas, love," said Halina kindly. "My first thought indeed was to move the Den. Yet there really is no other place for us. I have scouted the area and believe any other place will create problems with paladins. It's best they remain unaware of our group."

"Why?" asked Farinna. "Why should they care about us?"

"You are all aware of the story of man's blindness at night," said Halina. "They might still be interested in following us with their lights, and who among us wishes to be watched while we mate? The toms would avoid us, for they require discretion. We would be by ourselves and unhappy again."

"But alive, sister," said Syranosh. "The paladins don't kill us like krahstas do."

"The krahstas have killed none of us," answered Halina.

"Yet," said Syranosh.

"Still," said Halina, "there is something comfortable about this Den. And it's comfortable to be next to the Canyon. True, we are different from the animals in the Canyon. But not much different. In fact, I believe we could all live out there if need be. There is too much in our heritage to believe otherwise."

"I like this place too," said Mahri. "I agree about the paladins. I love my family very much, but I have no wish for them to know what we do here. They might not understand." Mahri was one of the few farries who believed the changes scar had nothing to do with divine intervention. She and Halina were the only ones in the Den who secretly believed the paladins had something to do with it, although neither would admit openly or even secretly to their belief.

As it turned out, all of the farries preferred the present location of the Den, krahstas or not. Even Syranosh, after some thought, went along with the others.

"What about the other farries?" Mahri asked Halina. "What can we do to protect ourselves against them?"

The thought of what was to follow still bothered Mahri. She knew she would have to raise Sharlo's idea of getting rid of Coron. She wondered what Halina would have to say.

"On this I have spent many hours of my life searching for the correct response," Halina said thoughtfully. She looked down the street away from the Canyon. As the sun was beginning to set, the toms would be starting to arrive soon. Any answers or decisions would have to be fast, or saved for another day.

"As we have discovered from our friends abroad, the problem can be traced to one farri," Halina said. Her words were greeted with groans from the group as each girl reflected her own personal distaste of Coron. "Truly, the elimination of Coron from their numbers could mean the end of their group entirely. Maybe not, but I might bet Mahri's beautiful fur on it."

Mahri smiled with the others, but felt mild surprise at the direction of Halina's words. The others in the Den had not yet caught on.

"Coron must be stopped," Halina said flatly. "We must do something to keep him from provoking the other group into violence. Without him they will forget about us."

"Does that mean letting him come back and mate with us?" asked Farinna. This question brought a chorus of hisses from the Den. The disgust was unanimous.

"None of you will be forced to do what I wouldn't do myself," said Halina. "And not that it matters, but you are all forbidden to mate with him anyway." Laughter was the response.

"What's the answer, then?" asked Mahri, who feared she knew the answer already, but wanted it out in the open for discussion. She was relieved she wasn't the one who had brought it up, but was surprised at Halina. She saw the questions in the eyes of the others and wondered what they would say.

"We might approach Coron as a group," said Halina. "All of us together might scare him out of the area." She scanned the faces of the Den before continuing.

"I fear the chances of this being a success are futile,"

she said. "We would even run the risk of him seeking an even more hostile revenge. An animal as unstable as Coron must be feared for their unknown potential. For this reason I have ruled this out as an option. I wish it could be so simple.

"There is always the choice of continuing on with our Den and facing the inevitable battle with the clan of the misled. They will certainly strike here if we do nothing, although their numbers will be less than before. That is, if they strike soon. The longer they delay, the more farries will forget the fateful night with Sarena and become brave again. How long they will wait, I cannot say. I would guess it would be sooner than later. Coron is impatient.

"The final option is to get rid of Coron completely," Halina said, and looked carefully at the group for reactions. "This will be quite a difficult task. Difficult and dangerous, I would dare to add. And as I see a pair of our tom friends coming toward us, I will leave you until tomorrow to think of what this might mean. We'll meet earlier than usual, for we have much to talk about. But until then, let's all have a good time tonight."

When Sharlo arrived and Mahri had still not been taken, she held her breath and hoped Halina had no other plans for her. When Sharlo asked, Halina wished them well and Mahri was relieved. Chasing around in the Canyon was fun occasionally, but chasing around with Sharlo was always a guaranteed great time.

They walked together toward Sharlo's house, which was on the street directly behind where Mahri lived. While the distance between their two houses was a drive or walk around the block for the paladins, it was an easy hop over two fences for the farries. Mahri wondered again why she saw Sharlo so rarely, considering the closeness of their homes.

"My paladin will be asleep already," said Sharlo. "I don't believe even your sweet cries will wake her if we hide in the bushes on the other side of the house." Noise and alerting paladins was always a concern of mating farries. Too much noise was a guarantee of interruption by an angry paladin. They seemed to have no respect for a farri's privacy.

"Anywhere with you is fine with me, dearest Sharlo," said Mahri. "Maybe you should visit me more during the day when you don't have such worrisome news."

"When the news is good, my love, I will bring you that instead," said Sharlo. "Unfortunately, there has not been much of late."

"Sure there has!" said Mahri. "This morning I was almost killed by a rattlesnake. The same one who got Melena, I think. If it was not for Treep, then I might not have seen you until you were called by Lady Farri."

"Treep?" asked Sharlo doubtfully. Mahri told the story of her adventure after leaving Sharlo earlier in the morning. At first he appeared concerned, but then he seemed relieved after giving the story more thought.

"These are strange days indeed," said Sharlo. "A farri saved from death by a hawk. Of course it would be a friend of Halina's! She befriends everyone who can help her, even if the help is in a way she could never have guessed."

"And only this morning you were doubting her for this," said Mahri. Sharlo's earlier questioning of Halina had been the first sore point she had ever felt toward him. Even though his questions seemed very valid, and indeed Mahri had raised them at the meeting a little earlier, she still took mild offense to the challenging of Halina.

"Halina always seems to know best," Sharlo conceded. "It's still strange to hear of dealings with birds, even if they are predators."

Mahri nodded but said nothing.

"Did you mention to her what we talked about this morning?" asked Sharlo.

"Yes," said Mahri. "We talked about it openly in the Den before the toms started to show."

"What did she say?"

"We all decided not to move the Den," said Mahri. "We're all comfortable there, even if it's dangerous. There's no place else for us to go, anyway."

Sharlo looked disappointed, but turned away too

quickly for Mahri to tell just how much. He began to groom the back of her neck, and she started to relax.

"What about the other thing we talked about?" Sharlo asked between brushes.

"Halina brought it up," said Mahri. "I was surprised. We didn't talk about it much. She just gave us all the idea to think about, although I daresay many of the girls didn't really understand. We're going to meet earlier than usual tomorrow to talk about it more. Halina thinks it might be our only choice."

"I would agree with you," said Sharlo. "Tell Halina I'll help with whatever you decide. Maybe I'll tell her. I'll try to find her tomorrow morning if I can get out. It seems like the wind has been changing in her favor. Now is the time to act on it."

"Let's not worry about it anymore tonight," said Mahri. "Don't we have sweeter things to talk about?"

"I would think so," said Sharlo. He stopped grooming her neck and bit down on it instead.

When Mahri left Sharlo, she decided to go back to the Den before returning home for the night. She wanted to discuss many things with Halina in private, and hoped the mistress was still around. This was unlikely, since Halina dated too, but there was always a chance.

Mahri crossed the sidewalk and stepped out onto the street. There was hardly ever any paladin traffic this late at night, so she walked openly on the road. The night was clear and warm, a good night for farries to be about. She kept an eye out for any of Halina's girls who might be on the prowl.

She turned the corner toward the street where the Den was. Another night she might simply have hopped fences and cut through yards, but tonight she felt wonderful and a longer walk seemed like a fun and relaxing idea. She walked from the street to the far sidewalk to cut across the corner yard from where she might be able to see the Den.

No one was there. Even from this distance, Mahri's excellent night vision gave her a clear view of the Den, and it sat empty in the night. There had been toms to spare tonight.

The movement in the bush caught her unawares. From the hedge along the side of the house he came quickly and deliberately. Before she could react he was in her face, bearing down with a fierce look of cold hatred and cruel satisfaction. It was Coron.

"Alone, are we, pretty one?" he asked, the contempt ringing in his voice. "Pretty young farries shouldn't be out alone at night."

"Leave here, Coron," said Mahri, trying to sound brave again. This was getting to be a habit, and she vowed to start practicing the art first thing in the morning.

"No need, pretty trash cat," said Coron. "In fact, I see every reason to be here."

"Fine," said Mahri. "Be here. Just let me pass, and there will be no trouble."

Coron's response was a laugh, but one so dangerous and crazy it sent terror throughout Mahri's system. Unless another girl from the Den was in the very close vicinity, Mahri was in deep trouble.

"If you touch me, Halina will come after you with the entire Den," Mahri threatened. "Let me pass."

Another laugh, even scarier than the first. If Coron could laugh at the thought of facing Halina, then there were no other threats.

"Let all the farries on earth come after me," said Coron. "What can they do? Will it heal your wounds? Will anything? I would guess not."

Mahri had no response. She wanted desperately to rip his lungs out, but this was not an option. Coron was twice her size and could tear her up at will. All she could do was run.

She turned and bolted instantly. Coron would have more speed, but there was always the chance of seeing one of the other girls. She dashed across the street and headed for her house. A little trickery and any luck at all could get her there before Coron, and he would never brave the trapdoor of the paladins.

He was behind her before she made the sidewalk, and

she knew the house was an impossible goal. As hard as she ran, she was no contest for the larger and stronger tom. No choice but to turn, fight, and make an awful lot of noise.

Her stop and turn were sudden enough to catch Coron off guard. He would have slammed right into her if she had not stepped to the right to avoid the collision. She even managed a swipe at his face as he went by. He growled and hissed and stopped, then turned to Mahri, who was wildly fluffed. Mahri began to cry out loud with threatening howls, hoping to be heard. Coron only laughed, oblivious to her intentions.

His eyes said it all; she could see now. He had passed beyond farri reason and into the frightening world of shattered minds. Too many nights as a wild and unwanted stray; Coron was quite mad.

He said something strange and she didn't understand, but it didn't matter. Mahri howled again, but it lost its meaning when she felt the presence of no others. This would be a sad and lonely battle.

Mahri struck hard with her left paw, scoring her claws deep into Coron's face. She crouched back and braced for retaliation, but there was none. He stood and looked at her, and then stepped forward. This was bad. He was not only a monster; she was fighting a farri who felt no pain.

She struck again, but was cuffed hard before she could deliver, and fell hard to her right side. She was on her feet instantly, but too late. Coron drilled her again, catching her hard in the ribs and spinning her around so she faced the other way. The second shot stunned her into losing her breath, yet she remained confused at the attack. Both blows had been without claws extended.

When Mahri tried to turn she was struck again, this time in the face. The pain ripped through her head as her teeth slammed together, making her head spin. Cries for help were now impossible.

Her tail was facing toward him, and when she felt the teeth clamp down on her neck, she understood. She lashed out hard with desperation but was no match for Coron's strength. He pushed her down hard with his weight, and her chin scraped the sidewalk. When she felt Coron start to force himself into the mating position, she began to retch.

Coron's grip tightened, piercing the skin. The pain was incidental. Mahri was already too overwhelmed with the agony of disgust and violation. She hurt everywhere, inside and out. Her soft, defeated whimpers only encouraged Coron, who crushed her with all of his strength and bulk.

For the first time in her life, Mahri was glad farries mated for only five seconds or less. And this one was less. Almost instantaneous. The spines at the end of Coron's sex sent one final spear of pain through Mahri's body as he pulled out, and her sob accompanied it with humiliation. Her spirit was broken.

But this was the time to act. Toms were always physically drained after mating, and queens often turned on them in the moment of weakness. Mahri pushed up to stand and was startled to hear the scream of another farri. This shocked her to her feet. She broke free from Coron as she heard the huge tom bellow with pain. It was Syranosh, whose teeth were clenched in Coron's flank.

Mahri began to step forward to help but instinct held her back. She saw Syranosh rip at Coron's face with a frenzy of extended claws. She tore with success at the unguarded face of the stunned tom, and followed up with bites to the nose and neck. Coron, still dazed from mating, could only step backward and take the punishment until finally snapping back to reality. What he saw was not to his liking.

Truly the fiercest queen in the neighborhood, Syranosh could hold her own against anyone. Coron at his best might pull a draw, but in his condition right now he was not ready for combat. The madness Mahri had seen in his eyes disappeared within moments, and he could clearly see the odds were no longer in his favor. He had no desire to mess with Syranosh by herself, let alone with the help of another. Without even a hiss, he turned and fled into the night.

Mahri crouched and cried softly. The stench from the filthy encounter clung as if it were fingers gripping into her soul. She shook violently and began to bathe, hoping the pain and humiliation could be washed away. She hurt all over. She looked up at Syranosh, who was sitting on the sidewalk, grooming her paws.

"He would have killed me," said Mahri. "Thank you."

"Farries don't kill other farries," said Syranosh casually. "You would have gotten away."

"No," said Mahri. "He's truly mad. You saved me from dying here on the sidewalk. I owe you everything."

Syranosh stopped grooming and looked over at Mahri, then stood and turned to walk away.

"Don't feel so privileged, sister," said Syranosh, looking back. "I only did it to get his ugly stink off my street. I'd never get any sleep with an awful smell like his around." She stepped out onto the street and disappeared into the night.

CHAPTER 32

Frustration was only one of the issues Roger wished to discuss. And the frustration with Laura was complex. So many lost directions.

He sat with her again—was this the third, or fourth time?—outside the home of Jerry Radcliff. Soft jazz from the stereo of her RX-7, and the soft voice of Laura expressing dissatisfaction with the news operation of the *Courier* filled the car. Roger was tuned in to neither, only to his own thoughts of how to approach the subject of complexity.

"I'm a little unhappy with some things myself," he began, using her words about the paper for a transition. He looked out at Radcliff's house and took a breath. "I know you've got your heart set on nailing this guy with something. But let's face it; we don't even know what he's into. If anything. This is the fourth time we've sat out here—"

"But you saw him drive into Mexico that night," Laura interrupted. "And you know as well as I do he's weirder than shit."

"Neither of which is a crime," said Roger. "I'm just bored, I guess. Well, there's more to it, I guess. There are other things. . . ."

"Look!" said Laura in a loud hush. It was Radcliff, leaving the house and getting into his pickup truck. "We'll let him get a good start like last time."

Roger rolled his eyes and bit down hard. He had counted on Radcliff not appearing at all, as was the case the previous two times. He watched the black truck pull out and head down the block, just as it had done on their first night as spies.

"He's probably just going to the store for some beer," said Roger.

"Tonight's the big one," said Laura. "I can feel it!"

"Sure," said Roger. "Why do you insist on taking me along on these joy rides?"

"Because you're so much fun," said Laura.

"You say that to all the boys."

"Yeah. So?"

Jerry Radcliff was not going to the store for beer. They passed the last convenience store and headed out onto the freeway—805 south, the same as before.

"Are we gonna follow him into Tijuana tonight if he goes?" asked Roger.

"Well, I've been thinking about it a lot," said Laura. "I was pretty sure about it until now. What do you think?"

"It's your car, not mine," said Roger. "I'd never drive my car down there." He hoped she would take the hint, but she didn't have to.

Radcliff took the E Street exit off the freeway and drove into Chula Vista, a city populated primarily by Chicanos. The only real stop between San Diego and the border, the small city was trying desperately to shake its reputation as a holding tank for illegal aliens. San Diegans referred to it unaffectionately as Chula Juana.

"What's going on with this guy?" asked Laura.

"Just be careful and don't let him know we're here," said Roger.

Laura stayed as far back as possible, although Radcliff had shown no signs of detecting them. He drove south a block to F Street and then west into the heart of town. When he pulled into the parking lot of a seafood restaurant, Laura continued for another half block and then pulled up to the other side of the street. She killed the engine and turned with Roger to look out the back windshield.

"What now?" asked Roger. He crossed his arms, resting them on the back of the seat, and dropped his chin to his wrists.

"How do I know?" asked Laura. "Let's just watch."

"He still hasn't gotten out of his truck yet," said Roger.

"Maybe he's waiting for someone," said Laura.

"Then why wouldn't he wait inside? They have a bar in there."

"Stop being difficult, goon," snapped Laura. "Let's just wait and see."

"What if he goes in? Then what are we gonna do?" Roger was starting to enjoy giving Laura a hard time. He could see how tense and nervous she was, and he was certain a few more questions would result in him getting slapped.

"Then we'll go in with him!" said Laura. "Now shut up and pay attention."

"But if we go in, we'll blow our cover," said Roger. "What the hell would we be doing in a restaurant in Chula Juana?"

"Oh shit," said Laura. "The same thing they are."

Jerry Radcliff stepped out of his truck and walked up to the passenger side of a late-model, maroon sedan that had just pulled into the parking lot. A woman got out, walked around to the back of the car, and opened the trunk. She reached in and pulled out a package about the size of a football. She closed the trunk, handed the package to Radcliff, and gave him a kiss. She got back into the car on the passenger side, and Radcliff watched them pull away.

Laura and Roger exchanged a long, wide-eyed look. The parking lot was very well lit. Lit well enough to make no mistake. The maroon sedan bore the words "Eyewitness News" on the door, and the woman was Rosemary Ogden.

They watched the eleven o'clock news at Roger's house. He had made popcorn, and Laura sipped a wine cooler while Roger worked on his second glass of Jack Daniel's. With both lost in their own thoughts, little had been said since returning from Chula Vista. They had not followed Radcliff after he left the parking lot.

When Rosemary Ogden's story about a Tijuana orphanage came on, neither of them was surprised. They stared at the set in silence, until long after the story was over. There was nothing to say.

CHAPTER 33

Halina was sharpening her claws, digging deep into the old stump near the Den, lost in luxury. When Mahri approached, she stopped immediately. Halina's look of pleasure dropped to one of openly expressed horror. She released the stump and bounded over to meet the young farri. Mahri looked almost dead.

"Dear Farri! What happened?" said Halina, now at Mahri's side. "Lie down, love!"

"Oh Halina," Mahri said, and fell to the blacktop. She wept softly at first, but then released a howl, blood chilling in its sorrow. It faded into light whimpers and labored pants.

"Relax, my love," said Halina.

Mahri ached all over. It was hard to breathe and she couldn't control her shaking. She rolled to her side and felt Halina grooming her face. The effect was comforting almost to the point of being scary. The pain began to melt away with each stroke of Halina's rough and gentle tongue.

Eyes clearing, Mahri began to focus on the delicate face of Halina. The mistress continued lapping at Mahri's ears, and then her neck, where she could no longer watch. Mahri closed her eyes and felt her shakes wash away. She almost fell asleep.

"You looked like death, dearest Mahri," Halina said when she finished grooming her. "I was afraid you might expire."

"I did too," said Mahri, opening her eyes and smiling

at how much better she felt. "Your magic saved me, I'm sure."

"Be still, love," said Halina. "Farries don't have magic. Only the Great Lady can do such things. Now tell me what happened, if you can."

"You are no ordinary farri, dear Halina," said Mahri. "How many times have you proved it to us? This is just one more case."

Halina crouched down on her elbows next to Mahri. She looked across the open street for intruders and saw none. The dark road near the dead end was still, save for the slightest trace of a breeze.

"It was Coron," said Mahri. "After I left Sharlo just a little while ago, he attacked me."

"Attacked you? Dear Farri, I feared such would happen," said Halina.

"I couldn't run," said Mahri. "He's so much bigger and faster. And I'm no match for him like you are." She felt another sob coming on, but bit it back and looked out to the Canyon. The shakes started to return, but not as badly as before.

"Be calm, my love," said Halina. "You have your freedom now, and no one can harm you here."

"I know," said Mahri. "I'll be all right, I think. Anyway, I was between here and Sharlo's house, too far to alert either of you with my calls. Coron knew this, of course, and planned his attack as such." She paused and bit down hard, wincing at the memory of what followed. "He forced me to mate with him," she said finally.

Halina stood up and hissed slightly. Even the mistress was not prepared for such abominations. She walked away from the Den and over to the edge of the Canyon. Stopping there, she turned back and faced Mahri. "Lady Farri will expect, no, demand us to punish him for this. And we will do all in our power to make sure he is punished. He has gone beyond evil and has violated not only you, but everything we hold sacred as the children of Lady Farri."

"He might have killed me if Syranosh hadn't been there," said Mahri.

"Syranosh was there?" asked Halina.

"She got there when we were finished mating," said Mahri. "She chased him off. Coron was happy enough to leave without a fight when he saw her."

"Indeed," said Halina. "Syranosh is a formidable opponent to anyone, should she choose to be. It's only too bad she didn't get there sooner."

"I think she did," said Mahri.

"What?" asked Halina.

"I think she watched from a distance, and then arrived at Coron's weakest moment to chase him off," said Mahri. "That way she could still be her rotten self and come off looking like a hero."

"Mahri!" said Halina. "You are very hurt and upset, which is understandable. Don't speak ill of anyone right now, save Coron. You will only regret it otherwise."

"You're right, Halina, but I feel like I hate everyone right now. And I feel almost certain about Syranosh."

"Be at peace, love," said Halina. "I will walk you home and you can rest comfortably with your paladins tonight."

Mahri stood and walked with Halina away from the Den. Besides her certainty about Syranosh, she was also sure that Halina was at a loss for words, possibly for the first time ever. This was a situation beyond even her capacity to understand.

When Mahri arrived at the Den the following evening, all conversation ended immediately. She thought this odd, since she knew they were all discussing her, anyway.

She saw the looks of pity and sorrow in the faces of the Den. Mixed in was the unmistakable undercurrent of fear, Syranosh being the only exception. She sat atop the old wooden stump and groomed her paws, paying no attention to Mahri's arrival. Halina stood and walked to the center of the group.

"Well, Mahri," she said, "you have found yourself the center of our attentions again. How sad that trouble follows the sweetest and most beloved of our Den."

Farinna was closet to Mahri, and she leaned over and touched noses with her. She then began to groom Mahri's right shoulder, listening as Halina continued to speak.

"You are all aware of the incident with Coron last night," said Halina. "I take full responsibility. It was my foolishness to ignore the warnings. We must now understand fully the evil intent of Coron and his followers.

"There are several things we must do from this day forward. We will no longer follow our dates to their homes, or anyplace out of calling distance from the Den."

"It might be hard to convince the toms of this," said Jassa. Her words were echoed throughout the Den.

"It is true," said Halina. "The toms love privacy and secrecy, as do we. All farries, for that matter. It will be as tough on us as it will be on them, but they must understand our situation. If they have concern for us at all, they will help us out."

"Won't they be offended?" asked Sina. "They might think we're accusing them of trying to lead us into a trap."

"If they know the story they will not," said Halina. "Clearly, Sharlo did not lead our Mahri into a trap. It was by tragic fate she happened to be the one to cross his path. It could have been any of you. The toms will either understand or go someplace else."

The girls answered Halina's last remark with a quiet giggle. There was no other place to go. Halina's Den was quite unique in the world of farries.

"They'll understand," continued Halina. "Most of our dates are good toms."

Suddenly the fur rose on nearly the entire Den. All farries were on their feet and fluffed, hissing at the unexpected intrusion from the sky. Standing before them was Treep, the great hawk from the Canyon.

"Be at peace, dear farries," said Halina. "Master Treep is our friend."

Although startled by the suddenness of his arrival, Mahri relaxed instantly upon recognizing the hawk. She was glad to see him, in fact, her face brightening and her heart racing with excitement. But she could see the apprehension in the eyes of the others. They previously had not met the majestic bird.

"They will be easy to pick out, Halina," said Treep. "They are the ones who greet their friends so cruelly."

"Maybe they are just cautious to see who their friends are," replied Halina.

Halina and Mahri stepped closer to Treep, but the other farries were still unsure. They remained fluffed, with their mouths open ready to hiss. One by one, however, they began to relax.

"I haven't had a chance to thank you for saving me, Treep," said Mahri.

"Save you from what, little Mahri?" asked Treep.

"The rattlesnake," said Mahri.

"He wasn't saving you," said Halina, answering the puzzled look of Treep. "He thought he was stealing your lunch."

"Oh, yes. Rattlesnakes," said Treep. "I guess they don't get along with farries too well. Never really thought about it."

"Treep is here to get familiar with us," said Halina. "I have talked him into assisting us in our dealings with Coron. He will need to be able to identify all of us should we be mixed up with other farries."

The girls who had been fluffed were now relaxed out of their battle stances, yet remained nervous for a different reason. The last time they had employed a predator from the Canyon to assist them against Coron, a puma had died. This time seemed more ominous than before, because Halina was introducing them all to the predator. And Sarena was supposed to have only been a show of force just to scare the other farries away. This time was very different. They could all read Halina's unspoken intentions. Treep meant business.

The farries of the Den spent several minutes talking with Treep, asking him questions about the Canyon and what it was like to fly. Treep was as confusing as ever, directly answering questions and then being evasive. Mahri noticed how attentive he was, however, and she was sure he would never confuse the girls in Halina's Den with any other farries.

"Dearest Treep," Halina said finally, "it is time for us to part company for now. Our dates will begin to arrive soon, and they might not appreciate your presence here. We will speak with you soon, and trust you will have an ear open for our calls.''

''As always, Lady Halina,'' said Treep, and bolted up into the setting sun. With two great strokes from his powerful wings, he crossed into the Canyon and was gone.

''I see three toms on the way,'' said Halina. ''Before they arrive, beware! Stay close enough tonight to be heard at the Den. Scream hard if you must, but never unless it's absolutely necessary. And remember, it is not our usual dates who we fear, but where they might unknowingly lead us. Take care and have fun.''

Mahri walked into the Den and hid in its tall, dry grass. She had no desire to mate tonight, not even with Sharlo. She hoped Halina or one of the others would stay behind. Every possible emotion was sweeping over her, and she needed someone to talk to.

Halina understood, and had other plans anyway. She shooed away the last tom, lying about how her stomach was bothering her. She complained about ingesting too much fur lately, and he scowled. All of the other girls were already gone. Disappointed and disgusted, he trotted off.

''Let's go and visit with Treep,'' Halina said to Mahri. ''He's expecting us.''

''But he was just here,'' said Mahri. ''He didn't say anything about meeting us. And besides, it's dark now. I don't want to go into the Canyon again after dark.''

''Treep will meet us at the Canyon's edge,'' said Halina. ''He is not a bird of the night, as is Dori, and is taking a risk by meeting with us. He must feel an urgency, or he would have waited until morning.''

''When did he tell you he wanted to meet?'' asked Mahri.

''When he was here visiting our Den,'' said Halina. ''Not in words, dearest. Remember, words with the most meaning are words never spoken at all. Listen without using your ears, my love. There is a whole world of knowledge to be told if you'll take the time to absorb it.''

Mahri was confused. She had seen no indication of

anything from Treep other than his few short words. But she wasn't surprised when the great bird landed on the short wooden fence at the edge of the Canyon. Halina was never wrong.

"Well, Master Treep," Halina said. "Is there news for us tonight?"

"Why would there be, Lady Halina?" answered Treep. "I wished only to see your lovely coats again."

"I see," said Halina. "Tell us of the Canyon."

"That could take a lifetime, Lady," said Treep. "You must be more specific, or I will only sit here and lose sleep needlessly."

Halina gave no answer. She stared hard at the hawk, pressing him with her eyes to get to the point. Her will was strong, and he broke her gaze and looked out to the Canyon. The farries were not in the mood for formalities, and he knew it.

"There are krahstas about," said Treep.

"Since when haven't there been krahstas in a Canyon, Treep?" said Halina, irritated.

"They are closer than ever to standing on your Den," said Treep. "I have seen them close by, and the demon leader eyes the street constantly. He lusts for your pelt, Lady Halina."

"Is this news, Treep?" asked Halina. "Don't I already know of the movements of the krahstas?"

"Don't be a fool, Lady!" screeched Treep. "You have been one for so long. The death of your Den is upon you now, and again you close your eyes!"

Halina did not answer. She stood locked in a terrifying gaze with the winged predator. Mahri carefully glanced back and forth between the two. The piercing silence of the moment made her heart thunder. Her fur began to rise involuntarily.

"There are other powers at work in the Canyon," said Treep. "Some may work to your advantage, others not. The wisdom you flaunt might help you determine your fate. You wish for me and scatterbrained owls like Dori to help you in your quest against other farries. I tell you this, Lady Halina: other farries are the least of your concerns, unless you move your Den far from the boundaries of what's wild.''

"What are the other powers in the Canyon?" asked Mahri. Seeing Halina's look of reprimand, she regretted the question immediately.

"You will see, young farri," said Treep. "There may be treasure in what was lost. All you must do is find it.''

Treep spread his wings and was gone. Mahri and Halina sat in silence for several moments.

"I'm sorry," said Mahri finally.

"Be at peace for now," said Halina. "We may have gotten the greatest answer of answers. Time alone will tell. But in the future, you must remember: a closed mouth is always hearing. You'll never learn a thing if your mouth is open.''

CHAPTER 34

Dahrkron did not need the exceptional night vision of cats to see the hawk leaving the edge of the Canyon. Nor did the three krahstas who stood with him. They were, however, surprised to see the two farries walking away from where the hawk had just been. Dahrkron was not.

"The bigger of the two is she," said Dahrkron. "Witness for yourselves how she conspires with predators of the Canyon. Have you ever heard of a farri doing such a thing?"

He didn't expect an answer. His words were only for effect, anyway. He had already turned the pack into believers.

"Can she be defeated, Dahrkron?" asked Khanval.

"She can if we are quick," he answered. "Before she can deceive others in the Canyon into assisting her in her schemes. Truly she wishes to destroy krahstas, and there are many others in the Canyon who traditionally have no love for us. They might be enticed by her treachery into aiding her against us."

The evidence was overwhelming. In addition to the hawk, there was the owl who had helped out the farries against Dahrkron and Trahna. And although not currently visible, there was the scent of many farries close by. Truly, there was something amiss. The group of four krahstas watched from the small, brushy Canyon hill as the two farries walked back to their Den. The krahstas dared not move against them, for certain ambush surrounded such obvious bait. There would be other nights.

''When?'' asked Trahna.

''When the pack is ready,'' said Dahrkron. ''We will need all of their strength, and all of their will. They will be no help at all without their hearts behind it. They will come around soon.''

''You can't blame them for fearing a demon,'' said Khanval. ''Maybe more coaxing is in order. I think if you told them we were planning a raid tomorrow night, they would follow, as they have followed you in the past.''

''Your words have truth, my friend,'' said Dahrkron, ''as they always have. They will follow and do well. After all, it is only a pack of farries. Your council will be taken, only on the night after tomorrow. The moon will be the fullest then, and the wild blood in our brothers and sisters will drive them fearless. Beware little farries of the street!''

Sharlo arrived at the Den only moments after Halina and Mahri returned from seeing Treep. His tail was down low and twitching very hard, the sign of an upset farri. He normally had it straight up when visiting the Den.

''We are not dating tonight, Sharlo,'' said Halina. ''Sorry, dearest, but Mahri and I don't feel up to it.''

''As you shouldn't, dear Halina,'' said Sharlo. ''I am aware of the tragedy of last night. Sweet Mahri, if only I had been with you! I am terribly sorry.''

''It's not your fault, Sharlo,'' said Mahri. ''If it hadn't been me, he would have gotten someone else.''

''These words are truer than you know,'' said Sharlo. ''I have not come here tonight for a date, but simply to relay news.''

Halina stepped closer at these words, concern flashing across her face for the briefest moment. Then it was gone, and she nodded for Sharlo to continue.

''It is Coron, of course,'' said Sharlo. ''He has doubled the size of your Den with angry followers. Not as many as before, but still enough to overwhelm your numbers. They are jealous females, mostly, which are the most dangerous of farries, as we know. But there are some large toms with them. None who ever come here, though. This time it seems the customers have remained strangely loyal.''

''They plan to attack the Den again?'' asked Mahri.

''Yes,'' said Sharlo. ''But no secret of such size can remain a secret. That is how I know.''

''As do I,'' said Halina. ''I have been trying to enlist the aid of friends from the Canyon. We will see how they will come through. If only one shows up, we will hold our own. And let's hope our krahsta friends will give us peace for a little while longer so we can finish with this trial and prepare for them later. I fear, however, we may expect to see them sooner than we hope.''

''When are Coron's farries planning to attack?'' asked Mahri.

''They plan to attack on the night of the full moon,'' answered Sharlo.

CHAPTER 35

Mahri awoke and stuck her claws into the blanket on Sweetie Pie's bed. The young girl continued to sleep soundly, and Mahri used care to keep from waking her. It had been rough lately. The young girl had wanted to play so much, and Mahri was in no mood or condition to oblige. Mahri went through her full stretch routine, and then hopped off the bed and trotted into the kitchen. Daddy grumbled something when she passed by his feet en route to her food. The grumpy paladin put his newspaper on the table and looked over at her intently.

"Is Your Excellency in a better mood this morning?" Daddy asked. "You been meaner 'n lizard shit lately. Thought you was gonna scratch the little sweetie pie yesterday. Damn finicky little bitch."

Mahri watched him as he spoke. She knew she was being lectured about something, but had no idea of what. She thought about how sad it was for the paladins to talk so much, yet not even comprehend the common language. It wasn't surprising, since it would be hard for humans to understand another species when they couldn't even understand each other. Very sad.

"Well, I hope you get your act together and lighten up a bit," Daddy was saying. "Woulda used your little tail for shark bait long ago if the sweetie pie didn't love your ass so much. God knows why she does. Maybe she'll grow out of it."

Daddy reached over and stroked Mahri behind the ears, adding to her confusion. He had sounded so irritated, but his actions were friendly. She wondered if paladins were oddly affected by the early morning. After all, the only time Daddy was remotely friendly was when the others were still asleep.

Mahri finished off the remainder of the dry food Mommy had given her the night before. She was relieved when Daddy opened the door to let her out earlier than usual. He made another remark about some crazy thing and closed the door behind her.

She walked down the street toward Halina's house. The two of them had decided to brave the Canyon yet again, today. For what, Mahri had no clue. As she approached Halina's house, she was surprised to hear the sound of a barking kriba. There were so few in this neighborhood, and none she had ever seen near this end of the block.

Nothing could have prepared Mahri for the sight she witnessed in Halina's front yard. There was the mistress, in the clear bright of an early morning of late summer, playing with a nearly full-grown springer spaniel.

The kriba was easily three times Halina's size. Yet, there they were, romping around and playfully nipping at each other. Mahri was amazed.

Halina saw her and then dove to the ground, rolling with a single motion to her back. Her paws were instantly over her face, pretending to ward off the imminent blows from the kriba.

"I surrender, dearest Bayne!" shouted Halina. "You have conquered again!"

The kriba jumped over to Halina and began licking wildly at her face. Halina gave a light hiss and stepped away, indicating playtime was over.

"My dear Bayne," said Halina, walking toward Mahri, "I have a friend for you to meet. Mahri, this is my next-door neighbor, Master Bayne."

Panting hard, Bayne gave a shout and danced around the two farries. Mahri was speechless.

"Bayne lives with the old female paladin who used to live with Melena," said Halina quietly to Mahri. Bayne settled down and approached Mahri for a sniff. Mahri fluffed out of instinct and hissed hard, despite the actions of Halina. And did Halina say she surrendered to a *kriba*?

Mahri didn't think there was a dog anywhere who could take on the mistress.

Bayne took it all well enough and laughed as he jumped around with a playful growl. Halina's new friend was simply a puppy in a very large body.

"Hey baby, wanna chase?" asked Bayne. In the few months of his existence, Bayne had gotten into the nasty habit of calling anything smaller than he was "baby."

"Not right now," said Mahri. "But I will." She relaxed instantly. The puppy kriba was all for fun.

"Mahri is one of my special friends I told you about," said Halina. "She'll be your best friend if you don't play too rough."

"No, Halina," said Bayne. "You'll always be my best friend."

"Of course," said Halina. "We need you to go back to your yard for a while. Mahri and I have some business to take care of. We'll be back later this afternoon, and we'll play chase with you then."

Bayne barked his approval and dashed back to the yard of Mrs. Grant. Equal energy Mahri had never seen in another animal.

"It's okay, my love," said Halina. "Bayne will be of great service to us. And let's face it, he is lovable in his 'baby' fashion."

"Yes, but what a huge baby!" Mahri smiled.

The two farries walked toward the dead end at the Canyon and stepped around the short, splintering fence. They paused momentarily for a look around and then for brief reflection on the coming venture. They both saw Treep circling high off over a distant part of the sage and took it as their cue to proceed.

A moderate wind gave the brush enough of a voice to hide their footsteps, even on the most brittle sage. Their paws hit mostly rocky dirt path, but an occasional stray branch found its way underclaw. Travel was easier than on the previous trips abroad; the air was pleasantly warm, unlike the stifling heat of the past.

They made good time, although to where, Mahri had no idea. They took a different direction than before, and

Mahri could see even Halina had no real course. They would find what they would find.

They walked for two miles. They went fast and slow, depending upon the footing. Mahri sensed a destiny with this trip, and could see the same feeling in Halina's eyes. There was a strange undercurrent of magic sparkling about them that Mahri could not understand. She began to feel light-headed and was pleased when Halina chose a soft patch in the shade to rest.

"We'll sit here for a while, love," said Halina. "You can rest your legs."

"I'm not really tired," said Mahri. "I was feeling a little dizzy there for a moment, but not because I was tired. It wasn't a bad feeling. I can't explain it."

"I felt it too, dear Mahri," said Halina. "It was as if Lady Farri herself was walking beside us. A good feeling, but very draining!"

"Yes, I felt it too," said Mahri. "She knows we're here. And she approves!"

"I approve too!" came the answer. The voice was wild and exotic, and came from behind Mahri, and not from Halina.

Both farries were on their feet and fully fluffed instantly. A wave of terror swept over Mahri. Her claws reached to their limit instinctively, although she still had not seen or identified the owner of the voice. But somehow in the back of her mind, the sensations attached to it were familiar. The brush began to move and Mahri took a half step back in response.

"Sarena!" cried Halina in a hushed, hoarse voice.

Mahri fluffed more and hissed, very confused.

"Still the uncertain one, pretty Mahri," said the puma. "And what kind of greeting is this after such a long time?"

Halina stepped toward the great cougar, but Mahri remained frozen in shock.

"It has been my great hope," said Halina, her voice and body trembling with emotion. "My great hope and wonder. Somehow I knew it couldn't be. The Lady would never let harm befall one of her line as wonderful as you."

"Halina, you are still so charming!" said Sarena. "It is truly a joy to see the daring innocence of my little cousins again. I had forgotten how darling you little dears are. And Mahri, are you going to relax yet?"

Mahri was frozen. She had never really gotten used to the feeling of Sarena before. And now, here stood the *spirit* of the great cat. This was too much. Mahri could barely breathe, let alone speak. Her mind was screaming at her feet to bolt in the opposite direction, but got no response.

"I still marvel at your gorgeous fur," said Sarena, and swooped down on Mahri with a swipe of the tongue across her shoulders and side. "Incredible!"she laughed. "Can I do it again?" And without waiting for an answer, she lapped at Mahri's other side, covering almost half of her body with the huge lick. "My, to groom such a pelt every day," she said in disbelief.

"Sarena, where have you been?" asked Halina. "Your tale must be a strange one, for we were convinced we had witnessed your death."

Sarena's smile melted into the stretches of sorrow. She looked back at Mahri and offered a sad smile. "The death of a puma is a dramatic and tragic thing," she said. Her face went sullen and she looked away into the tangle of sage. "And I believe you witnessed such a tragedy, although it possibly saved your lives. It was Sasho who died on the street near your Den. And his death was a blessing."

"How was it Sasho was there and not you?" asked Halina. "And how could his death be a tragedy and blessing at the same time? My farries often accuse me of speaking in riddles, yet this is beyond even me."

"It is always terrible when we lose a puma, for there are so few of us left in the world," said Sarena. "Sasho was the exception. He had the madness sickness, and was lost already. I grieve for him, because after his death I learned he was once a fair and friendly puma. His fall is true testimony to the evil of the madness sickness.

"He knew of our pact," she continued. "Somehow. By spying? I don't know and may never. But he knew, and he crossed me when I was on my way to your Den on the night of evil. He was mad, and truly directed by a pack of demons. He threatened to fight with me, ensuring I would be bitten and a demon would pass from him into me. There was no choice but to run." Sarena crouched and put her chin on her front paws. She remained motionless with her eyes closed for several seconds, and then slowly she opened her eyes.

"I knew he would die that night," she said. "If not from the man's thunder, then from the madness. He was awful. His eyes were on fire, and a foul-smelling foam poured from his mouth. He rambled like a crazed fool. There was nothing I could do. I could only hope for the safety of my little cousins."

Mahri was completely relaxed now. No spirits here; Sarena was real. Mahri stood beside Halina and watched the puma close her eyes again. The pain on Sarena's face ripped deep into Mahri's soul, and she stepped forward and began to groom the puma's face. Sarena responded by opening her eyes and offering Mahri a kind smile, while accepting the affection.

Sarena turned her head with a slight look of curious wonder at Mahri's purring, because although the huge puma was also capable of the happiness sound, she could not recall ever hearing it from the throat of another animal. Still, Sarena remained silent and let the little farri groom both sides of her face and the top of her head. For this, Mahri had to stand on her hind legs, resting her front paws on Sarena's left shoulder. When finished, she dropped down and snuggled against the puma's forearm. Mahri never stopped purring.

"Thank you, pretty Mahri," said Sarena. "Your kisses are more soothing than you know. They touched my heart and it is glad." She went silent again, closing her eyes for quite a while. "I heard the shots and I fled," she said finally. "I fled because I knew Sasho was gone, and I feared the men would chase after me. They didn't know there were two pumas near their homes, or surely they would have.

"I ran for two days. I was far from anyplace familiar, and I hadn't eaten. I was lucky not to collapse. But I made it okay. I lived scared and in hiding for all this time. But I am back now, and ready to reclaim my territory!''

"Reclaim?" asked Halina.

"Yes, darling little cousin," said Sarena. "I was barely out of sight when the krahstas moved in. They, of course, thought it was me who perished on the road that night. They might not have been so quick to move in if they had known the truth, and a real surprise awaits them when they find out.''

"They don't know?" asked Halina.

"No," said Sarena. "In fact, no one around here is certain yet. I met up with my two lynx friends yesterday. They fled in the same direction as me when Sasho died, although for different reasons. They are returning as well, and also have a score to settle with the krahstas.''

"Be careful with the new krahsta ruler," said Mahri. "Many animals in the Canyon think he's a demon.''

Sarena's response startled Mahri into fluffing her fur again. It was the suddenness and the volume of her answer, not the content. Sarena thundered with laughter.

"If the krahsta is a demon, then the world should fear nothing!'' the puma laughed. "Where was this demon when I visited their little pack with my lynx friends? They were all there; every one. And they all trembled right out of their hideous, stinking fur. No, my dear little Mahri, there are no demons within the krahsta pack.''

Mahri relaxed again and nestled against Sarena. The large cat responded with a giggle and a two-stroke grooming across Mahri's back. The small farri was soaked.

"But enough about me and krahstas," said Sarena. "Where is my friend the little black panther? Isn't her name Melena?''

Mahri exchanged a glance with Halina. It still hurt.

"Melena is with the Lady," answered Halina. "She died from the evil bite of a rattlesnake.''

Sarena took this news very hard. She closed her eyes again and shook her head. "A darker summer there has never been," she said.

"Things will get better," said Halina.

Sarena nodded. "They must.''

"Can we ask a favor of you?" asked Halina.

"Oh dear," said Sarena. "Some things never change!" Her mood changed instantly, and she laughed loud and free. "What trouble have you gotten your little furs into this time?"

"Just the same troubles you have," replied Halina.

"Oh?" asked Sarena. "And how may I help my little farries?"

"Don't let the krahstas know you're back until tomorrow night," said Halina.

CHAPTER 36

The situation with Radcliff had gotten just weird enough for Roger to agree to tail him one more time. He sat in the darkness of Laura's front seat, illuminated only by the few front-porch lights on the street.

It had been shortly after sunset when they pulled up to their usual spot down the block and across the street from the house under suspicion. It had been over an hour, and they had not seen any movement at all. It was very uncomfortable in the car. Even after dark, it was still very hot, and they kept the windows rolled up to keep out mosquitoes. Roger began to get restless when Laura switched the radio to an all-news station.

"I might be interviewing you," said Laura.

"On what?" Roger asked.

"I'm going to be doing a three-part series on the perils of living alongside canyons," said Laura.

"Perils?"

"Yes," said Laura. "You know how many people in San Diego live around canyons. There's all kinds of problems. Obviously the kid getting attacked by a mountain lion was a fluke, but it did happen."

Roger rolled his eyes. He didn't think the canyon was perilous at all.

"And of course, there are the coyotes you are always complaining about," Laura continued. "I've talked to several people who have lost pets. Cats seem to be the favorite. How would you feel if one of them got De Lilah?"

Roger rolled his eyes again with a chuckle. He had

seen his cat face down a full-grown German shepherd, who skulked away in humiliation. Somehow the idea of De Lilah ending up as coyote bait seemed absurd.

"Okay, so maybe *your* cat might not have to worry," said Laura. "But not everyone has a lion for a pet."

"True," Roger smiled. "Still, I think the idea is a bit farfetched for a three-part series. Literally tens of thousands of people live around wild territory in this county. It's nothing new."

"But look at all the new construction going on," said Laura. "All over. This is the fastest-growing city in the country. More and more people are moving in on what once was wilderness. We're pushing the wildlife into oblivion. Maybe this incident with the mountain lion and all of the noise the coyotes are making is their way of trying to tell us something. Maybe they're trying to tell us to stop. They're running out of territory."

"So, are you going to go ask someone who's just bought a brand-new, one-hundred-and-fifty-thousand-dollar house how they feel about moving in on what used to be the territory of coyotes?"

"Coyotes, deer, mountain lions, rabbits, birds," said Laura. "I'll ask them if they feel safe."

"I can see how they might be afraid to live next to rabbits," said Roger.

"And what about rattlesnakes?" asked Laura. "You told me Mrs. Grant's cat got bitten by one. It could easily have been a little kid."

"So?"

"It's a good story," said Laura. "It also gives me a legitimate reason to be hanging around your neighborhood. I want to keep an eye on Radcliff's house."

"And just what are you going to do if you catch him at something?" asked Roger. "Even if you catch him red-handed, what are you going to do?"

"I . . . Look!"

Radcliff had left his house and was walking down the driveway toward his truck. Both Laura and Roger leaned forward and gazed up the street. Roger became instantly tense and jittery, and he could tell Laura was feeling the same way. Laura reached for the ignition switch as Radcliff got into his truck.

Suddenly the two of them jumped as something rapped on the driver's-side window. Roger turned to his left and saw a man looking in at them, motioning with his finger to roll down the window.

"Who are you?" Laura demanded, obviously startled.

The man held up a badge to the window. Laura examined it, then glanced up the street at Radcliff's truck, which was pulling around the corner and out of sight. Roger also watched the truck, then turned to his right and saw another man standing beside the car just outside his door.

"FBI," said the man on Laura's side. "Please step out of the car."

"What the hell is this?" asked Laura, opening her door. Roger did the same.

"May I see some identification?" asked the man on Laura's side. Roger walked around the car to stand next to Laura. He was followed by the other man.

"No, you may not," said Laura, crossing her arms. "What's your name?"

"Special Agent Harvey Fischer, FBI."

Roger stood beside Laura and crossed his arms as she did. He decided to let her do the talking, since she was in the media and used to dealing with law enforcement types. Roger was also too nervous to speak.

Special Agent Harvey Fischer looked them over carefully. He was a short man with dark hair. Except for a tremendous nose, he appeared completely nondescript.

"What's this all about?" demanded Laura.

"I need to see some identification," said Fischer. The other man stood behind him in silence.

"No," said Laura flatly. She reached down into her purse and pulled out her small reporter's notebook. She wrote down the agent's name and badge number.

"Are you Miss Kay, I presume?" asked Fischer.

"It's none of your business," said Laura. "What do you want?"

"I want a little cooperation," said Fischer. "Believe it or not, I think I'm on your side."

"And just what side is that?" asked Laura.

"We both want Radcliff," said Fischer simply.

Laura was momentarily startled, but kept her composure.

"I don't know what you're talking about," she said.

"Listen, as much as I'd like to strangle both of you, I'm willing to play ball," said Fischer. "We've been after this guy for a long time. We want him bad. Obviously you want him too, or else you wouldn't have staked him out for at least the three times I know of."

"What do you want him for?" asked Laura.

"Here's the deal," said Fischer, ignoring the question. "You two back off, and I mean everyone at your paper, and we'll call you before we take him down. I guarantee it. We'll let you go along for the ride exclusively."

Laura looked at him as if he had just asked her to believe the moon was made of green cheese. She looked over at Roger and rolled her eyes for effect. "You can take your deal, and stick it up you ass," she said.

"Otherwise," continued Fischer, ignoring Laura's comment, "we arrest the both of you for obstruction of justice."

"Yeah, right," Laura laughed sarcastically. "I work for a newspaper, remember? They'd chop you up and feed you to the coyotes if you even thought about it. All of the media would."

Roger's heart began to race. This clown was talking about arresting him, and Laura was laughing at him. Roger reached up to his forehead to wipe off the newly formed beads of sweat.

"I suggest you take my offer," said Fischer coldly. "I give you my word, we'll let you in on it."

"You're just a glorified cop," said Laura. "You're word—"

"Listen, lady, you're beginning to piss me off. I suggest you take my offer, and take it now. I'll call you the minute we decide to move."

"Haven't you ever heard of the First Amendment, and freedom of the press?" Laura asked sarcastically.

"I don't give a goddamn about any of that crap," growled Fischer. "I've been working a long time to try

and nail this sleazeball, and you're not gonna fuck it up
for me. I'll worry about dealing with your two-bit, bull-
shit newspaper later, if I have to. But for now, you're
gonna get out of my way, either voluntarily, or force-
fully. Got it?''

CHAPTER 37

Mahri had never seen a lynx before. She had expected a smaller version of Sarena, but this was far from the case. In fact, the two lynxes looked more like larger versions of Halina. Their foreheads were higher and their tails shorter, but otherwise the resemblance was amazing. Any doubt Mahri might have had about Halina's wild lineage vanished instantly when the two lynxes stepped out of the brush.

They saw Sarena first, which was natural. Sarena would always attract more attention than two small farries. But the lynxes were more surprised at seeing the latter.

"Our little cousins," Sarena said to the lynxes. "Aren't they the prettiest little things?"

The lynxes stepped apart and looked over the two farries.

"We have met before, little Halina," said the largest of the two. He stood nearly twice the size of the mistress.

"Indeed, Wishous," said Halina. "I shan't forget the hospitality I received from you and Frahsh on our last meeting."

"Forgive us little one," said Wishous, who looked up at Sarena and then back to Halina. "You approached us when times were bad. Although they have not gotten better, until Sarena returned." There was a tense silence for a moment, while all of the large cats looked over the farries.

"Little Halina and Mahri have braved the Canyon to ask us for help," Sarena said to the lynxes. "Have you ever heard of such a thing? Farries from the street asking their wild cousins for help?"

"I believe Halina was here to ask for help before," said Frahsh. To Mahri's ears, Frahsh's voice was almost identical to the larger Wishous. Both were huge compared to Mahri, but their looks and sounds were identical. "We told her of our wish to avoid the street and all who live there."

"But how could you resist such adorable little fur balls?" Sarena laughed. "Look at the locks and colors on pretty Mahri!" She reached over and gave Mahri yet another swipe with her tongue. Mahri took it well, having gotten used to it.

"We almost didn't resist," said Wishous. He let his words hang, and everyone understood. Halina had almost been lunch. Mahri looked at the huge muscles and teeth of her large cousins and knew even though Halina had held her own against an even larger krahsta, she was no match for a lynx.

"Helping us is helping you," said Halina.

"And your little farri friends will chase off krahstas too?" asked Frahsh.

Halina was stunned. Before she had only asked for assistance in chasing off the other farries. She hadn't even told them what she needed now.

"Your actions are well known in the Canyon, little farri," said Wishous. "Too many times you have tracked the land where you do not belong. The Canyon has countless eyes and ears, and no secrets. The krahstas believe you are a demon, and there are others who have many questions. You are safe here when you walk with Sarena, but beware! The Canyon is not a place for one with so few friends as a farri."

"Little lynxes, why are you so harsh with our tiny cousins?" asked Sarena. "They are trying to chase off the krahstas, not you."

"Are they?" asked Frahsh. "In doing so, they have driven the krahsta leader mad with hatred for cats. Truly, there is no love between us to begin with, but traditionally we have lived in peace and respected each other's territory. No more in this Canyon; the krahsta pack has come after us numerous times. They steal our prey and chase us off our own land. And it is all because of these 'pretty little farries.' "

"Dear Wishous, how could Halina be responsible for such actions?" asked Sarena. "As you said, the krahsta leader is mad."

"And twice Halina has humiliated him," said Wishous. "The whole Canyon knows. So he takes it out on *all* cats. On all the Canyon, really."

"What would you have done, Wishous?" asked Halina. "Obliged the krahsta and spent the night in his belly? I think not."

The two lynxes stepped back and began to leave.

"Meet with us, Sarena, when you have real business to discuss," said Wishous, and they were gone.

"We met with Treep again, and tonight we hope to meet with Dori," said Halina. The farries had all shown up at the Den early again, although this time they had been told to. The girls sat around the mistress, some grooming, some sharpening claws, but all listening intently.

"The appearance of Sarena should be enough for a while," said Halina. "She will chase off the krahstas and scare the other farries to death. Unfortunately, I had hoped for more. I don't believe the lynxes will help us, despite the efforts of Sarena. She will see them again tomorrow, but for now we must plan on her alone.

"There are so many variables as to what might transpire. I wonder if we should just disappear and never have to worry about it, but I feel in my heart this is right."

"What if the puma dies again?" asked Syranosh.

"A greater concern I could never have," said Halina, "save for the safety of all of you. I have spent many nights thinking of nothing else. I believe we are doing the right thing."

"I think we're doing the right thing too," said Farinna. "But I thought so the last time too. And look what happened then?"

"It was the right thing," said Halina. "A puma fell, but he would have fallen soon anyway. And it was fortunate for all of us that he did. A puma with the crazy sickness is an unspeakable terror, and there's no way to know how much disaster he might have wrought had he not been stopped."

Mahri watched the girls all nod their agreement. Halina would tell them not to show up if they had any doubts about tomorrow, but they would all be there. Mahri knew, Halina knew, they all knew.

"Justice needs to be done," said Halina. "Coron needs to be stopped from terrorizing other farries. The krahsta pack needs to be stopped from disrupting the Canyon. I feel like Lady Farri is leading us. I can feel her presence here. She would never let Coron go unpunished."

The Den went silent. They all believed Halina. They all felt the presence of Lady Farri too. And the feeling was strong.

Roger pulled out the new, black leather tie one of his clients had brought him from Italy. It went well with the blue shirt and black suspenders one of his many women had bought him. He pulled up the tie—how different it looked from his work attire—and left the bedroom. He had twenty minutes to get to Tammy's apartment.

The doorbell rang. Roger kicked himself for leaving the door open again, or else he could have ignored it. He heard Mrs. Grant's voice through the screen and shook his head.

"Hello, Roger," she said when he got to the door.

"Mrs. Grant, what a nice surprise," said Roger. "Please come in."

"Oh, you're getting ready to go out again," said Mrs. Grant. "Such a busy young man. Is it your lovely girl Laura?"

"Not tonight," said Roger. When he saw how disappointed Mrs. Grant looked, he said, "Business."

"Oh. Well. My you look nice. I won't bother you while you get ready. I just came over to tell you about your little cat and my little Monty. He plays with little De Lilah all morning. They've become quite the friends, you know."

"Really?" asked Roger. "I'm surprised. De Lilah can be quite unfriendly with other animals. I don't think she even plays around with other cats."

"Well, she loves my little Monty. And he's so much bigger than she is, but she treats him like her little boy!"

"Monty is what kind of dog?" asked Roger, his interest now lost.

"A springer spaniel," said Mrs. Grant. "He has so much energy. It's good he has little De Lilah to play with."

"De Lilah's lucky to have a friend too," said Roger. "I'm not here as much as I should be. Which reminds me, I have to get going."

"Of course, dear," said Mrs. Grant. "Have a nice time." She gave Roger a wink, letting him know she didn't believe the business story, and walked away.

It was hot, and Roger was hot in his long-sleeved shirt, but went back to the bedroom for a jacket anyway. He was looking over the rack for a light one when the doorbell rang again.

Exasperated at having to talk with Mrs. Grant again, he pulled a jacket off the rack and walked to the door. He decided to just open the screen and step out, locking the main door behind. He would find out what she wanted as he walked to the car. He stepped into the living room and looked through the screen door. He stopped instantly and took a quick breath. It was Jerry Radcliff.

Very few toms made an appearance at the Den. Those who did were nervous and looked around a lot. Word had gotten out. Halina sent most of the girls home when it became clear they would not have dates. Only she and Mahri remained when Sharlo arrived. He walked up to where they were both lying in the soft grass of the Den and sat down between them. No one spoke for quite a while.

Mahri was happy just to look at Sharlo. He was so handsome, and so well groomed. It felt so good to be near him, romantic, even though Halina was there as well. It all seemed so natural.

"News for us, dear Sharlo?" asked Halina finally.

"Not much tonight," said Sharlo. "Tomorrow night is definitely on, which you knew already. I would guess not many toms showed up tonight."

"Only three," said Mahri.

"I'll be here tomorrow too," said Sharlo. "As always."

"There will be other dangers besides farries," said Mahri, concerned. She didn't mind facing krahstas and heaven knows what else, but she wanted Sharlo to be safe.

"Of course," said Sharlo. "But you will be here, my sweet Mahri, and I will be beside you."

"As always," Halina smiled. "We're going to go meet with an owl, Master Sharlo. Would you care to join us?"

"An owl?"

"How's the neyooz business?" Radcliff asked through the screen. Roger opened the door, deciding to use the same strategy he planned for Mrs. Grant.

"Just fine," said Roger. "How's the narc biz?"

"Can't complain. Say, where's the lovely lady of yours?"

"Which one?" said Roger as he closed the door behind him. He stepped out onto the porch and began to walk toward his car. "I'm running kinda late."

"Got anything planned for Saturday?" asked Radcliff. Roger thought it sounded like an accusation.

"The usual three or four dates," said Roger, reaching for the door of his Thunderbird.

"You're not such a bad guy after all," Radcliff laughed. He seemed relaxed and more congenial than he had in past meetings with Roger. "The reason I ask is because another mountain lion's been spotted in the canyon. I'm tryin' to get together some partners to go cougar huntin'."

"What time?" asked Roger, sitting into the car.

"Early as possible," said Radcliff. "Wanna see the sunrise. You game?" He pursed his lips and gave Roger a sideways, questioning glance. His eyes were squinted almost shut, yet open just enough for effect.

"I'll check my schedule and let you know tomorrow night," said Roger, and started the car. Laura would love to hear about this. He drove off, convinced Radcliff wasn't on to anything, and glad the paper had decided to cooperate with the FBI.

CHAPTER 38

This time Mahri was not surprised to see Halina romping around with Bayne. The only astonishment was seeing how young the mistress looked. She looked like a kitten, pouncing around with an oversized puppy. She fell to her back and slapped at his advances, showing no sign of claws. He barked and barked, jumping around her in zigzag patterns. Halina jumped up and dashed after Bayne, who pranced away and howled with delight.

Mahri walked out onto the lawn. Halina saw her but continued her pursuit of the puppy. Mahri took the cue and joined in the chase. Bayne barked recognition and then turned on the two farries. He chased them in circles around the yard until the two split up. He went after Halina first, who danced around until Mahri jumped in to give her a rest. They worked as a team, taking turns running with Bayne while the other rested, until the puppy was worn out. It took a long time. When the playing finished, Mahri was exhausted.

Bayne trotted up to the porch where his paladin had left a bowl of water. He began lapping furiously while Mahri and Halina looked on.

"He has unending energy," Halina smiled.

"Yes," panted Mahri. "To be a kitten again."

"He'll help us out, tonight," said Halina.

"I think he'd do anything for you," said Mahri.

Bayne trotted over and collapsed beside the two farries. Halina walked over and hopped up onto the kriba's side. Mahri was amazed at just how big he really was, and how well Halina had won him over. Halina crouched to her elbows, resting on the huge kriba.

"Can you sneak away from your paladin this evening, Master Bayne?" Halina asked.

"That would be easy," said Bayne. "My paladin sleeps in the afternoon, and then sits in front of the noise box late into the night."

"How would you like a whole big group of farries to play with?" asked Halina.

"Are they as nice as you, Halina?" asked Bayne.

"I'm afraid not, dearest Bayne," said Halina. "Actually, you might be the only one playing. But I think you'll have fun."

"Okay," said Bayne.

"You'll get to chase after some bad farries," said Halina. "There's a whole group of them who want to hurt pretty Mahri and myself."

Bayne growled and rolled over, tossing Halina to the grass.

"They won't hurt you," said Bayne. "I won't let them."

"I know you won't," said Halina. "I won't let anyone hurt pretty Mahri, either. But I must warn you; even though this will be a game of chase the bad farries away, there will be some risk."

"I'm big enough to not be afraid of baby farries," boasted Bayne.

"You're right," said Halina. "I think you'll be able to scare those bad farries right out of their furs."

Bayne panted with a smile. He licked at Halina, who winced with a smile, and let the huge puppy lick her head.

"The risk is from other kribas," said Halina, after the bath. "There will be many of them, and they will come from the Canyon."

Bayne's playful and happy expression became somber. He was old enough to know what might be in the Canyon. He had heard his cousins and their ancient, wild callings on many, moonlit nights. Their voices had both excited and terrified him, stirring up traces of wild feelings long forgotten to his breed. The possibility of seeing the faces behind the calls made his fur rise.

"You are a wise young kriba," said Halina, seeing Bayne's reaction. "And your wisdom will help you tonight. It will only be a game if none of us gets hurt. Even so, I dare not think about who the losers might be."

"Tell me what I'm supposed to do," said Bayne.

"My friends and I will be over there by the Canyon," said Halina. "The group of bad farries will pass by here. Let them pass. Indeed, hide so they never see you. The game will be more fun if there is a surprise. The bad farries will confront us near the Den. We will talk with them for a while, and you should remain hidden."

"What will I do?" asked Bayne. "And when will I know when to do it?"

"The bad farries want to fight with us," said Halina. "We will talk with them first. If you see us start to fight, then run as fast as you can, barking loud and hard. Farries will run toward you. Ignore them, and chase the ones who run away. Chase them toward the Canyon, and catch one if you want."

"What if you don't fight?" asked Bayne.

"When you smell the kribas from the Canyon, then you do the same thing," said Halina. "Even if we're not fighting, run after us, barking your little heart out. Your keen nose will smell the other kribas before we do, and you will be our warning. Again, ignore the farries who run to you, and chase the others away from you. But beware! The instant you see kribas from the Canyon, turn and run with the wind to your paladin's house. Don't chase the farries anymore and do not look back or slow for anything! Do you understand?"

"Yes, Halina," said Bayne. He understood, but wasn't sure about the running-away part. It might be fun to ask a few questions of the wild kribas. He was certain they were friends of Halina's, or else she wouldn't have arranged for their help. Bayne decided to wait and see what happened.

The sun was nearly overhead when Treep descended upon the Den. The entire area, Canyon and street, was quiet. Either animals from both sides of the imaginary line were hiding from the midday sun, or they remained hidden because of the impending doom. Very few knew the entire story, but everyone knew enough to keep out of the way.

Mahri was always impressed with Treep's appearance. He stood in the sun, so majestic and proud. The light gleamed off his shiny feathers, making him almost too bright to look at.

"Your cousins in the Canyon have met today," Treep said to Mahri and Halina. It was still several hours before the other farries of the Den were scheduled to arrive. Mahri and Halina had come by only to meet with Treep.

"Do you think Sarena will be able to talk the lynxes into helping?" asked Mahri.

"Pumas and lynxes are of no concern to me," said Treep. "I have told you this before, little Mahri. The puma walked away with the lynxes in the opposite direction of the street. I can tell you what I see when it interests you, but I have no time to bother with what it all means."

"Tell us of the krahstas," said Halina.

"They are near," said Treep. "As you have heard, they will strike here tonight. If you are fortunate, you will be alive tomorrow this time."

"If we're fortunate," echoed Halina. "Do you remember the looks of the farries of my Den?"

"Again, no concern of mine," said Treep. "From so high, all farries look the same. Even this close it is hard to tell your kind apart. I will recognize you, Halina, for you are not one of the street farries. You belong in the Canyon. But just in case, describe for me again the farri of your wrath."

"His name is Coron," said Halina. "He is evil beyond words, and he leads the group of farries who will oppose us tonight. He is large, and he is white. His fur is matted and dirty; his face is fierce."

"But Halina does not fear him," said Treep.

"No," said Halina. "But there are other farries besides me who walk the street, and have a right to walk free and unmolested."

"Is this part of the description?" asked Treep. "I am not aware of what that looks life."

"Use your best judgment, Master Treep," said Halina. "And do remember to be here on time."

"For what?" asked Treep. He stepped forward and spread his wings. "It's lunch time, now," he said, and was gone.

Mahri watched him fly off into the sun. He circled once around the area of the Den, and then flew on to deeper parts of the Canyon. Mahri looked over at Halina, hoping for some answers.

"He will be here, of course," said Halina. "He also knows exactly what our girls look like. He will make no mistakes."

"We forgot to tell him about Dori," said Mahri.

"I'm sure he knows," said Halina. "And if he doesn't, he'll figure it out immediately. Treep is very intelligent. In fact, a smarter bird you will never meet."

Dahrkron felt the sleep slowly escape. He opened his eyes and reached forward with a luxurious stretch. He looked over at Trahna, who remained asleep beside him. Most others in the pack slept as well, although Dahrkron noticed a few twitches. Afternoon nap time was about to end.

There was no hurry. Most of the day was gone; *tonight* was when it mattered. Dahrkron could feel the crazy pull of the full moon already, with the sun still overwhelming in the high western sky. Only a few more hours.

A few more hours and he would be eating farri. Tonight the pack would finally strike. Demon or not, the little bitch farri and her pack of rotten fur balls would be finished after tonight. Only a few more hours.

Trahna whimpered and began to stretch. She rolled over to her back and then all the way over to her left side. She opened her eyes slowly and looked up at Dahrkron. She smiled with warm affection, then crawled the tiny distance to where he rested on his forepaws.

"I feel good about it, my love," said Trahna. "Tonight we will follow you into a new tradition. It's just as we planned the night you took over the pack. A new tradition, with most of the pack not even realizing it. You've really won them over."

"We just told them what they wanted to hear," said Dahrkron. "They just needed a cause to follow."

"And full bellies," said Trahna.

"That helps too," said Dahrkron.

Most of the pack were now stirring, and Trahna nestled up to her mate. Dahrkron rested his chin on her shoulder, content for the moment just to be with her and the pack. Life was very pleasant right now.

When the pack was alert and standing, Dahrkron began to discuss strategy. The sun still boasted a couple of hours left of strength, giving the pack plenty of time for plans.

"There's a short fence at the edge of the road," said Dahrkron. "It doesn't stretch all the way across, so we'll crash through right at the edge of where it ends. Unfortunately, the farries meet on the other side of the road, so we'll have a small number of lopes to fill between the Canyon and their pack. They will scatter when they see us. We'll be in as wide a group as we can be when we leave the Canyon. We should be able to cut off any of their attempts to escape."

"What if we encounter the demon?" asked Brezni.

"Most likely we will," said Dahrkron. "She will be the only farri to hold her ground. Once we have killed off the others in her pack, we can all circle around her if we need to."

"Can the pack stand up to a demon?" asked Khanval. "Maybe we should take our kills and run. She will be crippled without her farries to follow her."

"Crippled but not dead," said Dahrkron. "There are many other farries who she might trick into following her. She must be stopped before it is too late. I believe we can do it."

"But you're not sure," said Brezni.

"I believe Lord Krahsta is with us," said Dahrkron. "He would never allow such evil to befall his race. And even a demon must accept the limitations of the body it takes. A farri cannot survive the attack of an entire pack of krahstas."

Most of them believed. Dahrkron could see it in their faces. Those who didn't would follow anyway, or else would live in shame if the pack returned victorious. *When* the pack returned victorious.

CHAPTER 39

Mahri looked down the street from where she sat in the dry grass of the Den. The other girls would arrive soon, she hoped. They would. For now, it was just she and Halina.

"What if Sarena doesn't show?" asked Mahri.

Halina sat in silence for several moments. Her eyes, like Mahri's, were fixed on the street. Finally she turned her eyes toward Mahri, and they were firm, yet thoughtful.

"Sarena will show, my love," said Halina.

"She didn't last time," said Mahri. "What if something awful happens to chase her away again? Treep said she and the lynxes were going *away* from the street."

"As you know, dearest," said Halina, "what Treep says and what Treep means are not always the same. He will be here, as will Dori, but they alone cannot fend off a pack of krahstas. If Sarena does not show up to help tonight, we are lost. Worrying about it will change nothing either way."

"You are right, of course," said Mahri. "But I can't help but worry. There is so much more to lose than last time."

"For everyone," said Halina. "The other farries will lose also if the timing is right. And you can take comfort in the knowledge of Coron's demise, for he will never survive tonight."

"How can you know that?" asked Mahri.

"Treep will never let him escape. Coron is the only farri we've really described to him. He won't forget. He will know even if Sarena doesn't show up, a huge, white farri is his main target.

"Which reminds me," continued Halina. "I questioned Syranosh about the night of Coron's evil attack. She came to your aid the moment she saw you with Coron. Your suspicions are unfair."

"I still wonder," said Mahri.

"You must believe it," said Halina. "I questioned her with much intensity. There was no lie in her eyes."

"Okay," said Mahri. "It doesn't matter anymore, anyway. We'll be standing side by side tonight, fighting the evil beast."

"The truth of all evil is how it divides what is good," said Halina. "The more we fight ourselves, the less we can fight what is truly wrong. Syranosh has her problems, but she is not our foe."

Syranosh was the last of Halina's girls to arrive at the Den. Mahri was actually glad to see her—if nothing else, for her tremendous fighting ability. Syranosh walked up to the Den with indifference and hopped onto the old stump.

The sun was close to losing its daily battle. The farries were tense. The hush was very loud.

When Halina finally stood up to speak, Mahri felt a rush of dizziness. Halina looked over the faces of her Den, pausing momentarily to study each individually, and in her eyes was defeat. The unfaltering confidence the girls of the Den had grown accustomed to was gone. Halina looked like someone who was about to die.

"There are things you must know," said Halina. "Many things I have kept from you, although most of you might have guessed already."

Mahri could see how nervous the other farries were. They were expecting a fight, but never had they imagined seeing the mistress this way. Mahri noticed the slightest undercurrent of fear start to churn within the group, and knew matters were about to get worse, although she wasn't sure how.

"We will face the misled farries of Coron tonight," Halina continued. "You all were aware of such stakes when you arrived. You were also aware of an attack by the pack of krahstas who haunt the Canyon. You may expect both of these events to occur as planned. Things only run as expected when they are not in your favor. And so it is tonight.

"Earlier today, Mahri and I spoke with Treep," Halina continued. "His words were not encouraging. Although we can certainly count on him to be here and help as he may, it might be up to us to decide our destiny. A hawk, an owl, and a barking kriba can do only so much in the face of hungry and angry krahstas."

It took a moment for everyone to understand. Mahri saw the tails of every farri twitching frantically. Every girl began to groom or sharpen claws, the true sign of nervousness.

"It's true," said Halina. "We must face the possibility of Sarena not showing. As we found out, she did not appear last time as we hoped and assumed. Better, of course, that she didn't, but a bad omen, nonetheless. There is the chance she may not appear tonight, and for this we must be prepared.

"She was seen traveling in the opposite direction of our street early this afternoon. Traveling with the same two lynxes whose favor we have not won. It could be she walked with them in hopes of persuading them to join us, but we can only assume the worst." Halina turned and looked behind her toward the Canyon. She spent several moments in deep thought, and then turned back to the girls.

"We mustn't blame her if she doesn't show," said Halina. "The last puma who stepped onto this street died within a very short time. We could never expect anyone to take such a risk for us, especially someone as great as a puma. There are so few of them left, we must understand if one chooses to avoid danger.

"Initially I had hoped for assistance from the lynxes. As you all know, these efforts have proved fruitless. They have not only refused, they appear to have talked our larger cousin into joining them. Again, we cannot blame them for their decisions. There are very few lynxes left as well."

"How will we escape the krahstas if none of our help shows up?" asked Naffa. As the youngest farri in the Den, she was the least experienced with the ways of Halina. Although her questions were annoying usually, this time she voiced the thoughts of the entire Den, including Mahri, who knew Halina the best.

"The krahstas will be easy," said Halina. "It will probably result in the end of our Den, but we should escape the Canyon predators without any problem."

Mahri heard the sudden gasp of the entire Den. It was finally out: tonight was probably the final night of their group. They all had suspected it, but none dared voice or even think it.

"We have another friend," said Halina. "He is a very large puppy. His name is Bayne, and when you hear his voice, run for it with all of your speed. His barks will warn us of the arrival of the krahstas. His keen kriba nose will detect their scent long before we can."

"Run toward him?" asked Naffa.

"Exactly," said Halina. "Jump over the farries of Coron if you must, but run for Bayne's voice with all of your might. It is our only salvation. Run past him, for he will be running toward us. He will run past us and chase the other farries. He will pay no attention to you if you are running in his direction. If you stay where you are, beware! Your life will end tonight.

"When you reach the lawn over there, stop and turn around. If any of Coron's farries come your way, hold your ground and chase them back if you can. If any krahstas come your way, get to a tree as fast as you can and forget the rest of us. You are no help to anyone if you are in the belly of a krahsta. Take no chances. Be brave, but don't be afraid to run either.

"You may see a hawk, and you may see an owl. Ignore them both. They know who you are and neither will do you any harm."

"What if Sarena does show up?" asked Mahri.

"I have told you the plan," said Halina. "It is the same should all or none of our friends appear. When you hear the barks of Bayne, run for them or perish." Halina paused for effect. She waited for her words to sink in, and then continued.

"A personal word," she said. "A finer group of farries there has never been. I love you all, and will forever. Should this be our final meeting, and I fear it might well be, remember you will be in my heart forever. You are my family, and I shall treasure our meetings always. If we go our separate ways, you will continue to know the bond of our Den. No matter where you might go, or what evil times might befall you, there is always someone who cares about you. And the someone is all of us. And you should remember, because if you don't, we won't be able to find you when you need us. After all we've been through, you should know what I mean."

Mahri did, and she could see understanding in the eyes of the Den. She believed in the strong bond between them all, and now she was certain Syranosh had acted in good faith the night of Coron's attack. They were being guided by Lady Farri; there could be no doubt any longer. The Lady had somehow tied them all together in the spirit of life.

"How will we know if the Den is to continue after tonight?" asked Sina.

"There will be no doubt," said Halina. "You will all know, just as you knew when to return after our last battle with the other farries. The feeling and knowledge will be part of the same we are experiencing now. I can see the feeling in all of your eyes. It is truly the feeling of Lady Farri, and if our Den shall fail after tonight, then look for Lady Farri in the eyes of the other farries you come across in your lives. Look for it when you are the most upset or lonely. I believe the uniqueness in all of you will attract it; you need only let it find you."

Mahri never flinched while watching Halina. The words of the mistress were comforting, but her eyes were full of sadness. Mahri read the speech as a calculated warning to the group to prepare for the absence of Halina. The mistress apparently did not expect to make it through this battle.

CHAPTER 40

Bayne could see the group of farries gathered near the Canyon. They were too far away to differentiate, but his keen sense of smell told him Halina and Mahri were there. They looked different from how he would have pictured such a large group of farries. They were all very quiet and still.

He thought about Halina and her request. The more he thought about it, the more he wanted to meet the wild kribas from the Canyon. Their mysterious life seemed so fascinating. Bayne considered scattering the bad group of farries before they even reached the Den and running to the edge of the Canyon to await the wild kribas.

The krahstas. Yes, he had heard that name today. It had so much more of a wild and throaty sound than "wild kriba." There were so many breeds of kribas, and Bayne wondered if the krahstas looked like him. They might be even more friendly if they did. They might take him for a romp in the Canyon.

Bayne smelled the other group of farries the same instant he first saw the full moon rising over the mountains in the east. The farries walked in silence, but Bayne could hear them anyway. There were many, many paws touching the ground. Far more than there would be in Halina's Den. No wonder Halina wanted help in chasing the bad farries away.

From where he sat, Bayne could now see the large group walking in the street. He sat on the front lawn of Halina's paladin's house and watched the farries walk past in the direction of Halina's Den. There were a lot of farries. He wondered if he should jump in now and save Halina the trouble, but a soft voice from somewhere in his mind convinced him to sit tight and watch for a while.

Like before, Sharlo had shown up to stand by the farries of the Den. He stood next to Mahri, just like before. Together with the rest of the Den, they watched the street for movement. They could not see the other farries yet, but knew they were on the way.

Sharlo leaned over to Mahri and whispered, "I need to talk to you when this is over. There's so much I've wanted to tell you, but have not had the courage. I should tell you now, but the advantage of time is not with us."

Before Mahri could respond, her internal warning system went on alert. The fur on her back raised just slightly, and she knew the other farries were very near. All of the girls from the Den responded the same way in the same instant.

They saw the faces of the other group start to appear. There were far more than the Den had anticipated, and Mahri's heart sank. She could feel and almost hear the morale fall in the line of farries who stood beside her. This was the first omen of the night, and it was very bad. A brief and startling thought flashed through her mind: was the presence of Lady Farri she had felt on the Den's side or with the other farries?

There were fewer toms than before. The toms who were there were very large, and there was a larger group of queens. The farries of the Den stood with tails up against the Canyon and faced the others who were circling just out of striking distance. Mahri looked around and did not see Coron, but knew he was there.

Roger sat on the couch in his living room and looked at Laura. She was on the couch too, with her feet up on his lap, where he was massaging them. This was unusual, because Roger rarely touched Laura other than an occasional hug. But this was an unusual night.

Laura had gotten a job offer. Someone from the *San Diego Union* had called, and Laura wanted to talk about it. A definite step up from the *Courier,* and she would not have to move out of town. Roger had secretly hoped for a move to help resolve things.

Neither of them was talking. They were silent in thought, drinking diet sodas and relaxing in the warmth of the August night. The doorbell rang.

"It might be Jerry Radcliff," said Roger. "You wanna talk to him?"

"Why? Why is he here?"

"He wants to go hunting for another mountain lion tomorrow," said Roger. "I told him I'd let him know if I wanted to go."

The bell rang again.

"Let's talk to him," said Laura.

It was Radcliff, and he was delighted to see Laura.

"Oh my, the married lady again," said Radcliff. "You're gonna get your boyfriend here in a whoopin' lot of trouble."

"I'm not really married," said Laura.

"Then no man is safe," Radcliff laughed. "Anyways, I was out and about to see if y'all want to hunt cougar tomorrow."

"We'd love to," said Laura. "What time?"

"I don't know if a pretty thing like yourself wants to stomp around in the canyon," said Radcliff. "Besides, it might be dangerous if we get close to a mountain lion."

"Nothing to worry about with big, strong men like you there to protect me," said Laura.

Narshi was there, and she stepped forward. Fahlo, the other one who had spoken before, was not there. Narshi stood alone. The large group behind her remained poised a few steps behind in silence, ready to strike when needed. Their faces looked eager for this to be resolved without a fight, although none expected Halina to agree to disband the Den.

Mahri noticed how clean most of them looked. They were from the homes of good paladins. They were many different colors, sizes, and breeds, but their faces all looked the same. Their faces were all lined with hatred and confusion. And fear.

"You are not welcome here, misled farries," said Halina. "Please go back, and live free and happy. We are not your enemies."

"Any evil farri who stands as an enemy to Lady Farri is an enemy to us," said Narshi.

"Then you must look within your own number for the evil," answered Halina. "It has deceived you into facing an opponent you do not even understand. Leave here and never return, or face the wrath of the wilds."

"You threatened us before," said Narshi. "By some trick we saw a monster appear from the Canyon, but Lady Farri struck it down."

"What you saw cannot be explained in such tense verses," said Halina. "You must turn around and leave now. Go and find the true evil, and destroy it. It has a name."

"And what name does evil have?" mocked Narshi.

"It is named Coron," said Halina. "And you are a fool to heed its advice."

"And is Master Coron evil simply because he opposes you?" asked Narshi.

"Evil is the harm he has inflicted upon us," said Halina. "And evil will be responsible for the harm about to fall on you if you don't leave."

Suddenly there was movement from behind Narshi. A huge, filthy white farri stepped forward and stood directly in front of Halina.

"So I am evil?" snorted Coron. "Am I the one who laughs in the face of Lady Farri by mating after receiving the changes scar? Am I the one who blasphemes in her face by calling strange beasts out of the Canyon in her name? Guess again, trash cat!"

His words were answered with the growls of every farri from the Den. Their tails were parallel to the ground, untwitching and fluffed. The farries from behind Coron were now beside him, also fluffed and baring teeth. Both sides stood frozen, waiting for the first movement that would send the entire street into a brawl.

Bayne could not hear the words exactly, but was smart enough to know none of the talk was friendly. He stood up and took the time for a good stretch, knowing he would have to run very soon. Halina had told him to run and bark if the farries started to fight. He was just finishing his stretch when it hit him. He bolted upright and put his nose to the air. The krahstas were near.

He took a moment to analyze it. The smell was wild and maddening beyond words. The fur on his neck rose involuntarily. The loud pounding of his heart felt like it was in his throat. The ground seemed to move, but he noticed it was the result of his front legs shaking out of control. And Halina expected him to bark and chase farries?

Mahri's eyes were on Coron. She had decided to go after him first, despite her disadvantage in size and strength. Considering the size of the crowd, she wouldn't have much time to fight anyway before the Den farries were overwhelmed. Mahri began to crouch back the slightest bit, trying not to let anyone else in the stare-down notice. She took a deep breath and braced to strike. Then the barking started.

The noise caught them all by surprise. Coron's group turned around immediately, giving the Den farries time to recover and react. Mahri raced forward, passing the stunned would-be assailants before they could even react. She ran hard for the barking, which was getting louder as Bayne ran toward her. She could feel the other Den farries beside her and knew the others would still be standing where they had been, not knowing what to do.

Bayne rushed by, barking and howling for all he was worth. He paid no attention to Mahri; his eyes were locked on the scene behind her. Mahri didn't even look back until she reached the lawn of the second house from the Canyon, where she stopped and turned around with the other Den farries. She watched Bayne run, then gave a quick glance across the group beside her. Halina was nowhere in sight.

Dahrkron was the first one to reach the street. Half of the pack was right behind him, the other half swarming around the fence on the other side of the street. Of all the possible scenes he had envisioned and planned for, none came close to what was occurring on the street.

There were more farries than he dared hope for, and they were running straight at him. His mind flashed with sudden panic as he thought they might all be under the power of demons like their leader. But Dahrkron realized immediately what was happening. They were being chased by a barking kriba, and when they saw him and the other krahstas, they went mad with fear. Without anymore hesitation, Dahrkron pounced.

He crushed the back of a farri with his jaws before it could even react. The other pack members were proceeding the same way. The farries had scattered right into the net his pack had formed around the end of the street. He could hear the howls of dying farries all around him. He could also still hear the annoying barks of the kriba. With a dead farri hanging from his mouth, Dahrkron looked to the source of the barks. Then he saw the young kriba reach the middle of the street and stop.

Bayne had seen enough. This was not a game, and now he understood Halina's words and warnings. He saw the faces of the krahstas. They were so wild and lonely and hungry. Their eyes were scary, cold beacons of fire. They looked like they had been that way forever. And each krahsta was in the process of killing a farri.

No romps in the Canyon with this bunch. Bayne turned hard and dashed for home, but stopped before he got there.

Almost everyone had a farri. There were a few farries who had broken from the main body and were almost to the sidewalk. Dahrkron watched two of the krahstas go after them, only to be stopped cold by a deafening scream. Dahrkron dropped the second farri he had killed, amazed to see an owl swooping down on the escaping farries. The cats turned and ran right back into the waiting krahstas. The owl broke its hover and flew off into the Canyon.

The entire pack was now successful. Each krahsta had at least one farri, with the majority having two. They all trotted, prey in mouth, into the middle of the street where Dahrkron stood. They turned toward the Canyon to lope off into the night and have dinner.

"Not so fast, filthy beasts," came the voice from behind.

The entire pack recognized the voice. It was a lynx. They all stopped and turned around. There were two lynxes, and they walked from the side yard of the house bordering the Canyon where they had obviously been hiding and watching the whole event.

"Each with a farri in its mouth," said the smaller one. "Didn't we warn you about harming the street farries?"

The lynxes stepped forward and every krahsta dropped its prey and began to growl. Dahrkron was so furious he ignored the danger of being on a brightly lit street and stepped forward to confront his enemies.

"Yes, you warned us," said Dahrkron. "But there are only two of you now. You are greatly outnumbered, and you stand no chance against my pack, as you have found out before. Your puma friend is no longer around to help you out."

His words were just leaving his mouth when he realized their untruth. He saw the group of farries standing on the lawn behind the lynxes. Why hadn't they run? Why would lynxes be on the street? Then he understood the folly of his success. It was a trap! He knew it and wanted to cry out in disgust and sorrow. Then it hit. Every strand of fur rose on his body as he felt her and then smelled her. His confirmation was the terrifying roar that dropped him to his forepaws.

"What the hell was that?" shouted Jerry Radcliff. He was just about to leave Roger's house when they heard the roar coming from the dead end.

"That sounded just like the mountain lion we heard before," said Laura.

"I have a shotgun in the truck," said Radcliff, and began to run toward the street where his pickup was parked.

"Oh God, here we go again," said Laura.

"Freeze!"

Suddenly there were men everywhere around the house with pistols drawn and pointed at Radcliff.

"Federal agents! Put your hands over your head and don't move!" yelled the man nearest the garage.

"What the hell?" yelled Radcliff. "There's a god-damn mountain lion on the street over there! Let's go after him, not me. I'm a state narcotics officer."

"We know you're into narcotics, Mr. Radcliff," said the man near the garage. "Now put your hands up."

Dahrkron whirled around to face the puma. It was huge, and the same one who had breached their camp a month earlier. How could it be alive? They had all heard of its death. This was the treachery of an evil demon.

The puma walked with slow confidence toward him. He quaked as it began to laugh. It was disgraceful to tremble like this in front of the pack, even though he knew their eyes were on the puma and not him. They were shaking harder than he was, but he was still feeling humilated.

"There stand the krahstas," said Sarena. "All with fresh kills at their feet. Fresh kills of my little cousins. Were you not warned to avoid such actions? Is there not enough prey in the Canyon for you filthy looters to destroy? Well?"

The krahstas shrank back from Sarena's growls. The lynxes had stepped closer to their flanks to prevent any attempt to turn and flee.

"Do the filthy looters speak?" asked Sarena. "I demand your leader step forward to answer for this atrocity. Now!"

The roar thundered over the pack, and Dahrkron fought off the terror and stood. It was anger and hatred now. He stood high and took a step toward the puma, fueled by hatred and anger. He might die now, but he would not die humilated.

"I am Dahrkron, and I am the pack leader. This is part of our territory. It is you who are here to loot from us what is rightfully ours. Leave us in peace, as we will do for you in the future."

Inspired by the words and strength of her mate, Trahna stood up and took her place at Dahrkron's side.

"The street is the territory of no animal from the Canyon," said Sarena. "Not yours, not mine. You have violated the warning you were given, and this I do not take lightly. Those dead farries at your feet were my friends, and I hold nothing on this land to be more sacred than friendship."

"I'm sure these farries will be even friendlier when they're in your belly," said Dahrkron. "You—"

The sudden, piercing screech ripped through Dahrkron's ears all the way through to his soul. But the screech's abrupt end was the most terrifying part for Dahrkron. It was a sickening impact of something hard and sharp with the solid part of an animal. It was Trahna. She was falling to the ground before the hawk had even reversed itself. The large bird screamed with triumph and raced back into the sky. Trahna was on the ground in a grotesque and twisted position, the huge, open gash on her head quite fatal.

The krahstas were stunned. They all stood and gaped at the fallen Trahna in disbelief and horror. They had barely taken a full breath when the lynxes attacked from behind.

The move was so quick and coordinated that two krahstas had their throats ripped out before the rest of the pack was even aware of the attack. The two nearest krahstas turned toward the movement and caught the lynxes head on, but were still too stunned and confused to react fast enough. Their dying howls alerted the others.

Dahrkron turned and lunged at the nearest lynx. It was battling with Prushtah, the former leader's mate. Dahrkron grabbed the lynx by the side and yanked hard, pulling it around enough for Prushtah to get a grip on the other side. The lynx grabbed Dahrkron's right shoulder with fierce teeth, but he held anyway, determined to rip the cat apart. But Dahrkron had forgotten about the puma.

He heard it first. The neck of a krahsta being crushed in the puma's jaws. Dahrkron held his position, but the sound was terrifying enough to distract Prushtah. In her hesitation, she lost her grip. The lynx bit harder into Dahrkron's shoulder and swung its body onto its back underneath him. Dahrkron had to let go to keep from falling, and felt the lynx kick rapidly into his stomach with claws extended. He tried to bite the cat again, but he was in too awkward a position.

The entire pack was growling and barking now. The puma had stepped between Dahrkron and the others, so only Prushtah could help. The lynx was still biting and kicking at him with a frenzy, and he looked up to Prushtah for help. He barked at her to assist, but she stood there, unmoving.

"Help me or we'll all die!" yelled Dahrkron.

"A true leader wouldn't let his pack die," said Prushtah, and she turned away from Dahrkron and ran. She dashed around the left side of the fence at the edge of the street and bounded into the Canyon.

Dahrkron was starting to be overcome by the pain. His stomach was a catastrophe of open gashes. The teeth in his shoulder seared hard and sharp down his side. And still, he could not maneuver enough to fight back. Suddenly the puma burst out with a thunderous roar, startling his assailant into letting go. Dahrkron jumped away and braced for another attack.

He spared a quick glance to the rest of the battle and saw only dismay. Khanval, his closest friend for many seasons, was struck in the side by the mighty forepaw of the puma and sent flying into the lynx Dahrkron had just fought with. The lynx turned on Khanval rather than pursue Dahrkron, so he had another moment to assess to situation.

There were dead krahstas everywhere. The puma was making sport of the event, and terrifying its victims before destroying them. This was giving the lynxes a chance to take on krahstas one at a time.

The pack was completely destroyed. Dahrkron could see no hope. The cats were positioned between the krahstas and the Canyon, and had now cut off the escape route. Dahrkron was witnessing a massacre. There was no chance left for anyone in the pack. Anyone except Dahrkron.

They had forgotten about him. He had a clear shot at the Canyon if he hurried. There was no other way. He was badly hurt and he might die anyway. He would without question if he remained where he was. But a leader could never abandon his pack. What pack? They were all as good as dead. He saw the body of his beautiful Trahna lying on the street and wanted to howl in misery.

He decided to run. There could be no revenge if he died tonight. There were many deaths to be avenged. He would start by going after Prushtah, the deserter. He would somehow destroy all of the cats involved. The owl. He would never rest until the hawk who killed his Trahna was ripped into small shreds. But first he had to escape.

The route Prushtah had taken was out of the question. He would only attract the puma's attention if he followed her. He began to limp toward the end of the fence on the right side of the street, where he could lope into the Canyon and be free. He hoped he would not be chased.

When he heard the dying howl of another krahsta, he broke into a bolt. He ran hard for the fence. He made it to the edge where the trail into the Canyon began and turned blindly around the fence toward it. His momentum carried him for two more steps before he forced his front paws into the ground to stop. There on the trail into the Canyon he stood, face-to-face with the same farri who had started it all two months earlier. He looked up at the stars in disbelief.

"How appropriate," he said. "I face again the demon who is responsible for the death of my pack."

"Only you are responsible for your pack," said Halina. "You were warned, yet you failed to believe. Lady Farri stands up for her race."

"Lies! Lady Farri wouldn't support the likes of you. You stand there masquerading as a simple farri, but I know. Yes, I know well who you are."

"You know nothing," said Halina. "You know not even of the Canyon you live in, for the animals here believed *you* to be the demon. They believed in a fool."

"And what did your pack believe in?" asked Dahrkron. "Almost all of them died at my feet. What kind of a leader are you?"

"Wise enough to lure my enemies into the hungry mouths of krahstas," said Halina. "My Den was never in danger."

Dahrkron's head swam with rage. Forgotten were the two previous incidents with this farri and the massacre of his pack. The wounds from the lynx held no more pain. He crouched back to strike.

He heard the growl, but it was too late. So intense was his gaze on the farri, he never saw the rush of the young white kriba with brown spots. He saw no face, but knew the voice to be the same as the barking kriba on the street, the one chasing the farries earlier in the night. He never saw, but felt the teeth as they clamped down on his throat from the side. He saw only the stars, and how they began to fade. Then he saw no more.

The battle on the street was winding down. Not much of a battle, thought Treep. He circled high above and was beginning to lose interest. Such an ordeal between dogs and cats was rare indeed, yet he knew the outcome before it had started and was no longer concerned. Rare too for a hawk to be involved in the death of a krahsta. Rare, but gratifying.

Halina would be happy. Maybe now she would leave him in peace. He had seen all of the enemy farries who had survived the krahstas run wildly into the Canyon. They would not live to see the sunrise. Nor would most of the krahstas, for that matter. Yes, indeed, Halina would be happy.

Treep continued his lazy circle pattern, keeping his eyes on the white farri who was now a block away from the battle. He had eluded the krahstas, the lynxes, the farries, and the owl, and was now quite confident of his escape. How did Halina describe the bad farri? Huge, dirty white, and fierce? He sure didn't look fierce from up here.

Treep began another circle. Halina's farri enemies were of no concern to him. He cared little for the quarrels of animals. But this was different. This one had broken the rules. Treep had seen the change in Mahri. And whether he cared about farries or not, some things could not be overlooked. This dirty white farri was quite dirty indeed.

The circle ended abruptly and the dive began. Treep loved the feel of the air at such speeds, especially in the dry heat of summer. It was strange to be diving over a street, but exhilarating nonetheless. The farri had stopped its trot and now walked in arrogant confidence. That would end.

Treep released his deepest scream of pursuit. The farri crouched, like all other prey, and Treep swooped in and grabbed him. A successful strike: his talons held fast to the back of the farri. Treep began to climb upward. He flew parallel to the street at first, getting used to the weight, and then made slow, gradual progress.

"Let go of me!" screamed Coron. "Let go now!"

Treep continued his ascent and laughed inside when the farri tried unsuccessfully to claw at him.

"Let go," said Coron. "You will not like the taste of another predator. You will not be able to kill me anyway."

Treep was now reaching the lowest of the man-made power lines, and his climb was beginning to get easier. He was amazed at how badly this farri reeked. Was this Halina's idea of payment for his services? The stupid farri in his grip was right. Treep probably wouldn't like the taste of him at all. He passed the highest of the power lines.

"Let me go!" screamed Coron in desperation. "I demand it!"

"As you wish," said Treep, and released his prey.

Mahri sat motionless next to Sharlo during almost the entire battle. She had cried out when Bayne darted past them the second time and ran into the Canyon, but otherwise had not moved.

The Great Battle for the Den was now over. Sarena roared with victory and then walked back to the Canyon around the left side of the fence. She was followed by the two lynxes, the smaller one limping. Mahri did not believe she would ever see any of them again. The lynxes she could live without, but she was already missing Sarena.

Mahri had heard the cries of Treep when the great bird snagged Coron. She also heard the howls of terror when Treep let go and Coron fell to his death. She heard the impact as well. A very sickening sound, but in this case, one Mahri found very gratifying.

The street was a mess with dead farries and dead krahstas. Both sides had been thorough in their killings. Mahri hoped the paladins would notice the dead animals soon and take them away to wherever they took dead animals.

The girls all began to leave the yard where they had watched the battle. Syranosh passed by Mahri and then stopped. She turned back and faced Mahri thoughtfully.

"You are the closest to Halina," said Syranosh. "I must apologize to both of you for doubting."

"Doubting?" asked Mahri, very confused.

"I didn't doubt, really," said Syranosh. "I knew Halina would pull us through. She knows everything. And you are a wise farri yourself, pretty Mahri. We all owe you the safety of the Den."

"It's nice to hear kind words from you, Syranosh," said Mahri. "But it's I who owe you the apology. I'm sorry for my ungratefulness when you chased off Coron. I owe you some fur."

"Chasing off that filth was a pleasure," said Syranosh. "And by the sound of things, we won't have to worry about him anymore. Thank Farri, although I dearly would have loved to have seen his death."

Mahri nodded. Syranosh walked off into the night, leaving Mahri alone with Sharlo.

"Is this the final end of the Den?" Sharlo asked her.

"I don't know," said Mahri. "I haven't seen Halina yet. If she is alive, then so is the Den. It will only die with her."

"I haven't seen Halina either," said Sharlo. "Do you think she is still alive?"

"Somewhere," said Mahri. "All great farries continue to live on somewhere, somehow. When we thought Sarena was dead, she was still alive in our hearts."

"You've only made it more confusing," said Sharlo.

"This was Halina's great test," said Mahri. "Her great plan. If she could not live through it, then no animal alive could ever come close. That's my answer. We will see her soon."

"Do you think she knew the lynxes would show up?"

"You heard Syranosh," Mahri laughed. "Halina knows *everything*."

"Will you continue to be part of the Den?" asked Sharlo. His expression was almost sad.

"Yes and no, dear Sharlo," said Mahri. "I love the girls so much. I would miss their company too much to part. And I wouldn't be able to stand not being with Halina after all of this. I will help the girls call the toms to the Den, but I will not date like the others anymore. That part I wish to save for you. I don't enjoy mating with other toms like I used to. I hope you feel the same way."

"More than you could ever know," said Sharlo.

CHAPTER 41

"Why haven't you ever made a pass at me?" Laura asked. She pressed against him so he leaned back on the couch, and she put her arms around him. "All of your girlfriends, and you've never even laid a finger on me. You know how that makes me feel?"

"No. How?" Roger couldn't believe any of this. She was leaning over and kissing him hard on the mouth. "I never thought you were interested," he said when he finally got a chance for a breath.

"You just never thought," said Laura. "Start paying more attention. Maybe this will help."

She began to kiss him again, and Roger started to feel delirious. He was just about to suggest someplace more comfortable than the couch when he heard the cat. He ignored it and began to speak, but was drowned out by the meow. Then he felt a sudden jolt to his chest, followed by a very loud meow. He opened his eyes and saw the eyes of De Lilah staring down at him. It was morning and she wanted food, oblivious to her destruction of Roger's dream. Another dream about Laura.

Roger wiped the sleep from his eyes and began to pet the cat. The dream dissolved into reality and cold memory. Laura had gone off to cover the Radcliff arrest for the *Courier*, her last big story before moving on, leaving him alone with a bottle of Jack Daniel's to sit and contemplate his existence. He vaguely remembered letting the cat in at about two o'clock.

He thought about Laura's new job again and hoped it would make things easier, not having to see her so much.

Then he thought about Tammy and decided it was time to give her the big dump. Another one of *those* nights ahead. Time to admit it: until Laura was out of his system, anyone else was a waste of time.

He looked at De Lilah and scratched behind her ears.

"Lucky little bitch," he said to the cat. "Why can't my life be as uncomplicated as yours?"

About the Author

Michael Peak is an Emmy Award-winning TV journalist based in San Diego, where he lives with a tabby named Lynxie. CAT HOUSE is his first novel.